Swapped

Carter hadn't called to send Jo anywhere else after she'd been to Fields and Lakeview, so she'd checked in with him while airborne, only to find that he was in the other Night Wing on his way to Gunter's current location in the Sawtooth Mountains. She grinned, remembering his voice. He was clearly hating every second of his helicopter ride, which she didn't understand at all but was more than happy to give him grief over. But that meant he was effectively out of the loop until he landed, so Jo was on her own. Once her chopper had lifted off again, she'd retrieved her car from its usual spot, checked in with Fargo and Zoe, and then headed home just to make sure everything here was in order. She'd also taken a quick shower—dealing with Gary's customers had been a surprising workout. Now, clean and freshly uniformed, she felt ready to face the rest of the day.

Jo was just unlocking her car door—not really necessary in Eureka, but old habits died hard—when a flicker of movement behind her made her stop, spin, and crouch, drawing her pistol in the same motion. Then she stared.

Her house was wavering.

Not waving, wavering. It seemed to be shimmering, its edges blurring and shifting, as if it were a grainy picture going in and out of focus. Then a bright flash of light blinded Jo, causing her hands to rise in front of her face by pure reflex. When she could see again and lowered them, she saw through the spots that her house had changed.

Or rather, it was no longer her house standing there.

"Great." Jo stood up, holstered her pistol, and brushed herself off. "That's just perfect."

EUReKA

SUBSTITUTION METHOD

CRIS RAMSAY

ACE BOOKS, NEW YORK

THE BERKLEY PUBLISHING GROUP
Published by the Penguin Group
Penguin Group (USA) Inc.
375 Hudson Street, New York, New York 10014, USA
Penguin Group (Canada), 90 Eglinton Avenue East, Suite 700, Toronto, Ontario M4P 2Y3, Canada
(a division of Pearson Penguin Canada Inc.)
Penguin Books Ltd., 80 Strand, London WC2R 0RL, England
Penguin Group Ireland, 25 St. Stephen's Green, Dublin 2, Ireland (a division of Penguin Books Ltd.)
Penguin Group (Australia), 250 Camberwell Road, Camberwell, Victoria 3124, Australia
(a division of Pearson Australia Group Pty. Ltd.)
Penguin Books India Pvt. Ltd., 11 Community Centre, Panchsheel Park, New Delhi—110 017, India
Penguin Group (NZ), 67 Apollo Drive, Rosedale, North Shore 0632, New Zealand
(a division of Pearson New Zealand Ltd.)
Penguin Books (South Africa) (Pty.) Ltd., 24 Sturdee Avenue, Rosebank, Johannesburg 2196,
South Africa

Penguin Books Ltd., Registered Offices: 80 Strand, London WC2R 0RL, England

This is a work of fiction. Names, characters, places, and incidents either are the product of the author's imagination or are used fictitiously, and any resemblance to actual persons, living or dead, business establishments, events, or locales is entirely coincidental. The publisher does not have any control over and does not assume any responsibility for author or third-party websites or their content.

EUREKA: SUBSTITUTION METHOD

An Ace Book / published by arrangement with NBC Universal Television Consumer Products Group

PRINTING HISTORY
Ace mass-market edition / September 2010

Copyright © 2010 Universal City Studios Productions, LLLP.
Eureka TM & © Universal Network Television, LLC.
Cover art by Syfy Network.
Interior text design by Kristin del Rosario.

ISBN: 978-0-441-01885-7

ACE
Ace Books are published by The Berkley Publishing Group,
a division of Penguin Group (USA) Inc.,
375 Hudson Street, New York, New York 10014.
ACE and the "A" design are trademarks of Penguin Group (USA) Inc.

PRINTED IN THE UNITED STATES OF AMERICA

10 9 8 7 6 5 4 3 2 1

To Aaron Rosenberg—
clearly we were switched at birth

ACKNOWLEDGMENTS

Writing is never a solitary profession. A lot of people are involved in making a book happen. In this case, I owe a huge thanks to:

- Peter and my evil twin, DaveDave, for serving as sounding boards during the initial process

- my Transatlantic Twin, Steve, for being a sounding board during revisions

- my genuine, adorable, arty family, for all their love and support while I was writing

- my amazing editor, Leis, for working with me throughout to really make this book as strong and tight and engaging as possible—and Ginjer for sending me to her in the first place

- Jaime Paglia, for making sure that this book was one hundred percent true-blue *Eureka*

- the rest of the *Eureka* fans, who love the show as much as I do—I hope you enjoy reading this story half as much as I enjoyed telling it

PROLOGUe

"The woods were calm, peaceful. Sunlight was just beginning to filter down through the leaves, tracing golden streaks across the lower foliage and dappling the tree trunks. Birds were rising from their nests, their chirps and songs filling the still-hazy air. Insects were on the move, rasping and buzzing and humming. Larger animals were stirring as well, creeping across leaves and dirt, sniffing the early-morning breeze.

"One small spider skittered out onto its web, testing each strand as always to make sure it remained taut. The web, strung between two trees, was the perfect mix of rigid and flexible—not so taut as to be torn apart by a stiff wind, but not so loose as to allow insects to pass through. Satisfied that its work remained intact, the spider retreated to one corner, its mandibles twitching slightly as it settled into a crouch and waited impatiently for breakfast."

Bill Early lowered his PDA and let his breath out—

slowly. He didn't want to spook the *Araneus diadematus*, or European garden spider. Not now, when he'd been so careful to ease himself up close enough to observe it clearly, and had kept so still and quiet that it hadn't felt a need to abandon its web and scurry for cover.

Bill smiled and resisted the urge to whistle. He'd wanted to study an *Araneus diadematus* in its natural habitat for a while now, but the clever, dime-sized orange-brown spiders were elusive. He'd lucked out in finding this one, and he planned to make the most of the opportunity. This would go a long way toward furthering his research and toward winning him a bit more respect. Let's see Taggart put together a presentation like this!

Then something changed. There was a hum in the air, but without sound. Bill looked around. It was clear that the spider had felt the shift through its web, vibrating along each strand, because it suddenly went perfectly still. There was a breeze, but nothing stirred, not even the tiny hairs along the spider's legs and body. The other anchoring tree seemed to shimmer all along its length, though the sunlight had not yet reached its lower half.

And then the spider's web went limp.

The spider reacted at once, leaping to its feet and racing along a web line in what Bill took to be panic. What had happened? The tiny arachnid skittered to a stop as it reached the end of that line—which now swung freely in the morning air. The very tip, where the spider had added extra material to anchor the line to the neighboring tree, was gone. From Bill's vantage point a few feet away, it looked as if it had been sheared off by a sharp bite.

But nothing had bitten it.

Nor was it the only one, he realized as he studied the situation more fully. All the anchor points along that side were gone. It was as if a massive claw had sliced down, removing the web from that tree.

But nothing had touched it.

The spider shivered, confused, and Bill felt a pang of sympathy for the little creature. It had seen no other life yet this morning, yet something had definitely done this. And now it would have to reattach the web, one strand at a time. It clutched the end of that line firmly between its mandibles and leaped onto the neighboring tree, its feet clamping onto the rough bark. Then it spat more web material and shoved the strand into that sticky glob, cementing it in place. *There,* Bill thought, fascinated. One strand reattached. A few dozen more to go.

As the spider continued its work, racing to complete the task before all the insects passed its location, Bill continued to puzzle over what had happened as best he could. But he couldn't come up with any answers. The web looked fine, except for those missing tips. The tree was fine, but the anchor points had vanished from its surface. He didn't even see traces of their sticky residue, which was surprising.

It was as if the spider had never attached anything to this tree before. But of course that was impossible. It was the same tree that had been here before.

Wasn't it?

CHAPTER 1

"Good morning, Sheriff Carter." The oddly melodious voice woke Jack Carter from sleep, just as it did every morning, and he smiled, rolling over.

"Morning, S.A.R.A.H."

The lights came up slowly, and music began to play through the bedroom—his favorite station, classic rock. Or "old stuff," as Zoe liked to call it.

Carter sat up and shook his head, trying to clear the cobwebs, then tossed aside the sheets and levered himself out of bed.

"Did you sleep well?" S.A.R.A.H. asked him.

"Not bad," he admitted, stretching to force both body and mind awake. "Just not nearly enough."

"That's what happens when you stay up so late watching football. I told you you should go to bed."

"I know, I know. And I should have listened. But it was the divisional play-offs! And the second game went into overtime! I had to see how it ended!" Carter made his way slowly toward the bathroom, the doors sliding open as he approached. He discarded his boxers and stepped into the shower stall, warm water immediately cascading down on him. With a sigh of relief, he reached for the soap and began lathering himself.

"I routinely record all major sporting events," S.A.R.A.H. said, continuing their conversation. "You can watch them at any time."

"Yeah, I know, and I appreciate that," Carter assured her. "But it's not the same as watching it live on broadcast TV, with commercials." S.A.R.A.H.'s programming automatically removed commercials while recording.

"I can add commercials."

"What, like that one time? No thanks!" Carter couldn't help laughing, though, as he remembered. He'd told S.A.R.A.H. that sometimes watching a movie with commercials made it more enjoyable—there was that forced pause between scenes, when you waited impatiently for the movie to return. So S.A.R.A.H. had added commercials for him as he watched *Rio Bravo*.

Unfortunately, she had decided to create her own.

After the third appearance of "Sheriff Carter's Brand of Justice cologne," Carter had begged her to stop. She meant well, as always, but sometimes S.A.R.A.H. just didn't know when to leave well enough alone.

Like now.

But what did he expect from a Self-Actuated Residential Automated Habitat?

Drying off, Carter grabbed clean underwear and his uniform and pulled them on. He was still buttoning his shirt as he made his way downstairs.

"Morning, sweetheart." Zoe had beaten him to the kitchen and was standing at the central counter, sipping juice and taking bites of a bagel. As usual she had a book open in front of her. It was like she'd never left for college.

"Morning, Dad." His daughter accepted a kiss on her forehead and smiled, but her eyes were still on the book. "Sleep okay? How late did you stay up, anyway?"

"Too late," S.A.R.A.H. answered, earning a glare.

"Late," Carter agreed, grabbing the plate S.A.R.A.H. had ready for him and digging into his eggs and bacon. "And I'll pay for it today. But it was worth it." He took a swig of coffee from his mug, then made a face. It was luke-warm. He knew he hadn't taken that long in the shower, so this must be another of S.A.R.A.H.'s subtle ways of getting back at him for staying up too late. It was like living with his mother—only she was everywhere at once.

"Can I get you a fresh cup, Sheriff?" S.A.R.A.H. asked sweetly.

"No thanks," he told her, carrying it over to the mi-crowave. "I've got it." He placed the mug in the center of the glass platter, closed the door, and hit the one-minute button—

—and nothing happened.

"You'll need to close the door properly, Sheriff," S.A.R.A.H. reminded him. "Otherwise the circuit is not complete and the machine will not activate, for safety reasons."

Carter looked more closely and realized he'd knocked a napkin aside when he'd swept the microwave door open— one corner had fallen inside the microwave and was block-ing the door from closing completely. He pulled it free and shut the door again, this time hearing the proper clack of the door latch catching. Then the microwave thrummed to life. His coffee was properly steaming a minute later as he carried it back to the counter.

Zoe glanced up finally. "Wow, you look awful!"

"Gee, thanks."

Zoe shook her head. "Y'know, S.A.R.A.H. could record the football games and show them to you anytime you want. It doesn't have to be the middle of the night."

"That's what I told him," S.A.R.A.H. agreed.

Carter sighed. "Neither of you get it."

His daughter wrinkled her nose at him and put her hands on her hips. "What, because we're girls, and girls don't get sports?"

Carter knew she was at least half-serious, but the fierce expression on his petite blond daughter made him laugh. "No," he assured her. "Because you're not dumb enough to stay up just to watch some stupid football game." That caught her off-guard and took the wind right out of her sails. Good thing, too—for all that he knew Zoe loved him, he knew better than to stay on her bad side very long.

Besides, right now he didn't have the time for one of their verbal sparring matches. Instead he wolfed down the rest of his food, grabbed his belt, and headed for the door, giving Zoe another kiss as he moved past. "Have a good day, sweetie."

"Thanks, you too." She barely acknowledged his departure, but Carter knew she had a physics lecture today, and he was always proud to see her so focused on doing well. That was his girl—goal-oriented. Even though she was now studying pre-med at Harvard, she'd decided to sit in on a few classes at Eureka's Tesla High during her midwinter break. Apparently even vaunted Ivy League professors couldn't keep up with the science breakthroughs Eureka's high school students came up with every day.

"Have a good day, Sheriff," S.A.R.A.H. said as she opened the front door for him.

"Thanks, S.A.R.A.H. You too."

"Will you be home for dinner?"

"Planning on it," Carter called back as he took the front stairs up into the bunker and out to his car. S.A.R.A.H.

was a little possessive, and she hated it when he canceled on her—when he'd first moved here, that had caused a few problems. But she'd gotten better about it since then.

It was amazing what a state-of-the-art smart house equipped with an adaptive artificial intelligence could learn to put up with.

Besides, Zoe was only home for a week, and he wanted to spend as much time with her as possible before she headed back. He still wasn't used to the idea that his little girl had grown up and left home, even temporarily.

Carter smiled as he opened the door to his Jeep—no need to lock it up around here—and slid into the driver's seat. The sky was clear, the sun was out, the day was still cool, and the breeze was pleasant.

Just another beautiful day in Eureka.

By the time he'd reached his office, Carter was prac-tically trembling with anticipation—and dread. Because you never knew what you were going to get in a town like Eureka. Well, that wasn't really fair, he thought as he parked in the *Reserved for the Sheriff* spot right in front and hopped out of his Jeep. It wasn't like there *were* any other towns like Eureka. At least, he'd never heard of any other towns created specifically to house supergeniuses and let them work undisturbed. Then again, if he had heard of them, the government probably wouldn't be doing a very good job of keeping them secret. He'd discovered Eureka only by accident, when he'd had a car accident just outside the town.

Funny how fate intervened sometimes.

Trying not to think too hard about that—or about the nagging possibility that someone in Eureka could have been messing with fate, because they messed with pretty much everything else—Carter took a deep breath and pulled open the front door. It was reassuringly quiet inside, but that didn't mean much. Most of the town's problems never made it into the sheriff's office. He usually wound up having to go to them.

He passed through the entryway and into the office proper. There was his deputy, Jo Lupo, sitting at her desk. She had her elbows on it and was engrossed in a book— probably something about different ways to kill a man at forty paces with random personal accessories. It was sometimes hard to reconcile her striking good looks with her no-nonsense attitude, and the fact that she was one of the most dangerous people he'd ever met. Fortunately, she liked him.

He thought.

"Morning, Jo," Carter called out as he approached her.

"Morning." She glanced up, gave him her usual tight-lipped smile, and gestured toward his desk. "Coffee?"

"Thanks." This was their tradition. Jo got up before he did—something about morning exercises and a three-mile run—and so she stopped at Café Diem on her way in to work and picked up coffee for them both. That was one thing they shared, along with their obvious devotion to law enforcement—the absolute need for caffeine to get the day started.

The other thing Jo usually had waiting was the first problem of the morning, and as always she was going to make him ask for it. She just couldn't do things the easy way, could she? But then, she wouldn't be Jo if she did.

"Okay, so what's on tap for this morning?" Carter asked, reaching for his coffee and taking a deep, long swig. Ah! Vincent certainly knew how to brew a good cup! "Metal turning to gold? Sunspots showing up in town? Gravity wells under the streets? People taking on whole new personalities? Signals from outer space?"

Much to his surprise, Jo didn't even glance up. "Nothing. All's quiet."

"Quiet?" Carter took another sip of coffee, then perched on the edge of his desk. "Really?"

"Really really."

"There's nothing going on?"

"Not a thing."

"Are you sure?"

That got Jo to look up at last—at least, long enough to give him one of her all-too-familiar *Are you a complete idiot?* glares. Of course she was sure. Jo could do his job ten times over. A fact she'd been trying to convince the town leaders of since before Carter had arrived on the scene. It had taken her some time to get past the fact that he'd been hired over her, and she still needled him about it occasionally. Especially when he questioned her ability.

"Okay, okay," he said quickly, raising both hands to ward off any weapons that might come flying his way. "So it's quiet." He didn't lower his hands until she returned to reading, just in case. "When was the last time that happened?"

"Three and a half years ago," Jo answered absently. Of course she would know. But that was well before Carter's time here, and he whistled softly as he scooted around his desk to sink down into his own chair. Three and a half years! Well, it looked like he'd finally caught a break. Nice! He leaned back, put his feet up, and sipped at his coffee again. A nice quiet day. Perfect.

Two hours later, Carter was going insane.

He'd already checked his e-mail. Four times. He'd gone over the recent arrest logs. Three times. He'd inventoried his desk. Twice. Why did he have seventeen No. 2 pencils, anyway? Was there some sort of test he didn't know about? He'd tried surfing the Internet, but that had never really been his thing—he was much more a go-out-and-toss-a-football-around kind of guy.

"Hey, Jo," he called over to his deputy, "wanna go outside and toss a football around?"

"No thanks." She'd barely moved a muscle since he'd arrived, except to turn a page or take a sip of her coffee. Carter wasn't entirely sure, but he was beginning to suspect that the rest of her body had been turned to stone.

In this town, that would hardly be a first.

"Aw, come on," he pleaded. "I'm sure I can rustle up a football somewhere around here." He had a sudden image of asking Fargo or one of the other eggheads at GD for a football, and the insane high-tech gadgets they might provide as a result, and resolved to only ask schoolkids. Their sports equipment was less likely to develop its own consciousness or attack random passersby. "It'd be fun. Let us stretch our legs, get some fresh air, work up an appetite."

Jo gave him another of her wintery smiles. "I wouldn't want to embarrass you *again*." He remembered how she'd clobbered him in baseball, when they'd started a virtual league shortly after he'd arrived, and shuddered. Why had he kept her on as his deputy, again? Oh, right, because she was perfect.

So what was he doing here?

That led to some thoughts Carter didn't really want to revisit. He'd been a federal marshal before he'd wound up here, and it had been a good job, maybe even a great one. He'd roamed all over the country, chasing down fugitives and working with other law enforcement agencies to coordinate operations. It had been exciting, and active, and dangerous.

And he'd loved every minute of it.

Working in Eureka was a lot like that, only more so. Here the problems were even crazier, because most of them stemmed from some breakthrough in science or technology. In the past two years, he'd seen things he wouldn't have thought possible before, including time travel and parallel dimensions. Every day had put his life in danger, usually in ways he only vaguely understood, and more often than not had risked the entire town as well.

Every single time, he complained about how crazy this town was, how crazy its residents were, and how he was risking his neck for a bunch of eggheads who could reverse-engineer a spaceship but couldn't tie their own shoes.

And every single time, he'd loved it. Not that he'd admit it.

But this —this was different. This was boring. This was . . . normal.

This was what it would be like to be the sheriff of a regular small town. One without geniuses behind every door. One that wasn't run by the military. One that didn't house the world's top research and development facility. One with normal, average, everyday folks.

Just like him.

In a town like that, the biggest problems would be things like hunters going out off-season, and neighbors arguing over property borders, and kids pulling pranks. Normal stuff.

Carter knew it would bore him silly.

What would he do, he wondered, if this quiet day stretched into two? Or three? Or more? What if it became an entire quiet week? Would he be able to cope? Or would it drive him bonkers?

It didn't help that Tess was in Australia. She was happy as a clam at her new job, overseeing the creation of a brand-new state-of-the-art radio telescope, which was great for her, careerwise.

But because she was Carter's first girlfriend since his divorce, it sucked. Big-time.

They'd been going out only a few months before she'd left, but things had been going really well. So well that

Carter found he didn't quite know what to do with himself now that Tess wasn't around. That fact had been partially to blame for his staying up so late the night before—watching sports took his mind off the fact that she wasn't there to share them with him.

At least for a little while.

The ring of the phone startled him out of his gloomy thoughts, and Carter leaped to his feet and scrambled to grab the receiver. Usually it was a battle of wills between him and Jo to see who would break down and answer first, but this time Carter was happy to lose.

"Sheriff Carter," he said as soon as he had the receiver to his ear. "What can I do for you?"

"Sheriff? It's Seth Osbourne," the man on the other end stated, and Carter stifled a groan and mouthed *Osbourne* to Jo, who rolled her eyes. They'd had more than their fair share of run-ins with Seth Osbourne, who dabbled in a variety of cutting-edge technologies and bent or broke rules in all of them.

Still, he was a Eureka resident, which meant he was entitled to assistance. Carter shook his head and cleared his throat. "What can I do for you, Seth?"

"It's that idiot Fargo," Osbourne complained, his voice rising to a whine. "He's messing with me again!"

That might or might not be true. Osbourne and Fargo, who were neighbors, had gotten into several disputes, including one that had endangered the entire town. But Fargo had been leaving things well enough alone lately. And more often than not it wound up being Osbourne who had started the trouble.

Still, Carter was duty-bound to investigate. And at least it was something to do. "I'll be right over," he assured Osbourne. Then he hung up and grabbed his jacket. "Wanna come along?" he asked Jo. He didn't expect her to, though, and sure enough she shook her head. She wasn't any more fond of Osbourne than he was. "Okay, well, hold down the fort until I get back, okay?" That earned a frown, though she didn't actually look up to direct it at him. "Right."

Carter hurried out to his Jeep, eager to be back on the road, even if only for a moment. Anything was better than sitting behind that desk for another hour. He'd started to wonder how many paper clips he had.

CHAPTᵉR 2

Carter pulled the key out of the ignition and hopped out of the Jeep. Seth Osbourne was already waiting for him, arms crossed, and once again Carter marveled at the fact that you could never judge a book by its cover. Tall and broad (and a bit round), with thick beefy arms and jowls and a menacing glower, all Osbourne needed was the too-tight black T-shirt, the jeans, and the club-sized Maglite to be the standard image of a bouncer. Instead he was a scientist, and a brilliant one. Cranky and difficult with a tendency to break the rules—like so many other Eureka residents—but brilliant nonetheless.

"What seems to be the problem, Seth?" Carter asked as he walked over. He noticed that Osbourne's car—a beautifully restored Mustang he'd reconfigured to run on nuclear power cells—was sitting off to one side of the driveway under a dustcover, and he felt a twinge of guilt. The last time he'd been out here it had been to confiscate those same power cells, which Osbourne had resisted turning in despite a GD demand. Of course, someone else had gotten to it first, but Carter still felt bad about being even peripherally involved with shutting down such an awesome car.

"It's Fargo," the heavyset scientist told him. He kept his arms crossed, which meant there would be no welcoming handshake. That was fine. The two of them had never been particularly cordial. Carter did his best to get along with everyone in Eureka—it was part of his job—but some residents were easier than others. "He's at it again."

"Yeah, you said that on the phone. What exactly do you mean by 'at it'?" Privately, Carter was really hoping Osbourne was wrong. He knew Fargo well, better than he knew most of the people here, and though they weren't exactly friends they did associate a lot. And Fargo was frequently very helpful in solving the problems Carter faced. Of course, he'd also been responsible for a few of those problems, but nobody was perfect.

Fargo and Osbourne did have a history, though. Fargo's trailer was just on the other side of Osbourne's property, and the two had gotten into a pretty nasty dispute about noise at one point last year—Osbourne had been blaring opera in the middle of the night to encourage the growth of his experimental plants and had refused to consider his neighbors' attempts to sleep. He'd also ignored Carter's cease-and-desist. The feud had risen to an all-out war, with Fargo sneaking in to sabotage Osbourne's speakers, and the two had actually come to blows—though admittedly that had been at least partially the plants' fault, because their pollen had released people's ids, causing them to act without restraint.

Carter was hoping to avoid such unpleasantness this time around.

But Osbourne was clearly out for blood. "Take a look!" he insisted, and led Carter around to the side of the house—and a field of colorful flowers.

"Oh, come on!" Carter couldn't help saying. "We talked about this, Seth! No more plants, remember?"

"No more *experimental* plants," Osbourne corrected him. "And I haven't. I've stayed entirely in other fields since then." Of course, one of those fields had been biolumines-cence, which had led to some other problems for the town, but Carter decided it wouldn't be politic to point that out just now. "These are just regular plants, entirely for color and fragrance and the natural calming effect such beauty produces." His brow furrowed. "Or at least they were!"

"Okay, then I'm not seeing the problem." Carter studied the flowers. "They all look healthy to me."

"That's not the point! Look at this one! And this one! And that one!" Osbourne was gesturing to one of the rows of flowers, and Carter tried to pay more attention. He re-ally wasn't a plant person. At all. In fact, back when he'd been married, his wife had accused him more than once of having a black thumb. Of course, the fact that she'd never remembered to water the plants might have had something to do with their dying, but try convincing her of that. Any-way, all he could tell was that these were bright and cheer-ful, with pretty yellow petals clustered around a thick stalk, and the smooth-edged leaves were a vibrant green.

"What's wrong with them, exactly?" he asked after an-other minute.

"Are you blind as well as stupid?" Osbourne burst out. This was exactly why they'd never gotten along. "They're *Linaria genistifolia dalmatica*!" Carter just stared at him. "Dalmatian toadflax?" Osbourne threw up his hands. "They're weeds!"

"So you have weeds? That's the big emergency here?" Carter was sure he was missing something, but for the life of him he couldn't figure out what. "What's the big deal? Can't you just pull them and plant something else in their place? And what does this have to do with Fargo?" He

couldn't exactly see the wiry little science geek out here
planting flowers—or weeds. No matter how much he hated
Osbourne.

But Osbourne wasn't about to be pacified. "I *did* have
something else there!" he replied, his volume rising as he
grew more agitated. "I had *Rosa rugosa* there! The entire
row is *Rosa rugosa*!" Now that he mentioned it, Carter did
notice that all the other plants around those three were very
different—they were wider and bushier, with shorter, thin-
ner, serrated-edged leaves, and their flowers were delicate
pale pink blossoms with small light yellow centers. "And
Fargo ruined it!"

Carter held up a hand to forestall any more accusations.
"Look, I can see that these plants are different," he agreed,
then ignored Osbourne's muttered "How astute of you!" and
continued, "but I don't see what any of this has to do with
Fargo. You said these Dalmatian plants are weeds, right?"

"Of course!" Osbourne looked personally offended.
"They're an escaped perennial ornamental from the eigh-
teen hundreds. Highly aggressive." Carter repressed sudden images of these plants breaking out of a greenhouse
and rampaging down the highway, shoving cars out of
their way and beating up pedestrians. No sense borrowing
trouble. This was Eureka, after all—stranger things had
happened. "Once their root system is established, they're
extremely difficult to remove," Osbourne was explaining.
"And most herbicides are ineffective. Though I have a few
that might do the trick."

"Uh-uh," Carter warned him. "The last thing I need is
you killing all the vegetation for a twenty-mile radius!" Osbourne actually had the decency to look embarrassed. "But
I still don't see how or why you think Fargo had anything
to do with this. Couldn't these weeds have simply blown
into your garden and taken root?"

Now the big scientist's discomfort switched to condescension, which was certainly more typical for him. "Do you have any idea what sort of growth cycle *Linaria genistifolia dalmatica* has?" he demanded. "No, of course you don't—look who I'm talking to. I'm surprised you even know they need dirt and water! It would take weeks for a *Linaria genistifolia dalmatica* to reach this height, much less flower. And these weren't here yesterday!"

Carter sighed and scratched his chin. Despite the insults, Osbourne had a point. There was no way the weeds had grown there overnight—well, not no way, but he suspected such phenomenal plant growth would have affected all the surrounding plants as well, and they were all neatly tended. So something had brought these Dalmatian plants here. But Fargo? Why would Fargo replace three of Osbourne's flowers with weeds? As far as Carter knew, the two had been keeping a safe distance from each other since that last incident—why stir up trouble now?

Squatting down, Carter studied the weeds—and the soil around them. "This doesn't look disturbed at all," he commented after a second, tracing the base of one plant with his finger. "The dirt here isn't loose, and there isn't any clinging to the lower leaves." He might not know plants, but he did know evidence. Or the lack thereof.

Osbourne crouched next to him and examined the spot he indicated. "No," he admitted after a second, though he clearly wasn't happy about it. "Whoever did this did a masterful planting job."

"Well, that rules Fargo out," Carter told him, straightening up. This time it was Osbourne who stared, and Carter got to explain. "Oh, think about it! You know Fargo! Sure, he's clever, but he's a total klutz! There's no way he could plant those things there without making a mess—he'd have dirt strewn all over your garden, and tracks everywhere!" He glanced around again just to confirm what he'd already noticed without registering it fully—sure enough, the only fresh tracks here were one set of his boots and several of Osbourne's extra-wide sandals. "You're looking at the wrong guy."

"Well, *someone* did this to my garden!" The beefy scientist insisted. "These plants didn't replace themselves!"

"Are you sure?" Carter asked him. "And are you sure there isn't anything you're not telling me? Like some new plant formula you're testing, or some hybrid seed you're developing?"

"No, of course not. I cultivate these flowers strictly for relaxation." But Osbourne didn't meet his gaze.

"Uh-huh." Carter brushed the dirt off his pant legs. "Well, I'll do some poking around—not literally—and see if any of your *Rosa rugosa* turn up anywhere else, and if anyone's been playing with these Dalmatian plants. But right now I'd say your best bet is just to pull the weeds, plant a few more of those other things, and forget about it."

"It's not that easy," Osbourne muttered as Carter turned to go. "It takes months for them to reach flowering height— though if I altered the formula by adding . . ."

Carter left the big scientist there mumbling to himself and returned to his Jeep. He would keep his ears open, but he had a feeling nothing would come of it. Osbourne had probably let a few of those weeds creep in unnoticed, and then watered them with some super-growth formula he probably wasn't supposed to be messing with, and now he'd rather blame Fargo than admit his own mistake.

Well, Carter thought as he pulled out and headed back to the office, at least it had gotten him out of his chair for a while. Maybe something else had happened while he was gone, something a little more exciting than some random weeds appearing in a garden. But if there'd been real trouble, Jo would have called him.

* * *

On the way back, Carter spotted a tall, lean figure walking along the side of the road. He was wearing tan slacks and a bright blue Hawaiian shirt, and the top of his head glistened in the sun. It was Dr. Baker—or one of the Dr. Bakers, at least. There were several of them, and they all looked exactly alike. In fact, Carter had no idea how many there were—he'd seen at least four of them together at one time, but he often suspected there were more because some days it seemed like everywhere he turned there was a Dr. Baker crossing the street or reading the paper or eating a bagel. It was hard to tell for certain, though, because it seemed like they always dressed exactly the same. Strange.

Carter slowed alongside him and rolled down his passenger-side window. "Morning, Dr. Baker," he called out.

"Morning." None of the Bakers were very talkative. At least not to him.

This one continued walking, and Carter kept pace. He'd already noticed that Dr. Baker wasn't wearing a hat, and in this heat that wasn't a good idea, especially for a man with so little hair. Plus he seemed rather flushed, and his shirt was soaked with sweat. "Out for a little walk?"

"Apparently."

Carter considered that one. Was Dr. Baker being sarcastic? He was used to that from so many of Eureka's residents, but he'd never seen the Bakers employ it, at least not in his direction. And it had actually sounded sincere—less of a *Can't you tell?* and more of an *I guess so.*

After another minute of driving alongside, he decided to make the offer. "Can I give you a ride back to town?"

He was more than a little surprised when Dr. Baker stopped, turned, and gave him a smile. The sunlight winked off his wire-frame glasses. "Thank you, I would appreciate that."

"Well, okay, then." Carter braked and popped the passenger-side lock, and Dr. Baker pulled open the door and slid into the seat, shutting the door firmly behind him. He buckled in conscientiously, and once he was ready Carter started moving again.

"I hadn't planned on taking a walk this morning," Dr. Baker informed him abruptly after they'd been driving a few minutes. "Actually, I thought my brother was taking a walk. That's why I don't have a hat on."

"O-kay." Carter wasn't really sure how else to respond to that. He'd thought his brother was taking a walk, not him? Did they take turns and this one had forgotten it was his day to walk?

"Yes, by the time I realized I was the one walking, I was already outside of town," Baker continued. "There was nothing for it but to walk back. Until you came along." He smiled at Carter again. "Thank you again."

"You're welcome," Carter assured him. He was more confused than ever about the Bakers, but that didn't surprise him. This one walked all the way out of town before realizing it, and that's why he didn't have a hat on? These guys were weird!

Carter tried to ignore the fact that the hair on the back of his neck was standing up. Somehow, in Eureka, whenever he noticed something was weird, it wound up becoming a problem. And usually a dangerous one at that.

CHAPTᵉR 3

"We've got a live one!"

Carter bolted upright from where he'd been dozing, his head nestled on his crossed arms, and looked around. "A live what, exactly?" Around here, a statement like that could mean anything from a metaphor to a sentient fungus to a state-of-the-art android in a box.

But Jo was just hanging up the phone, and she waved the receiver at him before she set it down. "That was Mrs. Allen. Her daughter Nora is missing."

"Nora? Nora Allen?" Carter made his way to Jo's desk and leaned on it, still trying to wake up.

"Yeah, you know her?"

"I do, actually." He dredged his memory. "Or at least Zoe does. Nora was in one of her classes last year. I think she came over once or twice—joint civics presentation or something." He could picture her now, a tall, athletic girl with auburn hair pulled back in a thick braid or a loose ponytail. A bit shy, not at all like Zoe, who could talk to anyone, but nice enough. A good kid. "You said she's missing?"

"Mrs. Allen said Nora went out hiking after school to collect some specimens for botany class," Jo explained, which made Carter glance at the wall clock. Six twenty-three! How had it gotten that late? "She hasn't come home yet."

Carter nodded. Tesla High let out at three thirty, so Nora had been gone for almost three hours. She might just have lost track of time, but it was long enough that he could see why her mom would be worried. "She isn't answering her phone?" Everyone in Eureka had cutting-edge PDAs that included cell phones, video cameras, and several other clever gadgets. They all tied into the central system, providing a cheap and easy way to stay in contact.

"Nope." Jo was already standing up and buckling on her gun belt.

"Okay." Carter shook his head, clearing out the last of the cobwebs. "Do we know approximately where she was going?"

"Her mom said something about the old gorge—apparently Nora thought the repeated cycle of erosion and flooding would produce more interesting plants."

"Well, that sounds like the place to start, then." Carter pushed away from the desk and headed for the door. "Call Taggart and have him meet us out there." He saw Jo nod as he turned away and heard her calling up a number on her PDA. Taggart was Eureka's foremost tracker, an expert on big game and tracking and animals in general. He was nutty even for the rest of the town, or "dashingly eccentric" as he'd referred to himself once, but if anyone could find traces of Nora in those woods it would be him. And if anyone could get him to set aside whatever animal experiments he was conducting these days and come help, it was Jo—the two had dated a while back, and Carter was sure the lanky Australian still harbored feelings for his deputy.

"He's on his way," Jo reported as she joined Carter outside a minute later.

"Good. Hop in—no sense taking both vehicles." Carter unlocked his doors, and Jo slid into the Jeep's passenger seat. He was buckled in and gunning the engine a second later. Missing kids were something he took very seriously.

"She probably got so engrossed in her plant collecting that she didn't realize how late it was until it got dark," Jo commented as they drove. "My bet is she's on her way back right now."

"I hope so," Carter agreed, concentrating on the road as it turned from paved to dirt. "But just in case, we'll look for her."

"Absolutely."

The rest of the drive was silent, and by the time the road petered out into a thin walking trail through the woods Carter was completely keyed up. Every time a kid wound up missing or in danger, he couldn't help thinking, what if it had been Zoe? He knew that was a natural parenting reaction, but he still had to fight against the urge to call and check that she was okay.

A battered old truck was parked up against a pair of nestled tree trunks, and Taggart climbed out as Carter parked right behind it. The scientist-tracker was clad in his usual gear: a mix of camouflage, khaki, and leather, his bush hat pulled down low over his long face. A tranquilizer rifle, complete with scope, was slung over one shoulder.

"G'day, Sheriff!" Taggart called out as they joined him. "Jo." Jo only nodded in reply. Which didn't mean much as far as any feelings she had toward him, Carter knew—he'd seen her behave exactly the same way with Zane, and he knew how deep those emotions ran. But she was in work mode right now, which meant everything was focused on the job at hand.

"Taggart, thanks for your help." Carter offered his hand and got a friendly slap on the back instead. Fine, close enough. "I don't know how much Jo told you, but we're looking for a high school student, Nora Allen. She came out here looking for plant specimens and hasn't returned home yet."

"Right, d'we know what kinda plants she was lookin' for?" Taggart asked.

"Mushrooms and lichen in the gorge," Jo told him.

"Ah, right, I know just the place t'look, then!" Taggart noticed the eyebrow Carter was raising at him, or more specifically at his rifle, and shrugged. "What? Y'never know what you might meet out here," he insisted defensively.

"Well, we're hoping to meet a girl who could be lost and frightened," Carter reminded him. "Let's try not to add to her problems by shooting her, okay?" Taggart nodded, looking a little sheepish, and beckoned for them to follow as he threaded his way quickly and confidently through the trees and vines and underbrush. That was another reason Carter had wanted him here—Taggart probably knew the outskirts of Eureka better than anyone. He certainly loitered out here often enough.

It took them a good fifteen minutes to reach the gorge, and Carter was gasping for breath by the time they stopped. He was used to running, but in some ways crawling and twisting and clambering were more difficult. Jo, of course, didn't even look winded. And Taggart was humming to himself.

The gorge was an enormous slice out of the woods, carved deep and wide so long ago that vegetation had crept in and coated it just like the rest of the ground out here. The foliage was slightly different, however, and between that and the change in elevation, it was easy to see where the gorge began.

"Now, if I were seekin' lichen," Taggart explained over his shoulder, "I'd look along tha' ridge first." He studied their surroundings. "Aha! Look 'ere!" He was tugging at a long stalk of something wheatlike, slender and golden brown. "See how it's been bent? Someone's been 'ere, and within the past six 'ours. I'm guessin' that's our girl."

Carter nodded. "She probably came in the same way we did," he guessed out loud. "It's the easiest way to the gorge if you're coming from the high school."

Taggart had dropped to his knees and was studying the dirt right in front of them, which was dark and moist. "Yep, here's her tracks," he announced, pulling some small creeper vines aside so Carter and Jo could see the crumbling footprints there. "Definitely female. About five foot ten, I'd say, and a hundred and sixty, hundred and seventy pounds. Wearing 'iking boots." That fit what Carter remembered of Nora.

"Great! Any idea which way she went?"

Taggart actually laughed at him. "Oh, now that I've found her prints, I can follow the little darlin', no problem," he stated, grinning as he rose to his feet again. "You leave 'er to me, Sheriff."

Hunched over so he could study the ground more easily, Taggart led them toward the ridge but by a circuitous route. "You're sure you're following a single set of tracks?" Carter asked after they'd circled partway back toward their starting point. "And not a bunch of kids out here spinning in circles?"

"She's not goin' in a straight line, that's for sure," Taggart agreed. "But that's probably about right for a young botanist—she'd keep seein' things she liked even more, so she'd want to get them all." He reached back and patted Carter on the arm. "Not to worry, Sheriff. I'll find 'er."

But ten minutes later, Taggart stopped and scratched his chin. "Well, that's bloody peculiar," he stated to no one in particular.

Carter sighed. "What is?"

"The tracks." Taggart went to a crouch again. "They're not there anymore."

"What, you lost them?"

But the hunter shook his head. "They're not like a pair of slippers, Sheriff. You don't just misplace one." He rested one hand on the ground before him. "Look 'ere." Carter stared where Taggart indicated, and after a second he spotted the footprint half-buried by vegetation. "That's her print, same as the ones I followed 'ere. But look just past it there." Carter looked where Taggart was indicating, but try as he might he couldn't find the tracks.

"I don't see anything," he said after another minute.

"Exactly!" Taggart beamed at him like he'd just won the science fair. "Nothin' to see 'ere. No tracks, no scuff marks, no anything. Her tracks just—vanish. Completely gone."

"So what made them vanish?" Jo asked from her position at the rear. "Could Nora have been testing an invention of her own?" Competition at the science fair could get vicious, and Carter admitted he could see a student working out here to get more privacy. And a device that let you become undetectable and removed telltale signs like footprints? That could be incredibly useful—or incredibly dangerous. The law enforcement officer in him cringed.

It still didn't make sense, though. "She's a good kid," Carter explained, trying to put his doubt into words. "She wouldn't stay out here this long, long enough to make her mom call us—if she really is doing secret experiments, the extra attention is the last thing she'd want. Besides, this is for botany class, right? So unless she's growing a plant that lets you erase your tracks, I don't think that's what she came here for."

Taggart nodded, though he still hadn't looked up from studying the ground. "She'd 'ave erased these other tracks, too, anyway," he suggested. "Why erase 'em at one end and not the other when you could just erase 'em all?"

"So what did happen, then?" Carter crouched down beside Taggart, and Jo moved to the hunter's other side. "Was there some sort of struggle? Did she get hurt? Talk to me, Taggart."

"I'm workin' on it, I'm workin' on it!" Taggart frowned and shifted his weight, pushing yet more foliage aside. "I don't see any signs of struggle, and no—'ang on!" He pulled a low-hanging vine out of the way. "Lookie 'ere!"

Carter stared, and Jo did the same over his shoulder. Where Taggart had indicated, there were more tracks.

Fresh tracks.

Different ones. Larger and heavier.

"That's a man, that is," Taggart told them. "Also about six 'ours ago. The question is, what was he doing all the way out 'ere? There's no sign of a struggle—the two sets don't even meet up! But two people way out 'ere at the same time? You ask me, it's gotta be connected."

Carter nodded, still looking at the footprints. It was highly unlikely Nora Allen had come to the exact same spot as a total stranger, purely by chance. But who did those second footprints belong to, and how did Nora know him? What had she been planning to do when she trekked out here?

"I've got another one!" Taggart shouted, drawing Carter's attention again and indicating another footprint a short distance away. It was more or less pointing back the way they'd come—back toward town.

"So we've got two sets of prints," Carter summarized aloud. "Nora Allen's, which disappear completely right there, and this man's, which just show up right near Nora's last tracks?" He turned to Jo. "Can you follow this new set?"

Jo studied it a second before nodding. "The ground's

still soft, so it took impressions well. Shouldn't be a problem." She started to walk away, then paused and glanced back. "What if whoever this is made it all the way back into town?"

Carter pulled out his keys and tossed them to her. "Take the Jeep," he ordered. "I can get a ride back from Taggart." Now it was his turn to slap Taggart, and the long-limbed tracker's turn to glower a bit. Taggart was very protective of his equipment, including his truck, and hated other people messing anything up. All this despite the fact that the truck was permanently a mess. The Australian was a bundle of contradictions.

"You want us to look for any signs of Nora past this point, yeah?" Taggart asked as Jo took off at a brisk walk back toward the vehicles. "That won't be easy, but I'm game—let's see if this young lady and 'er size nine hiking boots show back up somewhere nearby."

Carter nodded and followed as Taggart stood, brushed himself off, and began walking in wide circles, his back hunched so he could keep his face as close to the ground as possible without stumbling. This looked like it could be a very long evening.

Taggart didn't locate any other tracks, at least not fresh ones, but he and Carter did sweep the area in alternating, ever-widening circles. The good news was, they hadn't seen any blood, which suggested that Nora was fine. The bad news was, they hadn't seen anything to give them any idea where Nora was.

Until suddenly Taggart glanced up from the ground, looked back down, then did a small double take. "Well, well, well," he said, whistling through his teeth. "What 'ave we 'ere?" Carter spun about to see what had affected Taggart so strongly. At first he couldn't see anything but trees and vines and bushes and more trees. Then he heard a crackling noise, like dry leaves underfoot. Shadows shifted a short distance away, and he caught a glimpse of something reddish-brown moving just a little below his eye level.

"Nora?" he called out. "Nora Allen?"

"Yes?" came the reply a few yards away—right where he'd seen that auburn streak.

"It's Sheriff Carter," Carter told her. "Are you okay?"

"Me? I'm fine." A few seconds later, a head appeared behind some of the plants. The rest of her followed shortly thereafter. Nora looked exactly as Carter remembered, if a little sweatier and perhaps a bit flustered. "Sorry about that."

"Sorry about what?"

Nora made her way through the foliage to join them. "I was collecting lichen for a botany project," she explained. "I must have gone farther than I'd realized. Once I noticed that, I started back toward home. It's taken me at least an hour—maybe more like two—to walk this far."

"So you're saying you really did lose track of time?" Carter demanded. "Why didn't you call?" That came out in his "Dad voice," but he couldn't help it.

Now the girl definitely looked embarrassed. "I apparently left my PDA at home," she answered quietly. "Probably in the jacket I was wearing to school today."

Carter nodded. "Well, problem solved," he told her. "We'll call your mom, let her know you're safe, and then get you back home. Just try to be more careful in the future, okay?" She nodded quickly. "Maybe stick to plants in your own backyard for a little while?" That got a small smile out of her, and Carter relaxed further. She looked a little freaked out, and exhausted, but otherwise fine, and if she could smile at one of his lame jokes she was probably okay.

Just then Carter's PDA rang.

"Sheriff Carter," he answered.

It was Jo. "I found the owner of those second tracks," she reported. "It's Karl Worinko." Carter wasn't sure he knew that name. "He's a researcher at GD—alternate fuel cells, mostly. He says he was out on a nature hike and suddenly it was like all the landmarks twisted—the whole world looked different. So he decided to head back to town. It took him less than a third of the time it should have. He didn't see Nora at all, or anyone for that matter. I think he's telling the truth."

"Karl Worinko got back in a lot less time than he'd expected," Carter repeated softly after Jo hung up, careful not to let Nora hear him, "and Nora wound up a lot farther from town than she'd realized." He shook his head. It didn't make any sense, but he had a nagging feeling it should. Or would. Probably at the worst possible moment. That was the way things around here tended to work.

Still, the important thing was that—this time—he could actually give someone a happy ending.

"Mrs. Allen?" Carter said as soon as she picked up. "It's Sheriff Carter. I've got some good news—we found Nora! She's fine, just a little worn out, so I'll give her a ride home. You're welcome. Just doing my job." He listened for another minute, then hung up and turned back to Nora and Taggart.

"Time to head back," he told them both, and received completely different reactions: Nora looked thrilled, while Taggart looked annoyed, though only for a split second. The lanky Australian clearly would have loved to stay out here forever, just roaming the forest. And Carter might have let him stay out here a bit longer, except for one thing—

—Jo had taken his Jeep.

CHAPTᵉR 4

"What, are you kidding me?"

Jo shook her head and hung up the phone. "Nope. Larry says someone stole his car."

"Why?" Carter continued to stare at her from across the room, waiting for her to crack a smile and tell him it was just a joke, but of course she didn't—she just gave him that same little smirk she always did when something stupid came along.

That was one thing Jo did love about being the deputy and not the sheriff—anything she didn't want to handle herself, she could just tell Carter he was the sheriff so it was his responsibility. He'd tried the reverse on her, telling her that because he was her boss he could delegate to her. That hadn't worked so well.

"It's Larry, for Christ's sake!" he continued. "Who'd even want his car?" Larry worked as an assistant at GD, and from what Carter remembered he drove a beat-up old piece of crap.

"Maybe someone just wanted to mess with him," Jo suggested. That Carter could definitely believe. Larry was an annoying little twerp who was rude to anyone he considered his inferior and cloyingly sweet to anyone in a position of authority. But there was one person who hated Larry more than everyone else combined, and Carter and Jo said his name at exactly the same time:

"Fargo."

Fargo despised Larry, and the feeling was mutual—it had grown far worse when, for a brief period, Larry had been given Fargo's job as the GD director's personal assistant. Carter could definitely see Fargo trying to make Larry's life miserable.

But stealing his car? That wasn't really Fargo's style. He'd be far more likely to play some sort of elaborate, high-tech prank. Which would then backfire horribly, and put the entire town in danger. Yes, that was exactly Fargo's style.

And this was the second time in two days Fargo's name had come up connected to a problem. Not that that was anything unusual.

"Where did Larry say his car was when it was stolen?" Carter asked, hauling himself out of his desk chair and heading for the door. So much for a quiet morning—he still ached from yesterday's trek through the woods and had actually been hoping for a little peace and quiet to start the day. No such luck.

"Outside Café Diem." Jo glanced up. "And if you're going that way—"

"I know, I know—a chocolate-dipped raspberry cannoli and a vanilla caramel Vinspresso, double-strong. With whipped cream." Jo nodded and graced him with a slightly wider smile that lit up her face. He sometimes thought Zane was a lucky man. Sometimes.

Carter walked down the block to Café Diem, the town's

café and restaurant. It was a nice morning, and there were plenty of people out and about. He nodded hello to everyone he passed and said hi to those he actually knew. Before this job he'd never realized just how much of local law enforcement was about public relations. As a federal marshal he'd made sure he introduced himself to the local agencies and had done his best to play nice with their agents and officers, but knowing each resident's name? Asking after pets and children and recent injuries? It still felt a little strange sometimes.

Larry was standing outside Café Diem, arms crossed, foot tapping. He looked perturbed, which was a standard expression for him.

"Hey, Larry," Carter called out as he approached. "I hear you misplaced your car. Having a hard time waking up?"

"Yes, very droll, Sheriff," Larry replied impatiently. "I ducked in for a low-fat latte and a whole-wheat bagel with fat-free cream cheese, as I do every morning. When I came out, my car was gone." Sure enough, he had a to-go coffee cup in one hand and a brown paper bag in the other.

"Got it." Carter glanced around. "You're still driving a 1980 Olds Cutlass, right? Maroon exterior?"

"That's right."

"And where exactly were you parked?"

"Right here." Larry indicated the spot right in front of him—which had a car in it already.

Carter glanced at it, then at Larry, then back at the car. But Larry clearly wasn't kidding. "Right there? Where that car is now?"

"Yes."

"How long were you in Café Diem?"

"Barely a minute—Vincent knows what time I get here and always has my order waiting for me." Of course he did. Vincent was a model of efficiency and a marvel at food and drink. He could make anything for anyone and knew every customer's favorites and routines by heart.

Carter closed his eyes and rubbed the bridge of his nose for a second. "So you're telling me that, in less than a minute, someone stole your car—and this car pulled into the space it had left behind?"

"Apparently." Larry glanced at his watch. "Is this going to take long? I cannot be late for work."

"I have no idea," Carter admitted. He examined the car in front of them. It was a recent-model Honda Accord, also maroon, and for a second he considered asking Larry if he'd upgraded and had forgotten about it, but decided to keep quiet. Larry's sense of humor was iffy at the best of times. Instead he pulled out his PDA and dialed the office.

"Jo, it's me," he said after she answered. "Listen, run a check for me—plate number F-E-P-0-5-3-1. It should be a maroon Honda Accord, 2007 or later." He waited while she punched that in. "Got it. Thanks." He hung up and called Allison. "Allison? Hey, it's Carter. Listen, has a Nick Styvers checked in for work yet today? Great, thanks."

"So you know who did this?" Larry demanded as Carter tucked his PDA back in his pocket.

"Not exactly," Carter answered, "but I'm one step closer. Come on—I'll give you a ride."

"Thank you." Larry started toward the sheriff's office but stopped when he realized Carter wasn't following him. "Wait, aren't you parked over there?"

"Absolutely," Carter assured him. "You go on ahead. But if I don't get Jo her morning coffee, she's going to get cranky—and nobody wants that." Not surprisingly, Larry didn't argue.

* * *

Allison Blake met Carter as he and Larry walked
through GD's front doors. As the director of Global Dynamics, she was probably the single most powerful person
in Eureka, and at least partially Carter's boss. She was also
one of his best friends here. Their friendship had even bor-
dered on romance a few times, though that had never led
anywhere. But their feelings for each other aside, Allison
was incredibly organized and concerned about everything
that happened here at GD and in town in general. She knew
that Carter's call about a random employee wasn't simply
idle curiosity.

"What's going on?" she asked as soon as he and Larry
had passed through the security gates.

"It's not my fault I'm late, Director Blake," Larry began
whining immediately. "I'm the victim here!"

Allison looked to Carter for the answer, and he nodded
grudgingly. "His car was stolen, so I gave him a ride."

"That's fine—don't worry about it, Larry." Her tone was
a clear dismissal, and Larry got the message loud and clear.
He went scurrying off, bagel and coffee still in hand, to do
whatever it was he did these days. "Why were you asking
about Nick Styvers? You think he took Larry's car?"

"That's what I intend to find out. Where is he?"

Allison smiled. "On his way here. I figured you'd want
to talk to him."

Carter couldn't help smiling back. "Thanks. Yeah, that'll
make things easier." That was one of the things he'd always
liked about Allison—she went the extra mile to make everyone's life easier. Her predecessor, Nathan Stark—also
her ex-husband, and almost her husband again—had never
done that. At least not for Carter. Their rivalry over Allison aside, Stark hadn't liked the local law sticking its nose
into GD business and had cooperated only as far as absolutely required. Despite which, in the end, he and Carter
had reached a certain amount of reluctant mutual respect.

The fact that Stark had sacrificed himself to save all of Eureka—and possibly the world—on his own wedding day meant Carter couldn't really think badly of him anymore. Well, not much, anyway.

A short, round man with frizzy hair came hurrying across the lobby, lab coat askew, wire-rimmed glasses slightly crooked. "Director Blake, you wanted to see me?"

"Yes, Dr. Styvers." Allison's smile and relaxed posture clearly told the researcher he wasn't in trouble, and he visibly relaxed, though he looked surprised to see Carter standing there. "Sorry to take you away from your lab, but Sheriff Carter has something he needs to speak with you about."

"Of course, happy to help," Styvers agreed. "Sheriff, what can I do for you?"

"You own a 2008 maroon Honda Accord, is that right?" Carter asked. No point beating around the bush. "License plate F-E-P-0-5-3-1?"

"That's correct. Upgraded to hydroelectric power. Completely green." The researcher pushed his glasses back up his nose. "Is there a problem with it? My registration is up to date."

"Did you drive to work this morning?"

"Of course. I got here at seven fifty-eight precisely."

"And have you moved your car since then?"

"Certainly not. I went straight to my lab, entering it at eight oh-nine, and was there until I received Director Blake's summons."

Allison turned to Carter slightly. "Dr. Styvers works in relative chronal physics," she explained. Then, seeing his expression, she added, "Time science. He's very precise."

"I kinda got that." Carter glanced over at the researcher. "Could you show me where you parked your car?"

Styvers looked confused and glanced at Allison, who

nodded. "Of course." He led them out of the building and into the parking lot, down one row—and stopped, mouth falling open.

"That's not my car!"

"No, it isn't," Carter agreed, looking at the beaten-up Olds Cutlass parked there. "But I know whose it is." He sighed. It looked like he'd need to talk to Fargo after all.

"I have no idea what you're talking about," Fargo replied, eyes still intent on the screen in front of him. "Now if you'll excuse me, this experiment is at a critical stage."

Carter stepped forward and put himself between the wiry little scientist and his monitor. "It'll be a lot harder to finish if you're stuck behind bars," he pointed out, though he didn't bother putting an edge to his voice. He actually liked Fargo, despite the trouble he often caused. "Just tell me the truth, Fargo—did you swipe Larry's car?"

"Why would I want to go anywhere near that thing?" Fargo asked, finally giving Carter his full attention. "I try to avoid anything Larry's touched on general principle."

"Well, somebody swapped his car for Nick Styvers's," Carter explained. "And it looks like they did it literally— one car for the other, in exactly the same place."

"Really?" Fargo adjusted his thick black-framed glasses, clearly intrigued now. "That is interesting! Any idea how they did it? I'd love to examine them, see if they have traces of radioactivity or anything else that might provide a clue."

Carter frowned. He hadn't even considered the possibility that the swapped cars could be dangerous somehow. "Do you really think that's a possibility?"

"No, probably not," Fargo admitted after a second. He smiled. "But it would make things more interesting."

"They're already plenty interesting, thank you. So you had nothing to do with it?"

"Not a thing." He could tell Fargo was telling the truth—he was a terrible liar. "But I'd have loved to see Larry's face!"

"Yeah, it was priceless." Carter shook his head. "Okay, thanks." He moved out of the way and headed to the door, but stopped at the last second. "So, any idea how whoever it was managed it? And who it might have been?"

Fargo shrugged, already focused on his experiment again. "Not really. If it's actually matter transference, the list is pretty short—that's real high-end stuff. If it's just someone playing a prank, using something to make the switch without being seen—any number of people. I can put together a list, if you like."

"Yeah, you do that, Fargo. Thanks." Carter wandered back out of the lab and down the hall to Allison's office.

She was sitting at her desk, scrolling through reports on something or other, but minimized them and gave him her full attention as he approached. "Anything from Fargo?"

"He didn't do it," Carter told her. "No idea who did."

"Well, I'm sure you'll figure it out. And at least nobody got hurt."

"No, you're right," Carter agreed. "You're right, I know you're right. It's just—"

"What?"

"I don't know," he admitted. "Something about all this is bugging me. It just feels like there's something bigger going on."

Allison laughed. "You're paranoid, Carter." She didn't say it meanly, however, and after a second she added warmly, "It's what makes you good at your job. But this is probably just a prank. That's all."

"Yeah, I guess." He rubbed the back of his neck, trying

to figure out what about it was bothering him, but nothing came to mind. He was sure it would, though. Eventually.

Carter nodded. "Guess I'll head back to the office, see if Jo's got a kitten in a tree somewhere or something." That got another laugh out of her, and he smiled in return. "See ya." Despite the inanity of the day and the nagging feeling that he was forgetting something, he was in a good mood when he headed back to his car. Talking to Allison tended to have that effect on him.

A part of him had to wonder, though—was this really all his job had become? Silly pranks and little games and foolishness? He'd fought long and hard to get his job back after General Mansfield had fired him, and eventually had (with a lot of help from Henry, and a surprising assist from his temporary replacement, Sheriff Andy, as well). Now he was starting to wonder if coming back had been the right choice after all. This sort of thing was exactly what most people would expect a small-town sheriff to spend his time handling, and that would make perfect sense. Anywhere but Eureka. It had been only a few days, but Carter was already starting to get bored with these mundane little situations. He knew Sheriff Andy probably would have been perfectly content to handle stolen cars and missing kids. Of course, for a cutting-edge robot, Sheriff Andy was surprisingly happy to put up with the most deadly dull assignments possible. Apparently no matter how high-tech it is, a robot is still a robot, and deadly dull isn't a problem for a machine. But Carter wondered how long he could be happy handling such minor problems.

Still, he had to admit it was nice to have a break from life-threatening emergencies. Sheriff Andy had quit because he'd decided Eureka was too dangerous for him—a robot that could repair itself from almost any injury, lift cars barehanded, and channel a couple of million volts of electricity without lasting damage! Andy had wanted something quieter and safer. Carter laughed at that, his good mood returning. Leave it to him to take the job a robot felt was too risky! Made you wonder which one of them had the faulty wiring, didn't it? He was still chuckling about that as he drove away.

CHAPTᵉR 5

Carter wasn't smiling that evening, however. He was groaning.

"Oh, come on!" he said to Jo, his voice shifting up to a whine. "This is getting ridiculous!"

"You want some help on this one?" his deputy asked, rising from her chair and grabbing her gun belt. "I wouldn't mind getting out of the office myself for a bit."

"Sure, why not?" Carter was still grumbling as they headed for the door. "But really, this is just silly. Stealing a car I can see, though using"—he glanced at his PDA and the text Fargo had sent him a little while ago—"a portable hologram generator to mask the vehicle so no one notices the exchange still sounds like overkill to me. But 'overkill' might as well be Eureka's middle name, so I guess that fits." He shook his head. "But stealing a carport?"

"It is more of a challenge," Jo pointed out. "Cars are easy—you hot-wire them and go." The way she said it,

Carter was sure she'd seen her fair share of auto theft, presumably from her days before the military, but he didn't pry. Prying with Jo was a risky business. "Carports? Tricky."

"Yeah, great, so we've got a thief who likes to stretch himself," Carter muttered. "Where're you going?" That was because Jo had turned toward her own car instead of toward his Jeep.

"I figured we should each drive," she told him, opening her door and sliding in with that same deadly grace that fascinated so many of the men in Eureka. "This time there won't be a Taggart to drive you home if we have to separate." The grin she gave him said clearly that she knew how much he'd hated having to get that lift yesterday, but she had a point, so Carter just gave her a token laugh and let her go. A minute later he was right behind her.

"Hey, Aaron," Carter called as he pulled up at the address and hopped out of his Jeep. Aaron Finn was standing there waiting for them.

"Sheriff, good to see you again, though I can't say I'm happy with the circumstances," Finn replied, stepping forward to shake Carter's hand. He repeated the gesture with Jo. "Deputy Lupo."

"Mr. Finn." Carter wasn't surprised that Jo knew Finn—she seemed to know everyone in town, whereas even after two years he was still learning names and faces. But he and Finn had met before, when there'd been a problem involving space debris and a high school science project gone horribly out of control. Finn was an astronomer at GD and had been the high school science fair winner almost ten years before. That prestigious award had apparently been the high point of his career, though since their meeting Allison had privately told Carter that Finn was showing more enthusiasm and initiative again. Tall and slender and sandy-haired, Finn was a quiet man, and it was only the slight furrow of his brow behind his glasses that revealed how annoyed he was right now.

"So this is it?" Carter asked, studying the carport. "Or rather, isn't it?"

He could already see the problem. Finn's house was much like the man himself—tidy, carefully tended, not pristine but well maintained. The carport, however, was a completely different story. It was barely standing, two of its support beams askew, rot visible all around the edges, the roof barely held together, the ceiling buckling. It was a disaster.

"Definitely not," Finn confirmed. "I actually wouldn't care so much except that I just finished remodeling my garage—new diamond-plate flooring, corkboard walls, retractable storage bins and bike racks, solar cell lighting, the works." He glanced down at his hands. "It's part of my attempt to clean up and move forward."

"Makes sense," Jo agreed, glancing at Carter. "An orderly home is the reflection of an orderly mind, and restoring one can rejuvenate the other." Carter wasn't surprised at her statement. He'd never seen Jo's house, but if it was anything like her desk at work it was immaculate, everything precisely in its place. Once military, always military. Personally, he liked a little bit of clutter, though he could never convince S.A.R.A.H. of that.

"So, can you get my garage back?" Finn asked them. "And get this . . . thing . . . removed somehow?"

"Well, let's concentrate on finding your garage first," Carter warned him. "Though I can't imagine they got very far with it." As often happened, neither of his two listeners smiled at his joke. "Okay, Jo, we'll need to canvass the town, look for—"

"I know where it is," Jo interrupted. She loved doing that.

"You do?"

"Absolutely." His deputy gestured at the pathetic carport in front of them. "I recognize this structure. It belongs to Victor Arlan. Or at least it did."

Ah. That explained the carport's sad condition. Victor had been GD's storage vault supervisor, maintaining the secure containment area where GD kept all its old failed experiments. Unfortunately, he had also been pocketing devices and selling them on the side. They'd discovered his larceny while trying to save Fargo's life—ironically because Victor, afraid someone would realize what he had been doing now that he was retiring and the vault was being shut down, had planted a device on Fargo to use him as a scapegoat and Fargo, being Fargo, had turned the thing on instead—and Victor had been arrested and removed from Eureka to serve time in prison. Eureka's very existence was classified, and stealing anything from it, even failed experiments, was considered the theft of classified military technology. Needless to say, Victor wasn't coming back anytime soon.

"Okay, so you figure if Victor's carport is here, Aaron's garage must be at Victor's house." Jo nodded, though of course she couldn't resist giving him that *You just figured that out?* look.

"We'll check and make sure," Jo was assuring Finn.

"Great! Thanks!" Finn scratched his head. "But how are you going to get it back here?"

"One step at a time," Carter answered. "Let's make sure we have it first. Then we'll talk to Henry, see what we can come up with. Okay?" Finn nodded and shook hands with both of them again as Carter and Jo returned to their respective vehicles. It was easy enough to call up Victor Arlan's address. Jo already knew it, of course. And, not surprisingly, she beat Carter there.

"You know, it's not really an emergency," he told her as

he joined her in front of the abandoned house. "You don't need to speed. Or run the siren."

She responded with a playful hip check. "You're just annoyed that I won." Which was probably true.

They both studied the house. It was a nicely built wooden structure, a two-story A-frame that blended into its surroundings. Now probably more than its builders had intended.

"Youch, this place has seen better days," Carter commented.

"That's the problem with wooden buildings," Jo agreed. "Leave them untended for even a few months and they start to fall apart. This one's been untouched for almost a year now, and I suspect it was in need of repair even before that."

It showed, too. The exposed wooden frame had obvious rot, the front deck was crumbling to pieces, and one of the windows had cracked, most likely as the frame bore down upon it.

The house's wretched appearance stood in stark contrast to the pristine garage beside it. The garage was squared and solid, with a weathered but clean brick exterior. Its door was up, and they could see the gleaming metal floor inside and the tools and equipment and bikes all neatly stacked and stored. It was like night and day.

"I'd say we found Aaron's garage," Carter declared. He sighed. "Why don't you go let him know, and then head back to the office? I'll go check in with Henry, see what we can do to return this place to its rightful owner." He rubbed the back of his neck, thinking.

Jo nodded, and they parted ways.

As he headed to Henry's garage, Carter thought about the events of the last few days. First Seth Osbourne's flowers, then Nora Allen and Karl Worinko, then Larry's and Dr. Styvers's cars, and now Aaron Finn's and Victor Arlan's garages. There was definitely a pattern developing here, and he didn't like the shape it was starting to take. It was beginning to look less and less like random pranks and more like a planned progression. What would be next, whole houses? That was crazy, he knew, but in Eureka *crazy* didn't mean *impossible*. At best it meant *unlikely*. At worst, it meant *so much worse than you could possibly imagine*.

He hoped this wasn't one of the latter.

Pulling up outside Henry's garage, which was also his machine shop and lab, Carter was relieved to see Henry's fire truck parked outside. Henry Deacon was the town's mayor, but also its mechanic, fireman, coroner, and basically any other job no one wanted to handle. He was a brilliant man, a top-notch scientist, an eclectic genius—and Carter's best friend in Eureka.

"Henry? You in here?" Carter opened the door and stuck his head inside cautiously. You never knew what someone might be working on in this town, and Henry's interests were even more varied than most.

"Over here, Jack!" For once, Henry was actually doing what the garage supposedly did all the time—fixing a car. Only his legs, clad in his "work" uniform of grease-spattered coveralls, were visible beneath the vehicle, but he slid out as Jack walked over, and accepted a hand up. Pulling off his cap and shaking his head to let his short dreads loose, Henry smiled and patted the car's hood.

"Good as new," he proclaimed proudly. "Just a clogged fuel line. Sometimes it's nice to work on the little things. Now, what can I do for you?"

"Did you hear about Aaron Finn's garage?" Carter asked, following Henry as he moved to the utility sink to wash the grease and oil off his hands. News sometimes traveled obscenely fast in Eureka, so Carter was almost surprised when Henry shook his head. "Well, it's been moved."

"Moved?" Henry dried his hands off and then led Carter back over to the nest of computers and scanning equipment that served as his office. "Moved where?"

"To Victor Arlan's old place."

"Really?" Henry perched on one of the stools clustered there, and Carter did the same. "Who moved it?"

"I have no idea," Carter admitted. "Nor do I have any idea how. And it's not the first time, either." He explained about the other recent switch, and about the incident with Nora Allen and Karl Worinko, then the one with Seth Osbourne's flowers, and how it had occurred to him that they might all be connected. "Seems to me they're getting worse."

"Well, certainly bigger, anyway," Henry agreed. "Matter transference is no laughing matter."

"Thank you!" Carter banged his hand on the worktable. "I've been saying that, but both Jo and Allison think these are just harmless pranks!"

"They may be," Henry warned. "At least, nobody's gotten hurt yet, and they're things that can be easily put back to their proper locations. But there's a difference between harmless and unimportant." He frowned. "I'd be a lot less worried if it were only inert matter, like cars and garages. The fact that both plants and people have been moved, however—that worries me."

Carter leaned forward. He could guess what his friend was thinking. Not too long ago Henry had faked a biological emergency at GD to set up a situation where he could sever the link between Allison's autistic son, Kevin, and the alien device known only as the Artifact—a link that was killing Kevin. Henry had deduced that the only way to cure Kevin was to rebuild his body, cell by cell, and map it on his original DNA patterns before they were altered by the Artifact. To do that, he needed the SRT, or Subatomic Reconstructive Transport, a teleportation device that had been built at GD and placed in the director's emergency bunker as a last-ditch escape route. The SRT had worked and Kevin had been saved, though Henry had been jailed for fabricating a catastrophe.

"That thing was destroyed, wasn't it?" Carter asked quietly.

"It was decommissioned," Henry corrected. "Not fully destroyed. But yes, it should still be offline. I hope." He was still frowning. "That's the only device I know of that can transport people intact, however."

Something on the worktable buzzed, and Henry rummaged through some papers and circuit boards and wires until he came up with his PDA. When he saw the screen, he leaped up from his stool. "Is that the time? I've got to go!"

"What's the big rush?" Carter asked, following as his friend grabbed a jacket from the coat rack and pulled open the main door. "Hot date?" He immediately wished he hadn't said that—the love of Henry's life, Kim Anderson, had been killed in a tragic accident less than a year ago, and he knew Henry still grieved.

But to his surprise, Henry smiled. "Yes, as a matter of fact! With Vincent and Fargo. We're watching an advance screening of that new science fiction movie, the one set on that alien planet! Care to join us?"

Carter laughed. "No thanks, I get enough science fiction around here to suit me plenty. Try to keep the noise down though, okay?" The guys got a little carried away sometimes, and around here a "killer sound system" really could be a killer!

"Not a problem," Henry assured him. "And I'll think on ways to get Aaron back his garage, too. We'll come up with something. 'Night, Jack!"

"'Night, Henry." Jack laughed as he climbed back into his Jeep. The garage—and other questions—could wait until tomorrow. It had wound up being a long, strange day, which was nothing new, and right now he just wanted to go home, grab some dinner, spend some time with Zoe, and maybe watch a game on TV. They'd sort out the rest in the morning.

CHAPTᴱR 6

"La vendetta, oh, la vendetta! È un piacer serbato ai saggi. L'obliar l'onte e gli oltraggi—"

BLARK! CLANG! THHHHRRRRUMMMMM!

"What the bloomin' 'ell?"

Taggart startled upright, yanking the headphones off his ears as he blinked and glanced around. He'd been listening to *The Marriage of Figaro*, one of his favorites, when suddenly Bartolo's beautiful aria had been interrupted by that—noise. Had something corrupted his digital recording somehow? That would be a shame—it was from the 1981 London Philharmonic version, with George Solti directing, and he considered it one of the finest versions ever performed of the Mozart opera. But as his eyes adjusted after being closed for so long, Taggart realized the purity of his beloved music might in fact be the least of his problems.

When he'd closed his eyes perhaps twenty minutes ago, he had been at home, reclining in his favorite chair, unwinding by listening to opera before having dinner. Now, however, he found himself in completely different surroundings. Gone was his cherrywood paneling, his top-flight stereo system, his collection of Impressionist watercolors, his Oriental rugs. Gone, too, were his ergonomic zero-gravity relaxation chair and his Bose headphones. Instead he found himself sitting in what, unless he missed his guess, was a Herman Miller Aeron chair, a cheap pair of headphones now dangling from his hands as he stared at a dizzying array of computer monitors and parts mounted to a tall desk like some sort of techno-flower.

Taggart levered his long frame out of the chair and studied the computer collection more closely. He recognized some of the monitors and hard drives and servers, but others were unfamiliar, and more than a few looked like they'd been hand-built. All of them were high-end, however, and all of them were currently on. He counted at least four simulations running simultaneously, though he couldn't begin to guess what they were about—Taggart was a renowned animal geneticist, but this looked like theoretical physics and that was something he'd never been able to wrap his brain around. Give him animals and recombinant DNA over string theory any day!

But what was he doing here? He glanced around, studying the rest of this unfamiliar room. The decor was grad student at best, a mismatched assortment of cheap furniture clearly purchased simply to fill space and serve a basic function. The walls were bare or covered in sprayboard, and both surfaces bore scribbles and notations and lengthy computations. A rough, unbound carpet covered the floor, the kind you bought from a rug company because it'd been miscut and so was sold at a discount. Everything about this place screamed that the owner didn't care what it looked like, only that it fulfilled the basic needs and provided shelter for his work.

But who was the owner? And how had Taggart wound up here instead of at home?

The room had a set of sliding wooden doors and a regular paneled wood door. Taggart ignored the sliding ones—those were almost certainly a closet, and he shuddered to think what he might find lurking behind them—and tried the other door instead. It wasn't locked and led to a short hallway. From there he discovered a bathroom, a kitchen, and a bedroom.

The bedroom was where he thought he'd find the most answers, so that was the room Taggart examined first. Besides, the smell from the kitchen had been horrifying, a mixture of old burnt coffee, moldy food, and stale bread. Obviously whoever lived here didn't do much cooking. Or entertaining.

Entering the bedroom, Taggart saw that the decorating motif matched that of the computer room. The bed looked decent enough but plain, the sheets and blankets and pillowcases were mismatched, there was a lone nightstand that actually looked like it was probably a nice piece of furniture under the garish green paint someone had splashed on it, and a rickety dresser stood against the far wall. Clothes were strewn everywhere, mostly T-shirts and sweatshirts and jeans, and Taggart selected a shirt and held it against himself. Hm. Shorter than he was by several inches, but possibly a bit broader. Not that that narrowed the field much, he admitted as he picked his way through the piles toward the nightstand—he was one of the taller and skinnier people in Eureka.

Scattered across the nightstand were tissues, loose change, Post-it notes, crumpled business cards, old mints—clearly the owner emptied his pockets and just left the debris to accumulate there. A stack of magazines sat below that detritus, all of them scientific in nature—most seemed to focus on mathematics, physics, or computing, but a few were on chemistry and even genetics instead. So the owner had broad interests. And a short attention span, from what Taggart had seen before. He flipped over one of the magazines, but there was only a GD address label on the back. Damn! He'd been hoping for a name, but these were just part of GD's general subscription base to all major scientific magazines, and those could be borrowed by any GD employee at any time.

Since the nightstand was a bust, Taggart switched to the dresser. More magazines and several books occupied its top, none of which were any help. With a sigh, Taggart resigned himself to invading his mysterious host's privacy still further and pulled open the topmost drawer. The clothing stuffed within didn't look any cleaner or neater than the articles strewn about the floor, but he ignored that and began rooting through it, checking for anything that might give him a clue as to where he was and whose home he was in.

It was the third drawer that finally yielded an answer. "A-ha!" Taggart said softly, yanking a photo out from under a snarl of socks and holding it up to the light. The picture showed a man and a woman standing together, most likely married by their stance and proximity, with several other people arrayed around them. She was short and buxom and had black hair and straight features, while he was taller, with dark skin and short dark hair and a heavy brow. Many of the children clustered around them looked like theirs, but Taggart immediately zeroed in on a second man standing just to the woman's side. Average height and build, with short black hair and the same straight features, a broad grin showing amid the stubble, he was immediately recognizable.

Zane Donovan.

GD's current wunderkind. And Jo's current boyfriend.

"Great," Taggart muttered, shoving the photo back under the socks and slamming the drawer shut. He looked around the explosion of a room again. "She left me for this?"

"—è bassezza, è ognor viltà. Con l'astuzia . . . coll'-arguzia . . . col giudizio . . . col criterio—"

"What the hell?"

Zane sat up, yanking the headphones off, blinked—and stared.

"Oh, this can't be good," he muttered.

Where the hell was he? He'd been working on that static phase-testing array Allison had asked for, listening to some atonal technopop while he let the latest simulation run, and suddenly his music had been replaced by—opera?

But the music wasn't the only thing that had changed.

It took him a second to clamber out of the chair he found himself in, because it seemed permanently locked in a full horizontal state, and then Zane forced himself to breathe deeply and examine his surroundings.

It was like being in one of his professors' houses back in school. Or some of his ex-girlfriends' parents' places, for that matter. The rich ones.

He was in a living room, obviously. But it was the kind you only saw in movies about rich and famous people, elegant people with taste and the money to satisfy it. There were beautiful paintings hanging on the wood-paneled walls, fine carpets on the floor, handsome leather furniture, shimmering curtains, and soft lighting. The music was pouring from a pair of expensive headphones connected to a stereo system that looked like it probably cost an entire year's pay—and GD wasn't exactly stingy with salaries for its top employees.

And what was that smell? Zane glanced to the left, where the room continued into an equally impressive kitchen.

Food sat cooking on the stainless steel stove, and the aroma drew him toward the pots and pans, his mouth watering. Was that chicken tetrazzini? It certainly looked—and smelled—like it! So whoever's place this was, he or she was an excellent cook as well as a classical music buff. And an art collector.

And a wine connoisseur, Zane added, noticing the refrigerated wine rack taking up one corner of the kitchen. The thing was massive, as big as the stainless fridge standing nearby, and through its glass doors he could see the rows of wine waiting in their neat wooden racks. He'd known a few people who collected wine seriously enough to have one of these, but he couldn't think of who in Eureka might be that hardcore. Vincent, maybe? He was a foodie, certainly, but surely he'd just cook at Café Diem if he wanted to make something fancy? Allison? Zane wouldn't put it past her to love good food and fine wine, but when would she ever have the time to cook? And this place showed no signs of children, so that seemed out—he was sure she had Kevin's drawings and photos up all over her house.

So whose home had he found himself in? And how?

Zane paced through the kitchen, examining everything, and resisting the urge to sample the food or the bottle of Chardonnay waiting open nearby. There was only one glass with the bottle, he noticed, which meant whoever it was lived alone. And clearly wasn't here right now. He studied the fridge, which had several notices and notes and papers tacked to it, and then spotted a photo among them—and froze.

"Oh, no way," he whispered.

But photos didn't lie. Usually. And there was no mistaking this one. That was Jo—*his* Jo—standing there grinning. And next to her, with one long arm draped possessively over her shoulder and a goofy grin on his long face—

—was Jim Taggart.

"That can't be right," Zane muttered. He looked around again. This place was Taggart's? How was that possible? Taggart was a tracker and an animal nut—well, a bit of a nut in general, really. He seemed happiest wallowing in the mud or crawling through bushes, rifle in hand, covered in dirt and grime and bugs. How could a man like that have a home like this?

But the photo clearly belonged to the home's owner. And Zane knew this place wasn't Jo's—he'd spent enough time at her place to be sure of that.

Well, whatever, Zane decided. He knew where he was now. He'd never been to Taggart's place, of course—the tall Australian still held a grudge for his stealing Jo away—but he had a rough idea of where it was in town. Which meant he could get home from here.

Shaking his head, Zane started toward the door. Then he stopped. Quickly, he hurried back over to the stove and lowered the burners to simmer. Then he made his way out.

Taggart had left Zane's house and, once outside, got-ten his bearings quickly. They lived almost on oppo-site sides of Eureka, so it seemed quickest to cut straight through downtown. He was a block from Café Diem when he spotted Zane walking toward him.

Zane saw Taggart at the same time and stiffened slightly. If he'd been in Taggart's home, had Taggart been in his? And if so, what had the Australian thought about it—and what had he learned?

The two men approached each other warily.

"Zane," Taggart called out, stopping a few paces away.

"Taggart."

They eyed each other for a second without speaking.

"I turned down the flames," Zane said finally. "Didn't want your dinner to burn."

Taggart nodded. "Thanks, mate—I appreciate that."

"I take it you were—" Zane didn't finish the question, but he didn't really have to.

"Yeah." Taggart glanced back the way he'd come. "No idea how or why, though. You?"

"Not a clue. I'll look into it, though. First thing to-morrow."

"Right." They stood there a little bit longer, neither sure what to say. The subject of Jo hovered uncomfortably be-tween them, as did the new knowledge they each had of the other.

For his part, Zane now knew how much more there was to Taggart than the face he presented to the world at large. Clearly the man was a lot more complex than he'd realized. And that explained a lot about why Jo had been with him.

On the other side, Taggart was even more confused—but simultaneously more impressed. Zane was an utter slob, and yet Jo had chosen him anyway. Which suggested that the young man had other qualities to offset such poor living conditions. Because Jo was nothing if not an as-tute judge of character, and she wasn't about to settle for second-best at anything.

"Did you—?" Zane started, then stopped. "I mean, while you were—I suppose you—?"

"Yeah, I did," Taggart admitted. "Sorry, mate—needed to know where I was, which meant findin' out whose place I was in."

"Right. Yeah, of course."

"I put it back where I found it," Taggart assured him. He took a step closer and lowered his voice. "But some friendly advice? Family's too precious to hide away in a sock drawer."

Zane found he couldn't reply past the lump in his throat, so he just nodded again. Taggart returned the gesture, then stepped past him and continued on home. After a second Zane did the same. He was eager to check on those simulations, and eager to put this strange encounter behind him. But somewhere inside he knew that he'd never look at Taggart the same way again, and that the man had now risen in his estimation—as much for that last friendly gesture as for the state of his home.

CHAPTER 7

"Hm. What?" Zoe rolled over, grimaced, tried to get comfortable again, and finally gave up. "S.A.R.A.H., lights," she mumbled, stretching and stifling a yawn. There was no reply, however, and the room stayed dark. "S.A.R.A.H., lights!" Still no answer.

Now Zoe was wide awake. She hopped out of bed, threw on the clothes she'd laid out for today, ran a brush once through her long blond hair, pulled it into a quick ponytail, and raced downstairs. Her watch read eight fifteen, ten minutes past when she had planned to wake up for school, but the whole house was dark, cold, and quiet. Usually by this time S.A.R.A.H. had the lights coming up—gradually, to let Zoe's eyes adjust—Zoe's favorite radio station playing, and, if Zoe's dad had already left for work, coffee brewing. If he was still here, it was tea or hot cocoa. There were definite perks to living in a fully automated house, things she missed at Harvard. But this morning Zoe didn't see, hear, or smell any of those, and it had her worried.

"S.A.R.A.H.?" she called as she reached the living room. "Is everything okay?"

"I'm sorry, Zoe," S.A.R.A.H. finally answered, and Zoe relaxed a little. But only a little, as the house continued, "We are in full lockdown mode. Only essential functions are active, and only defensive commands will be acknowledged."

"Right." Zoe frowned, took a deep breath, and marched over to the far wall. There she opened a small panel, reached inside it, and pulled a lever. A portion of the ceiling slid open, and a ladder dropped down. Whew! At least she could still get out! After the time that S.A.R.A.H. had somehow been replaced by an earlier, military-grade personality and had locked several people inside, Carter had installed a manually operated ladder and ceiling hatch. Zoe had been on the outside at the time, and the altered S.A.R.A.H. had almost vaporized her. Zoe was glad she wouldn't have to go through that again.

"I'll go find Dad," she assured the house as she started up the ladder. "He'll fix it." That was his job, after all—being sheriff in Eureka meant fixing all the strange problems that occurred as a result of being in an entire town of eccentric geniuses. Of course, in this case he would probably call Fargo, who'd designed S.A.R.A.H., and tell him to get his scrawny butt over here to take care of the situation. But whatever worked.

Zoe reached the top of the ladder, stuck her head through the hatch—and froze. This wasn't S.A.R.A.H.'s surface bunker! Instead she was looking into a cramped space, long but narrow, with a low roof and a single window on each of the two long sides. A freezer took up the entirety of the far wall, and the near one had some sort of grill and what looked like a soda machine.

And there was someone else in here.

He looked to be about Zoe's age, skinny with spiky black hair, acne, and several piercings. His hat and apron had *Burger Run* printed on them, with a logo of a burger on wheels. He was sitting on the floor, arms around his knees, quivering slightly. When he saw Zoe, he jumped, and she could see he was holding back tears. She'd never seen him before, and her dad hadn't said anything about anyone new moving to Eureka while she was in college, which in a town this size meant the guy definitely wasn't from here.

But first things first. Now that she was safely above-ground, Zoe was able to put her own fear aside. This kid, however, looked like he was still ready to freak out at any second. And who could blame him?

"It's okay," she assured him, climbing the rest of the way into the little room. "It's going to be okay." She gave him a friendly smile, the same one she'd turned on the patrons at Café Diem when she had been waitressing there. "I'm Zoe, by the way."

Then she pulled out her PDA.

Carter had just settled in behind his desk, coffee in hand, when his phone rang. He checked the Caller ID and smiled.

"Good morning, sweetie," he said as he answered the call. "Welcome back to the land of the living! Guess you hit the books pretty hard last night, huh?"

As Carter listened to his daughter, however, the smile disappeared from his face. "Don't move," he urged her, already up from his chair. "I'll be right there."

"Problem?" Jo asked, glancing up from her monitor across the room.

"Yeah," Carter replied, grabbing his coat, his coffee,

and his keys. "Zoe's got herself a situation. I'll fill you in when I know more."

"I'll just take care of things here, then, shall I?" Jo called after him, but Carter was in too much of a hurry to reply.

"Oh, this can't be good," Carter muttered as he turned off into what should have been his own driveway. But wasn't. Normally this was a stretch of grass with a patch of bare dirt in the middle, leading up to the bunker that was S.A.R.A.H.'s surface appearance—the automated house was actually belowground. And, unless something special was going on, the only cars here when he pulled in were Lexi's and Zoe's.

Not this time.

Instead Carter found himself pulling off the road and into . . . a parking lot. A typical asphalt parking lot, complete with paint marking the spaces. And cars filling many of those spaces. Cars with Idaho plates, he noticed.

But Eureka wasn't in Idaho. The town was in Oregon.

The cars were the least of his worries right now, though. Because S.A.R.A.H.'s bunker was also missing. In its place was a tiny fast-food joint, the kind that only offered drive-through because there wasn't any place to sit or even to walk up to a counter. It had a sign above it, a cartoon of a hamburger on wheels, clearly racing somewhere. Across that were emblazoned the words *Burger Run*.

Burger Run? Carter pondered that as he pulled his Jeep right up next to the place, shut off the engine, and climbed out. He'd seen the small chain once, back when he'd been a federal marshal. Good burgers, actually, and great curly fries. Pathetic milk shakes, though.

But Burger Run was strictly statewide—he'd checked after that first visit, the fries had been that good.

Still, that was all secondary. His first concern, as always, was—"Zoe!"

"Dad!" Carter felt his guts unknot as his daughter's heart-shaped face popped up in the drive-through window. "I'm okay!"

Carter stepped over to the window. "What happened, honey?" He glanced inside and saw the boy huddled in the corner. "And who are you?"

"Bobby—Bobby Markess," the boy answered quickly, climbing to his feet. He looked relieved, which wasn't surprising—people in trouble often reacted like that to the uniform. It meant they were safe and could let Carter take charge. Too bad most of Eureka's residents didn't see things that way.

"You work here, Bobby?" Carter kept his voice friendly but concerned. The kid was clearly terrified. He also wasn't anybody Carter knew, and after two years he knew most of Eureka's residents—and after almost two years of Zoe attending Eureka's Tesla High, he could at least recognize most of her fellow students. That, plus the license plates and the restaurant name, suggested that Bobby was a long way from home. He'd have to break the news gently.

"Yes, sir. Six months now."

"And—I know this is going to sound completely crazy— but where is 'here,' exactly?" Carter held up a hand. "Humor me."

"Burger Run," Bobby answered slowly.

"I know that. I meant, where is this particular Burger Run located?"

"Oh. Cedar Point Mall." When Carter motioned him to continue, Bobby broke into an uneasy grin. "Boise, Idaho. This is a joke, right? Or one of those hidden camera shows?"

Carter sighed. "Something like that." Then he turned

back to Zoe. "So you woke up and this was just here instead of the bunker?"

Zoe nodded. "S.A.R.A.H.'s in full lockdown mode. I used the ladder."

"Good girl." Carter glanced around. "What about your aunt?" Lexi had shown back up a few days ago, appearing out of the blue as usual for a quick visit. Her boyfriend, Duncan, wasn't with her—apparently he was helping with some epidemic the CDC was handling—and though it was nice to see Lexi again, she always created a whirlwind of chaos around her. Still, she was his sister and he loved her, which was why, when he saw the look of horror creeping onto Zoe's face, he felt his stomach clench again. "Zoe? Where's Lexi?"

Just then, Carter's PDA rang again. He snatched it out of his pocket and clicked it on even as he raised it to his ear. "Lexi? Is that you?" He turned away from the booth window so he could focus. "Yeah, I know. I know. You okay? Don't worry about that right now. Are you okay? Good. Yeah, Zoe's fine—I'm here with her. Look, I'll figure it out, okay? I will—you know I will. What I need you to do is just stay put." He sighed. "No, probably not in the middle of the parking lot. Yes, the mall would be a better choice. Fine. Go in there, find the food court"—he turned back toward Bobby, who nodded—"find the food court, get something to eat, and stay there."

Something occurred to him. "Where did you get a phone?" She explained and he sighed. "Yes, that was very nice of him. You can return it now. When you get to the food court, find a pay phone—call me and give me the number, then stay by it. Yes, I know you can probably get back here on your own, but I don't want to take any chances. I'll come and get you, or send somebody to get you, as soon as I can. Okay? Okay." He hung up.

"Is she okay?" Zoe asked immediately.

"She's fine," Carter assured her. "She was leaving S.A.R.A.H. this morning when everything got blurry and she got dizzy. When she recovered, she was in the middle of a mall parking lot somewhere, and the bunker was sitting on solid ground—fortunately she was already up the stairs, because I don't even want to think about what would've happened if she'd been halfway up instead." Of course that meant he did think about it, and Carter shuddered.

"So somebody swapped S.A.R.A.H.—or her bunker and our driveway—with a burger joint from a mall in Boise?"

"Sure looks that way. Come on—I'll drop you at school on my way back to the office. I'll send somebody to go get Lexi, and in the meantime I'll try to figure out what happened." He looked at Bobby. "You should come with me, Bobby. You're not in any trouble, but this isn't Boise and it's best if you don't wander around on your own. Oh, and," he added before Bobby could exit the booth, "while you're in there, could I get a combo meal number two? Heavy on the pickles. What?" he asked as Zoe gave him one of her *I can't believe you!* looks. "I haven't had breakfast yet! And this place makes great curly fries!"

Carter popped the last fry in his mouth as he finished parking the Jeep and shut off the engine. The food had helped calm him down.

These definitely weren't pranks anymore! And this was exactly the sort of thing he'd been worried might happen, after the carport incident the other day—something was going on, and it had escalated to houses! And—because that was how things always went around here—it had started with his! And he had a bad feeling S.A.R.A.H.'s bunker wasn't the only home that was going to be moved around. But Boise? That was a hell of a lot farther than across town!

He forced himself to stay in control. Getting angry wasn't going to solve anything. And it would probably scare his passenger.

"Okay," he said to Bobby, who was sitting beside him— he'd put the boy in the front seat after dropping Zoe at school, so the kid wouldn't feel like he was a criminal or anything. "We'll just head inside and get you situated, then I can work on what's going on and how to get you back home."

"Sounds good," Bobby agreed as they climbed out of the Jeep. "But where's your office?"

"Hm? Oh, it's right*—" Carter started to gesture right in front of them, then let his hand fall to his side as he finally registered what he was seeing. "Oh, come on!" Because the sheriff's office wasn't there. It had apparently been re-placed.

By a gun shop.

CHAPTᵉR 8

"All right," Henry said as he pulled out a chair and dropped onto it, "I'm here. What's going on?"

"Hang on a sec," Carter told him, holding up a hand. "Allison's on her way, and it'll be easier if I only have to explain this once." He looked at his friend. "Did you figure out a way to swap the garage and the carport back yet?"

Henry shook his head. "Nothing I can be sure won't damage their integrity," he admitted. "But I'm still working on it."

"Work faster."

Carter glanced up as Allison approached their table, and he smiled, gesturing toward a third seat. "Hey, Allison. Pull up a chair."

"This had better be good, Carter," she warned as she sat. "I've got a stack of reports to get through, and I still need to finalize next month's budget."

"Oh, it's good," he assured her. "Or, rather, it's bad.

Very, very bad. See that kid over there?" He gestured toward Bobby, who was sitting at the counter demolishing a Philly cheesesteak. Apparently that was the teenager's absolute favorite food in the entire world, last consumed on a trip to Philadelphia when he was fourteen, and his eyes had lit up when Vincent had assured him he could make one every bit as good. "Well, that's Bobby Markess. He's from Boise. He works at Burger Run—it's a local chain up there, great curly fries. Only he's here right now because his particular Burger Run is now in Eureka. Where S.A.R.A.H.'s bunker used to be!"

Allison and Henry were studying him, and Carter let them. Finally both of his friends nodded.

"This is related to that garage switch yesterday, isn't it?" Henry asked.

"A garage?" Allison looked confused. "I thought it was two cars—Larry's and Dr. Styvers's?"

"The answer to both those questions is yes," Carter told them. "It's related to both of them—and they're both connected. I just don't know how yet." He rubbed a hand over his head. "But I think it's actually been going on for a while now, I just didn't realize it at first." He told Allison about Seth Osbourne's flowers, and about Nora Allen and Karl Worinko. And finally about S.A.R.A.H. and the Burger Run.

"Thank God Lexi's okay," Allison said after he'd finished. "Can she make her way back on her own, or do we need to arrange for someone to pick her up somehow?"

"She's not my biggest concern at the moment," Carter admitted, "which I know sounds terrible, since she's my big sister. But Lexi can take care of herself—she always has. Besides, somebody's going to have to run this kid home again—Philly cheesesteaks are only going to hold his attention for so long—and when that happens we can get Lexi back as well." He sighed. "I'm more worried about what's going on here, and how we're going to stop it before someone does get hurt."

"We'll need to contain the situation," Henry pointed out. "Keep an eye out for any other switches, track them down as soon as they happen, and put any people involved in safe custody." He looked around. "You should get Jo in on this—and maybe deputize a few others, if necessary."

"Well, that's another problem," Carter said, leaning back in his chair. "Jo's gone. And so is the sheriff's office."

"What?" He definitely had Allison's attention now. "Where? When? How did this happen? And why didn't you tell us?"

"I have no idea where, though I plan to find out," Carter replied. "*When* would be between when I left the office about an hour ago and when I got back maybe ten minutes ago. How is what we need to figure out. And I didn't tell you yet because Jo can take care of herself, too."

"We have no idea where she is?"

"I'm betting the gun shop will give me some ideas." He smiled at their expressions. "Oh yes, the office was replaced by a gun shop. A closed one, fortunately—I guess they have better hours than we do. Good thing, too, or we might have a half dozen trigger-happy strangers wandering Eureka, partially panicked and fully armed." His half-hearted joke didn't change the gravity of the situation, and all three of them knew it.

"It's definitely from outside Eureka, then," Henry commented. Their quiet little town didn't have a gun shop—why bother when most of the residents were smart enough to build their own weapons out of standard household items, if they really wanted? Henry pulled out his PDA and switched it on, scrolling through the numbers in its database before selecting one and holding it to his ear. "I'm getting an out-of-area signal from Jo, which means she's well beyond Eureka as well." He gave Carter a rueful smile as he put the little gadget away. "But I guess you already tried that."

"First thing," Carter agreed. He'd whipped out his own PDA the second he'd seen the gun shop, but he'd already figured he wouldn't get an answer. "And that's the only phone Jo carries—hell, it's the only one any of us carry unless we know we're going outside of town." And for good reason—the Eureka PDAs Henry had helped design and every Eureka resident carried provided better sound, a better picture, real-time video, one-touch dialing, voice recognition, and a whole bunch of other features. Plus they didn't require their own batteries—they drew off the broadcast power the town supplied. As long as they were within the town's borders. "But she'll get in touch. Jo can handle herself." He frowned. "I just hope she doesn't have to shoot too many people to do it."

"Yes, but what about the gun rack?" Allison asked. Carter had been trying not to think about that. The gun rack in their office was fully automated and ceiling-mounted and held more than two dozen different weapons. Only a few of them were standard issue—the rest were all high-tech wizardry. There was enough firepower there to take over a decent-sized nation. And Jo was an expert with all of it. Carter couldn't even remember half their names.

"Jo will keep that under control," Carter assured her. "Remember, she's got the remote for the rack." It was still a bit of a sore point for him, actually—it had been months before Jo had even allowed him access to the rack or its weapons, saying that he couldn't be trusted with them until he knew each weapon by heart. He had learned them—and had promptly forgotten half of them within a few weeks. He'd never mentioned that last part to his overzealous deputy, but he suspected she knew anyway. Right now, however, the fact that she guarded that remote so closely was a good thing. "Our biggest problem is, who keeps stealing or at least swapping parts of our town, and how do we get him to stop?"

But Allison leaned forward. "That may not be our biggest problem either," she corrected. "Think about it. You said that boy over there was from Boise, Idaho, right? Which means whoever's doing this, they can exchange parts of Eureka for parts of other towns—towns that don't have the sort of special equipment we do. Can you imagine what would happen if some of the things the people here have in their homes fell into the wrong hands? There's a reason this entire town is classified!"

Henry was rubbing his chin, deep in thought. "It's not just a question of the wrong hands, either," he added after a second. "That at least suggests that people with comparable training and intellect are acquiring our inventions for their own ends. But those people would be careful with them—they'd understand how dangerous even daily-use items here in Eureka can be, and they'd take proper precautions." He sighed. "But the average man on the street, anywhere but here? He'd have no idea what he was looking at. He'd think it was the nearest normal equivalent and try to use it that way, with potentially disastrous results." He leaned forward, elbows on the table. "Can you imagine, for example, what would happen if someone used the fire hose on my truck as if it were a normal one?" All three of them groaned. Henry's fire hose used sonic vibration to produce pressure waves that could batter any fire into submission. But what if those waves were turned on people, in the same way firemen sometimes hosed kids down on hot days? Anyone caught in those waves would be crushed instantly!

"Then there are the unexpected and uncleared visitors, like your friend over there," Allison pointed out, indicating Bobby with a toss of her chin. "We can't just have strangers wandering around Eureka. You know what sort of clearances are required just to visit this place!" Did he ever! When Carter had first arrived here, purely by accident, he'd wound up at the sheriff's office, and not just because he'd been transporting a fugitive. Only his credentials as a federal marshal had persuaded them to grant him temporary visiting status. And for good reason—just taking a stroll through Eureka could expose you to more than a dozen new inventions, all of them cutting-edge and all of them classified by the military.

"That's why I brought him here," Carter reminded her. "With my office gone, it seemed the safest place." And it was. For the most part, Café Diem looked like a normal diner. As long as Bobby didn't take a tour of the kitchen, or pay too much attention to his fellow patrons, they'd be okay.

"That's fine," Allison agreed, "but that's just one kid. And you were lucky to find him so quickly. What if some other building gets swapped, though, and whoever's inside steps out before you can get there?" She leaned back and took a deep breath, clearly contemplating the potential problems that would cause.

Carter nodded. "So we need to not only stop this from happening again, but also contain the people who wind up here by mistake, since they can't see any part of Eureka without the proper clearance, which none of them have. And then we need to make sure nobody goes into any transplanted Eureka building, wherever it wound up, and that both the transplants and whatever experimental doo-dads they have with them remain safely in their homes." He sighed. "Well, this should be a whole world of fun."

Allison reached across the table and rested her hand on his. "You don't have to do this alone, though," she reminded him. "I can task GD security to you for the duration—I'll keep a few back to patrol the building, put the place on general lockdown, and give you the rest. That should help."

But Carter shook his head. "Thanks, but I don't want them."

"Why not?" Now Allison removed her hand, and banged it on the table instead. "Damn it, Carter, I know you don't like working with them, but we are all on the same side here!"

"No, we're really not." Carter held up his own hands. "Listen, I trust you, absolutely. But GD as a whole answers to the Department of Defense. All of your security guys are soldiers. Which means, although they report directly to you for now, they ultimately answer to Mansfield. And I can't risk his finding out about this and trying to take control."

Henry nodded. "That's a fair point, actually. Mansfield would declare martial law and send in troops, which would only create wide-scale panic. If we can handle the matter ourselves, we should." He grinned. "After all, we usually do."

Allison sighed. "Okay, fine, no security personnel. Yet. But what about transportation? You're talking about getting to each house or building that's been moved, right? Doing that by car would take hours! We've been developing some new stealth helicopters for the military, and we've got two working prototypes now. I can have them prepped and ready in twenty minutes. That way you can get wherever you need in a fraction of the time."

Carter gulped. "Yeah, that sounds great, thanks," he said. "But let's keep those in reserve, okay? I'll stick with driving for now."

Allison's frown softened. "Oh, right—sorry." She was one of the few in Eureka who knew about his fear of heights, and the fear of flying that went with it. "I'll have the pilots stand by anyway, just in case."

"Thanks."

"Okay, so you take care of the containment," Allison

told him, pushing her chair back and rising to her feet. "Let me know if you need any help. I'll grab Zane. We'll try to figure out who and what exactly is performing these substitutions." Her frown made it clear that she would also rain down some holy hell on whoever was responsible. Allison took her job as GD's director very seriously.

"Don't take too long," Carter warned as she walked away. "We've been lucky so far, but the longer this goes on, the more chance there is our luck'll run out." She nodded and waved a hand at him, then pushed open the door and was gone. "Well," Carter said, turning back to Henry, "looks like we're on our own."

Henry nodded as they both stood. "As the town's mayor, this is certainly my problem as much as yours," he agreed. "What should we do now?"

Carter thought about that. "First things first." He fished in his pocket and pulled out his PDA. "Can you forward the office's calls to here? That way I'll at least know when someone needs help." Normally people either called the office's landline or showed up in person with any complaints or requests they might have. Obviously, at least for now, neither of those was very feasible.

"Shouldn't be a problem," Henry agreed, holding out a hand. Carter dropped the slim device into it, and within seconds Henry was calling up programming menus at lightning speed. As always, he worked carefully but quickly, and in as much time as it would have taken Carter to dial a number Henry had his PDA working again.

They knew it was working because it immediately began ringing. Only the ring tone sounded like an old-fashioned phone, rather than the buzzing Carter used as his default.

"I set that for the call-forwarding ring," Henry explained as he handed the PDA back.

"Thanks." Carter opened it and answered the call. "Sheriff's office. Hi, Mrs. Radcliffe. Yes, I know the office isn't there right now—what can I do for you? You want to report a missing building? Shocking." He fished a pen out of his pocket and pulled a napkin toward him, ready to start writing, but stopped as the caller continued. "Yes, Mrs. Radcliffe, the sheriff's office is missing. No, you don't need to report it—I'm already well aware of that one. Yes, it does make it difficult to report things missing if the building where you go to report it is one of the things missing. I agree. No, thank you for calling. Yes, I'm sure you'll know when we manage to restore the office."

He glanced at Henry after he'd hung up. "Any chance you can set a new ring tone for just the crazy calls? Actually, can you do that with the regular office phone, once we get it back?"

"I think that would just mean changing your default ring," Henry told him, laughing. "Besides, it could be worse. She might have been calling to tell you about a new building that's gone missing."

"Yeah, I know, it's just that I—" The PDA rang again. "Hold that thought. Sheriff's office. . . . You have new next-door neighbors—house and all?" Carter glared at Henry as he readied his pen. "What's the address again? I'll be right over."

He had the feeling it was going to be a very, very long day.

CHAPTᵉR 9

"Thanks for your cooperation," Carter told the Merkels as he stepped back outside, pulling the front door shut behind him. "We appreciate it. And I'll let you know the minute it's safe to go outside again."

He let out his breath as he walked back toward his Jeep. That had gone better than expected. The Merkels, a nice young couple from Lakeview, had bought his story about a strange gas leak that was causing hallucinations and other problems. They'd agreed to stay safely indoors until the danger passed, despite having two small dogs that liked to roam around the fenced-in backyard. Of course, their fence wasn't there anymore—or rather, they weren't by the fence—so it had been important to stress that pets could be affected as well.

Carter hoped any other encounters like this went as smoothly. But somehow he knew that was asking too much.

His PDA rang as he pulled away, and he answered it while maneuvering his Jeep back onto the road. "Carter."

It was Henry. "How'd it go on your end?"

"Fine, actually. Nice folks, and they bought the whole gas leak story. How about you?" There'd been another building switched, a small office building that normally housed a hardware store—Eureka-style, which meant it included a lot more than wrenches and screwdrivers—and a small accounting firm. Henry had offered to deal with that one while Carter handled the house.

"Same here—claiming a gas leak was brilliant, actually. It's vague enough that it can cover a lot of different situations, and potentially dangerous enough that people respond quickly to the request that they stay inside and away from the windows."

Carter smiled. It was always nice to have one of his ideas appreciated, especially around here. "Yeah, well, we'll see how many times we can get away with that one. Where's the building from?"

"Fields. What about yours?"

"Lakeview."

"Well, that's not too bad, then." Both cities were in southern Oregon, not too far from Eureka. "I take it we're heading out to both places right away?"

"Yep. Just one quick stop first." Fortunately, Carter kept a duffel bag in his trunk, an old habit from his marshal days, when he never knew how long he'd be away from home. The bag contained two changes of clothes, spare shoes, basic toiletries, a paperback novel, a few power bars—everything he needed to keep him going for a short trip.

"No problem. I should gather a few things myself. And probably change." Henry had still been wearing his coveralls this morning, this time with the *Mayor* patch over the breast pocket. He had one patch for every job he performed in Eureka. There were a lot of patches. "Meet you at Café Diem?"

"Perfect." Carter hung up and headed back downtown. Time to see about some guns.

"Hello? Anyone here?" Carter peered around the gun shop. He'd never much liked places like this, actually. Too many guns all in one location made him nervous, especially after he'd had to raid a small militant group. Their stockpile had looked almost exactly like this, with rack upon rack of shotguns, rifles, and assault rifles. It still made him cringe.

The fact that the gun shop's door was unlocked didn't help matters any.

But the lights were still off, and no one had seen anybody exit or enter the building since it had arrived. He hoped that was a good sign.

"This is the sheriff," he tried again. "Is anyone here?"

"Sheriff?" The voice was coming from the back somewhere—it was hard to see through the gloom, despite the big glass windows along the front. All the guns were blocking the light. "Is that you?"

"Yeah, it's me," Carter answered, not sure what else to say. "Where are you?"

"The office," came the reply. "Hang on."

A minute later a dark shape appeared against the shadows across the back. It grew larger as it approached, and slowly Carter was able to make out details. The guy was built like Seth Osbourne, broad and beefy, and he had a neat, graying black goatee and a silvery-gray buzz cut. The T-shirt stretched tight across his chest said *Gary's Guns!* in big, blocky letters.

"Sheriff?" The man—presumably Gary—stopped about

six feet from Carter and stared, suspicion clear across his face. "You're not Sheriff Winslow!"

"No, I'm not—I'm Sheriff Carter." Carter could see the big pistol in Gary's hand and made sure to keep his voice even and his own hands in sight. This could go very, very badly if Gary got upset. "Sheriff Winslow's dealing with things elsewhere, and I got called in to help."

"You got ID?" Gary demanded, raising his pistol slightly.

"Absolutely." Carter reached—very slowly—into his pocket and pulled out his ID. "Right here."

"Let's see it." Gary edged closer, close enough to snatch the ID from Carter's hand, and then stepped back again quickly, squinting to read it in the dim light. His pistol remained half-raised the whole time, and Carter had no doubt the man could aim and shoot in a heartbeat. Even at the rate his heart was currently beating.

After a few seconds Gary lowered the pistol, then holstered it, and returned the ID. "Eureka?" he asked. "Never heard of it."

"It's a small town," Carter agreed, relaxing a little now that the gun was safely put away. "That's why they figured they could call me in—not too much going on where I'm from."

The gun shop owner nodded. "Yeah, okay. Sorry about that." He offered his hand. "Gary Miller. This is my place."

"A pleasure, Gary." They shook, and Carter glanced around. "Nice shop."

"Thanks. So what the hell's going on? I was getting ready to open and suddenly the power went dead." Gary scratched at one cheek. "I got a little dizzy, too. Fine now, though."

"That's why I'm here," Carter told him. "There's been a gas leak. We're going door-to-door, warning everyone to stay inside until we can make sure the danger's passed."

"What kinda gas?" Gary puffed out his chest. "I was a Marine—we were trained to handle gas attacks."

Crap. "I don't know all the details," Carter fudged. "I heard something about it being an experimental new thing, though. Nasty stuff. And potentially flammable," he added, figuring anything that kept Gary from pulling the trigger was a good thing. "Have you been experiencing any hallucinations?"

The other man grimaced, then nodded slowly. "Things outside don't look right," he admitted.

"That means the gas has definitely been here," Carter warned him. "You need to stay inside where you won't get any additional exposure. Lock the door behind me, and don't let anyone in until I or Sheriff Winslow or some other officer tells you it's okay." He could already see that the aftermath of this was going to be an unholy mess.

Gary considered for a minute, then nodded. "Yes, sir." For a second it had looked like he was going to offer to help, and that was the last thing Carter needed—a jumpy vet, armed to the teeth, going door-to-door in Eureka? Yeah, that'd go over well.

"Great! Thanks for your cooperation." Carter turned to go, then stopped as if he'd just thought of something. "Hey, this is going to sound really stupid, but I still don't know my way around very well—what's the street address here again?"

"104 West Elm," Gary answered. He grinned. "Got lost coming off the highway, huh? Happens all the time."

"Yeah, I feel like an idiot," Carter agreed, going with it.

"Well, here, this'll help." Gary walked over to the main counter—Carter could tell because it had a large cash register on it—and picked up a sheet of paper, than returned and handed it over. It was a flyer for the gun shop. And it included a small map showing its location.

In downtown Denio.

"That's great—thanks!" Carter assured him. And it

was. Now he knew where Jo was. In Denio, at the very northern tip of Nevada.

Of course, Carter thought as he said good-bye to Gary, making sure the gun shop owner locked up behind him, getting hold of her was still going to be tricky.

"Carter?"

"Jo?" Carter had hoped it was her when his PDA had shown an unfamiliar Nevada number. "Are you okay?"

"Fine, fine." As usual, his deputy sounded mildly perturbed but otherwise unruffled. "I'm not sure all of Gary's regular patrons can say the same, though. A few of them got a mite . . . pushy. I had to push back." He could hear her grin.

"What happened?" He was still walking over to Café Diem, but slowed outside it so he could listen more easily. Fortunately Vincent had tables set up out here for nice days, and Carter plopped himself down by one of them.

"I don't know, exactly. You'd just left, and suddenly I felt dizzy. That passed after a second, and then a bunch of guys came barging in through the front door, demanding to know where Gary was and why we'd remodeled and whether the new assault rifles had arrived. I tried to tell them they were in the wrong place, but they all insisted this was Gary's Guns—one of them even told me if I couldn't remember the name of my new place of employment, I probably shouldn't be here. They didn't seem to care about the uniform, and when I drew my pistol on them they actually laughed and told me I was cute." Her voice got sharper. "I don't like being called cute."

"I'll make a mental note of that," Carter assured her. Not that *cute* was how he'd have described Jo anyway.

"I had to take down a few of them, and then the rest backed off. I locked the front door behind them and threw the troublemakers into the cell, but we're full up now and it's not like the doors were made to withstand gunfire. Carter, what the hell is going on?"

"I don't know yet, not completely," he admitted, "but someone or something is swapping buildings from Eureka with places in other towns. You're in Denio, Nevada, by the way."

"I figured that out. And Gary's Guns?"

"Is currently where our office should be. Complete with Gary."

"Everything okay there?"

Carter leaned back. "Relatively. I've been telling people there's a gas leak and they need to stay inside. And the leak can cause hallucinations. So far they're buying it."

"Okay. Do you want me to head straight back? I'm sure I can come up with a vehicle." Jo's own car was still parked outside Gary's.

Carter had already thought about this. "No, actually, I think I need you in the field right now, keeping things contained there," he answered after a second. "Henry and I are about to head out, too—somebody's got to get to each of our transplanted Eurekans and warn them to stay inside, too. And not to let anybody else in."

"Got it. Where do you need me?" That was Jo—the very model of efficiency. She didn't bother complaining about the situation, she just accepted it and moved on. For the thousandth time Carter wondered how he'd gotten so lucky as to wind up with her as his deputy. Not that he usually told her that—she was smug enough as it was.

"I don't know yet," he answered. "So far you're in Denio, Lexi's in Boise, and we've got an office building in Fields and a house in Lakeview. But I have the feeling there are going to be more." He thought of something else. "What about the office? Is it is safe to just leave it unattended? I know you've got the gun rack's remote, but is there any risk of those guys jimmying it somehow?" The idea of a bunch of gun nuts running around with that particular firepower left him cold.

But Jo was quick to reassure him. "Nah, it's fine. I'll just put the office into lockdown. It'd take a tank to get through the armor plating."

Carter sat up. "Wait, we have a lockdown mode? Why didn't I know about that?"

"Oh, the list of things you don't know." Yep, definitely smug.

Now wasn't the time to get into that. "Fine, whatever. Lock it down. Then stand by. I'll call you as soon as I need you—wait, whose phone is this?"

"One of the guys I locked in the cell," Jo answered. "I figured he wouldn't be needing it anytime soon."

"Yeah, probably not. Okay, hang on to it for now and just be ready to move. We'll need to get to our people as soon as possible, to keep anyone from wandering outside and creating even more trouble than we've already got." That reminded him of something Allison had said. "Oh, Allison's put the new GD stealth copters at our disposal."

"The GD-3 Night Wings?" Jo sounded positively giddy. "Really?"

"Yep—if you want, I can have one of them pick you up."

"Definitely!"

"Okay, I'll let Allison know. And I'll give her your cell number, to pass along to the pilot—they'll call when they're close by. After that, just be ready."

"Not a problem." Jo signed off, and Carter pushed back from the table and rose. Well, at least that was one less thing to worry about—if Jo said it would take a tank to break into the office once it was locked down, she wasn't exaggerating. So as long as Gary's customers didn't have a spare Sherman or Pershing stashed somewhere, the office would be safe. And he had an extra pair of hands to help corral their displaced residents.

Which reminded him, he was going to need someone to take over for him here. But who? Allison would be busy trying to stop whatever was causing this, Jo was already out of Eureka, Henry was coming with him—for a second he considered asking Henry to stay behind but decided against it. Not only did Henry know absolutely everyone, he was also one of the smartest guys here. If they needed to shut down some device that had gone haywire by being moved, Carter wouldn't have a clue what to do except maybe kick it or shoot it. He needed Henry with him.

But that didn't leave him a lot of options. There were plenty of people in town he liked, but not many he could trust.

But as he stepped into Café Diem, he spotted one of them. Someone he trusted completely.

"Zoe? Why aren't you still at Tesla?" He walked over and gave his daughter a quick hug and a peck on the forehead.

"Hey, Dad. School let out early—some GD initiative or something." Allison, Carter realized. And she was absolutely right. Better to send the kids home—this way, if the school wound up on the list of places that swapped, they wouldn't have Eureka's entire teen population transported to some suburb somewhere. Zoe shrugged. "S.A.R.A.H.'s still nonresponsive, so I came here instead."

"I'm glad you did," Carter assured her. "I've actually got a job for you."

"For me?" She broke into a smile, and Carter marveled again at how amazing she was, and what a beautiful, smart, capable young woman she was becoming. Moving to Eureka had been the best thing for her, absolutely.

"Yeah. And it's important." He led her over to a table and quickly filled her in on the other building exchanges.

"There are going to be more, I'm sure of it," he finished. "I need you to keep an eye on them—I'll give you my PDA, so you'll know whenever anyone calls one in—and get to them before they can step outside. Tell them there's a gas leak and it's not safe, and that it can cause hallucinations. Just don't let them loose in Eureka."

"Gas leak, hallucinations. Got it." Zoe nodded, then shook her head. "Shouldn't I have a gas mask or something?"

"Probably, but I've only got the one in my bag and I might need it." He seriously hoped not, but he could just see leaving it behind and then needing it after all. "Tell people"—he racked his brain—"tell them you've got people out sweeping the area and alerting you to danger zones, but that it's clear where they are for now. Things could change at any time, though, which is why they need to stay inside." He debated getting a hazmat suit from GD but decided it was better to keep things simple. No props.

Zoe frowned. "But what if two places show up at once? I'll get there as quick as I can, but it's a lot to handle by myself." She brightened. "What about Lucas? He could help!"

Carter repressed a growl. Lucas was Zoe's boyfriend, and he was a good kid—and terrified of Carter, which was exactly the way he liked it—and also back in town on midwinter break, but Carter shook his head anyway. "He's not all that good at the whole talking thing," he reminded Zoe. "I need a people person for this." He could see that she wanted to argue but couldn't. Lucas was a genius like most of the people in town, but he was shy and awkward. He'd probably send people into a panic rather than calming them down.

But Zoe was right about one thing—this could wind up being more than one person could handle. Carter glanced around and saw two things at once—Bobby Markess, still sitting at the counter but now stacking empty water glasses into a pyramid. And the wiry little guy talking to him.

"Fargo!"

Fargo jumped. "I'm not doing anything wrong, I swear!" he insisted immediately.

Carter rolled his eyes—he couldn't help it. "I know that, Fargo. Come here." He deliberately ignored Zoe's *Are you kidding me?* look. "Listen, I need your help with something."

As always, Fargo looked pleased to be useful. "Really? Great!" He pulled out a chair. "What can I do for you?"

Carter explained the situation, only being interrupted when Fargo shouted triumphantly, "See, I told you I had nothing to do with Larry's car being stolen!" When he'd finished, Fargo adjusted his thick black-framed glasses and nodded.

"I'll be happy to help," he said gravely. "You can count on me, Sheriff."

Zoe was the one rolling her eyes now, but Carter nodded. "Good. The two of you will need to work together—coordinate so you don't go after the same place. Try to keep everyone in their own home or office or whatever, but if they have to go anywhere, bring them here." He rose to his feet. "Got it?"

"Got it." Fargo saluted. Zoe shook her head but stood as well and gave Carter a hug.

"Be careful, okay?" she warned.

"I'll be fine," he assured her. "This is basically just rounding up strays—they just happen to be stray people and buildings." He handed her his PDA. "I've got my old cell still, and the number's already in there, so you can call me if you run into any problems." He smiled and kissed her forehead. "You'll do great."

"Thanks." She pocketed the gadget, sighed, and turned back to Fargo. "Okay, let's get started. I think we should divide the town up into quadrants, and each take two . . ."

Glad that was taken care of, Carter headed over to Bobby. "Hey, Bobby, how's it going?"

"This place is weird, Sheriff," Bobby answered. "You know there was a guy in here earlier who was talking to his laptop—and it was talking back? And these"—he indicated the water glasses he was playing with—"feel like glass. But I dropped one earlier, and it didn't break. It bounced." He shook his head. "Weird."

"Yeah, it's a funny old town," Carter agreed. "Listen, I completely forgot to ask you earlier—how do you get to work? Do you bike, or take the bus, or—?"

"I drive," the kid answered proudly. "Got my license just before I started working there."

"Really? That's great!" It was exactly the answer Carter had been hoping for. "Was your car still in the lot when we left, by any chance?" He held his breath.

"Sure was," Bobby replied, making Carter let out a sigh of relief. "It was the little silver Datsun hatchback just in front. I got her from my uncle—she's a little beaten up, but she still drives great."

"I believe it." Carter took another deep breath. "Listen, I know this is a lot to ask, but if I get you back to your car and give you directions, do you think you can make your way home on your own? It's going to be a lot farther than your usual commute, unfortunately."

Bobby was studying him suspiciously. "How much farther? And where am I, anyway? That guy"—he gestured toward Fargo, who now seemed to be arguing with Zoe—"said Eureka, but I've never even heard of it. How'd my whole restaurant wind up in a different town? With me inside?"

"It's complicated, and classified," Carter answered, resting a hand on the boy's shoulder. "I really can't tell you. But you're in southern Oregon right now. I can get you back to 95, which'll take you straight to Boise. It's a few hours' drive, though."

Bobby thought about it. "Can I get another one of those Philly cheesesteaks to go?"

"Absolutely." Carter nodded to Vincent, who'd been hovering unobtrusively behind the counter, and Vincent nodded back and headed into the kitchen. Bobby grinned, and Carter left him waiting for his sandwich and stepped off to one side. Then he pulled out his old cell phone—good thing he'd kept it for out-of-town travel!—and called the number Lexi had given him.

"Lexi?" he said once she'd picked up. "Yeah, it's me. You doing okay? Good. Listen, we're still working on getting the bunker back, but there's been some other stuff going on, too. Your car's out there with you, right? Great. Listen, I need you to do me a favor . ."

"So we've got Lexi and Jo out here as well?" Henry asked as they turned onto the highway and headed out of town. They'd already dropped Bobby off at his car, made sure he had directions back to Boise, and seen him take off ahead of them.

"Yeah, I figure we should use what we've got," Carter answered. "Lexi's good at making friends, and she puts people at ease, plus most people in Eureka know her." *And know she's my sister,* he thought, which might make them more likely to do what she says. "She's not good at sitting idle, either. This way we get extra help and she keeps busy."

"Sounds good to me," Henry agreed. "Too bad Tess is Down Under. She'd be perfect for this."

"Yeah, if she didn't make people want to kill her first!" Tess was a people person. She liked to talk. A lot. All the time. And when she got flustered, she often said whatever came to mind without stopping to think it through first. That could create all kinds of problems in a situation like this, but Henry was right, she was good at putting people at ease.

And Carter wished she were here, too.

"So," Henry interrupted his thoughts, "Fields or Lake-view?"

"Lakeview—I sent Jo to Fields. It's right by Denio, so it'll save us the trip."

"Nice." Henry settled back into his seat and closed his eyes. "Wake me when we get there, hm?" And within seconds he had dozed off.

"Lot of help you are," Carter muttered, but he didn't mind. He'd always liked driving, and had no problem being by himself. It gave him time to think.

Unfortunately, right now that meant thinking about the current situation—and whether he was really going to be able to take care of it. Sure, Allison was going after the root of the problem, and he had Zoe and Fargo to help back in Eureka and Jo and Lexi and Henry to help out here. But he was still the one who had to coordinate all of them. Time was, he'd have a dozen different agents and officers, from almost as many agencies, all taking his orders. But that had been two years ago. He hadn't done anything like that since— most of Eureka's problems came down to him, Jo, Henry, and maybe one or two others, and it was a less formal arrangement than interoffice cooperation. Plus it had been two years since he'd had to leave Eureka on official business. Was he really still equipped to handle problems in the outside world?

"Of course I am," he told himself softly. Certainly the Department of Homeland Security had thought so—after he'd been temporarily fired from Eureka he'd applied for a job with the DHS and they had made him an offer almost immediately. So they considered him still competent. But what if they were wrong? What if he was no longer cut out for anything but being a small-town sheriff, even if it was a small town like Eureka?

He thought of Zoe then, and how happy she was in

Eureka—and how much their relationship had improved since they'd moved there, and he'd been able to stay in one place and see her every day instead of shuttling around the country. He smiled. She was absolutely worth it.

But she was going to college now—on the other side of the country. It had been only a few months, so it hadn't really sunk in yet, but eventually he'd realize she'd moved on. Eureka was Zoe's home for only a few months a year now. Did he still want to stay here without her? And if not, would he be happy doing anything else?

Carter pushed those thoughts to the back of his brain and concentrated on the road and the problem at hand. Now wasn't the time to worry about what he'd be doing in a year or two. He had a situation to handle.

He just hoped he was up to it.

CHAPTᵉR 10

"... started happening to whole buildings now as well," Allison finished.

"So that's what happened!" Zane said, banging one fist against his leg. "Well, that explains it!"

Then he realized his boss was watching him closely, one eyebrow raised. "Explains what, exactly?" she asked in her *There had better be a good explanation for this* schoolteacher voice. Which was at least better than her *Do it now or I'll have you arrested!* military commander persona. "Zane, if you experienced a swap, it's important," she continued, leaning forward. They were in her office at GD, which meant she was sitting behind her desk and he was standing in front of it. As if that didn't reinforce the whole schoolboy-sent-to-the-principal motif! "We need every scrap of data we can get if we're going to figure out why this is happening and stop it before anyone gets hurt."

"It was nothing," Zane insisted. "I got swapped with

Taggart last night, I made my way back home, I never left town, it's all good. Moving on." He perched on the edge of her desk, which he knew amused her as much as it annoyed her. "So first things first—we need to figure out what's causing all this, right?"

"Right." She accepted the change of subject—for now—and stood, then began pacing around the office, hands clasped behind her back. The very picture of a modern executive deep in thought. "There's a good chance it's here at GD, though we shouldn't rule out other possibilities."

"Might as well start here," Zane agreed, "and work our way out." Most of Eureka's residents were GD employees anyway, and given the choice between building experiments in their garage or in GD's state-of-the-art labs, well, he knew which one he'd choose.

Most of the time.

"Okay, so what do we know?" Allison asked.

"We're dealing with a matter transporter," Zane offered. "A really advanced one." He remembered his little trip to Taggart's home. He'd been wearing headphones, and he'd realized he was in different surroundings as he'd removed them, only they were no longer his. They were Taggart's. He'd be willing to bet the Australian had also been wearing headphones at the time, and had wound up with Zane's on instead. He'd have to remember to clean those.

"Right," Allison agreed. "Only it's not just transporting matter, it's switching it, trading one thing for another."

"Which means it's basically performing two teleportations at once," Zane pointed out. "That's got to take a ton of computer power—and a ton of power in general. Enough to light up the entire town and then some." He scratched his jaw. "That kind of power output should be easy to trace."

"Absolutely!" Allison rushed back to her desk and tapped several commands into the keyboard. "Looking for recent energy usage spikes," she explained as she worked.

An activity log appeared, but swiveling around to peer over her shoulder Zane could see that it showed very little variation. "Nope, nothing. Either it's not here or it's not drawing as much power as we thought."

Zane frowned. "That doesn't make sense—maybe it's got some kind of alternate energy source." He raked his fingers through his short but unruly black hair, focusing on what little they knew. "It can transport matter up to the size of a building. It can keep the matter's structure perfectly, so perfectly the people inside barely notice the change. It's got a range of at least, what, two hundred miles? How far is it to Boise from here?" Now he was the one pacing, and he forced himself to stop and perch on the desk's edge again. "Really, I don't see how anyone could do something like that without gigawatts at their disposal, whole great big bunches of them."

Allison nodded and typed in a new command, then angled the monitor around so he could see. "I asked for energy usage spikes in Eureka, and there are a few minor ones but nothing big enough to account for any of this." She sank back into her chair. "How're we supposed to stop it if we can't even figure out what's causing it?"

"Okay, let's assume for now that it's here at GD," Zane suggested. "That way we can go through the files, see if we find anything that seems like a good match, and if we can't, it must be somewhere in Eureka proper. Sound good?" Allison nodded. "So we're looking for something that can transport matter."

"Living matter," Allison added.

"Right, living matter. Complex living matter. Hell, people!" He scratched his jaw again. "How many actual, working human teleportation systems have we developed over the years?"

Allison's eyes were wide, and her naturally tawny skin had gone a bit pale. "Only one."

"Really? That's it?" Zane would have thought there were more, but he'd only been working for GD a little over a year now—there were still whole wings he'd never seen. "Well, that makes it easy, right? What've we got on it?"

"It's the SRT," Allison told him. She wasn't looking at her screen, he noticed, and as soon as she said the name he understood why. This was something she'd experienced firsthand.

"Well, that sounds about right," Zane agreed. He knew about the SRT—and why Henry had used it on Allison's son, Kevin—but that was it. Only Allison, Henry, Kevin, Carter, Stark, and the traitorous Beverly Barlowe had been present in the executive director's emergency bunker, a mile underground, when they'd operated the machine. "Do we have anyone still working on that?"

Allison was already pulling up the file. "No, it's a closed project," she replied after scanning the information as it scrolled down her screen. "The SRT prototype was deemed functional, but the one-kilometer maximum range was deemed too limiting and the power drain too prohibitive to bother developing further. They installed the prototype in the bunker because they decided not to waste its potential, but it was never going to be for anything but absolute emergencies. Besides, the Stockholm treaty banned teleportation research, along with miniaturization and invisibility."

Zane thought about it. "Maybe somebody continued the research on their own?"

"Maybe." Allison zeroed in on the project's initial details. "The developers were Warren King, Walter Perkins, and Arnold Gunter."

"I don't know any of them," Zane admitted. "Do you?"

She gave him one of her looks. "Of course. It's part of my job. Anyway, Warren King is an astrophysicist, and he was in charge of GD before Nathan. Last I heard, he'd been reassigned to a lookout post in Alaska and was happy as a clam up there, with his VR rig and his radio telescope. Walter Perkins was studying the space-time continuum. Unfortunately, he was experimenting in his own basement on the side, and triggered a time-space anomaly that we first thought had killed him but later discovered simply changed his body into a fluctuating energy state. He was recovered eventually, and is still undergoing treatment to stabilize him completely."

"Could he be our guy? Sounds like he's willing to work off the reservation."

But Allison shook her head. "He's under house arrest, and has been since his return. No tech allowed."

"Okay, what about the third guy, Gunter?"

Allison frowned. "I don't really know Dr. Gunter well," she said after a second. "We've met, of course, and I've seen him at various briefings, but I haven't seen him recently." She called up the personnel files and selected Gunter's record. She and Zane both studied the photo at the top of the page, which showed a tall, angular man with a prominent nose, a weak chin, and a mass of graying black curls. "He's been working on alternate energy sources," she read. "With some success, too."

Zane stood and moved around the desk to lean over Allison's chair, where he could see the screen more easily. "That could explain the lack of energy spikes. He's got a way to fuel his project unnoticed."

"It could." She was still reading the rest of the file and stopped on a section. "Hang on. Take a look at this."

Zane read where she'd indicated. " 'Previous project management: MRS.' Okay, what's an MRS, and don't tell me it's what girls go for in college."

That at least got a half smile out of her. "I have no idea," she replied. "He's been working on energy sources as long as I've been running GD, which means the MRS must have been under either Walter's or Nathan's tenure." She clicked on the project name and entered a password as a new screen came up. Zane pretended not to memorize the keys she'd hit. "Here we go."

Both of them saw the project title at the same time: "Project 5-3413: Matter Relocation System (MRS)."

"That's it!" Zane rapped his knuckles against the screen, creating a momentary ripple in the display. "That's got to be! Gunter continued the SRT project under a new name! And he found a way to solve the energy problem by creating an alternate energy source!"

"It certainly looks that way," Allison agreed. "It says here the MRS was designed to relocate designated items or structures by mapping a target area, confirming sufficient space was available, and then transporting them using 'reconstructive technology.' That's definitely the SRT at work." She read over some of the more technical details. "Looks like he found a way to beat the range problem, too. Why wasn't this a top-priority project? If Gunter actually figured out how to teleport people and objects safely, with no standard energy expenditure, it could revolutionize travel!"

"There's your reason." Zane pointed to a line on the screen. "Classified as Double Top Secret. The military found out what he was working on and decided they wanted it all to themselves." Zane had never been too fond of authority figures in general, and military ones even less. Things like this reminded him why. Here was one of the greatest potential achievements known to man, and the military had deliberately kept it from being discovered, just so they could move troops and tanks around the world more easily!

"It's never been cleared as operational, though," Allison pointed out. "In fact, it was shut down three years ago for 'insufficient progress and prohibitive cost.'" Which also

explained why she hadn't known anything about it before
this—three years ago Warren King had been in charge of
GD, and he hadn't been big on sharing information. Nor
had she had any reason to dig through old files on canceled
projects. Until now.

Zane stepped back to lean against the wall now that
he'd finished reading the file. "That must be when Gunter
switched to energy research," he mused. "The MRS needed
too much energy to power it conventionally, so he had to
find another source. The military shut him down, but he
must have continued working on it in his spare time."

"And he obviously solved the energy problem," Allison
agreed. "We know of at least four buildings he's transported already!" Her brow was still furrowed. "But that
doesn't explain why we're getting other structures in their
place. The MRS looks like it's only supposed to relocate
objects to open areas. And why would he have selected
S.A.R.A.H.'s bunker, or the sheriff's office, or an office
building, or a house? It doesn't make any sense."

"Maybe not," Zane said. "But at least now we know who
to ask." He grinned. "And I'm betting Gunter was working
on the MRS either in his basement or somewhere here at
GD near his regular lab."

Allison nodded and returned to the personnel file. "He's
in Section Five, of course," she pointed out. "Lab number
five twenty-seven. That's one of the outlying locations—
plenty of space." She rose to her feet, pulling out her PDA
as she did so. "We'll look at the lab, and I'll ask Carter to
stop by Gunter's house and check for him there."

"Hey, Carter?" she said a second later as she shooed
Zane toward the door. He turned, however, at the note of
surprise that crept into her voice at the next word. "Fargo?
What are you doing answering Carter's phone?" Fargo—it
figured. Zane had worked out some of his differences with
the little researcher, but still didn't like or particularly trust

the guy. Especially not around Jo. Not that she couldn't take care of herself, and she'd certainly never shown any interest in Fargo, but it was still annoying watching him follow her around like a little lost puppy.

Apparently Fargo was providing a detailed explanation, because after a second Allison closed her eyes and held up a hand. "Okay, okay, stop!" she ordered. "You can explain it all to me later. Right now I need you to do something for me. You know Arnold Gunter? Right, I need you to go to his house and see if he's there. He may be responsible for all this, so if he's home bring him here at once. He's at 417 Rosedale. Call me and let me know what you find. Thanks."

She hung up, pocketed the PDA, and looked at Zane. "Carter and Henry left already," she explained. "He charged Fargo and Zoe with containing any non-Eurekans who show up here, and gave them his phone." She shook her head. "They're both bright, and Zoe's a good kid, but she's a freshman in college! Carter couldn't have found somebody else to help out?"

Zane stepped aside to allow her through the door first. "I assume we're trying to keep quiet about all this, to avoid as much panic as possible? Zoe already knew about it because of S.A.R.A.H., and Fargo seems to know about everything, so Carter probably figured he'd put them to use." He set aside his own dislike for the guy. "Fargo's certainly . . . goal-oriented."

Allison laughed and led the way to the elevator. "Well, right now he's got a simple enough goal—bring Gunter here so we can talk to him in person." She shook her head. "Assuming he's not still in his lab, in which case I just sent Fargo on a wild-goose chase."

Zane grinned back at her. "Couldn't happen to a nicer guy."

CHAPTᵉR 11

"At last! A chance for Douglas Fargo, acting sheriff of Eureka, to show his quality!" Fargo noticed the look Zoe was giving him. "What?"

"Not a thing," she answered, shaking her head, but he could see she was laughing at him.

"I'm paraphrasing," he pointed out, but she only arched an eyebrow at him.

"Yes, I'm well aware of that." Her tone was a bit sharper than before. "I do go to the movies, you know. You're hardly the only *Lord of the Rings* fan in Eureka." Still, he suspected she was one of those Arwen-Aragorn worshippers, while he preferred the more manly action scenes. "I just think it's funny that you're comparing yourself to Faramir and giving some scientist a ride to capturing the One Ring."

"Both are instrumental to preventing a major catastrophe," Fargo defended himself. "One could even argue that they are both the key to their particular situation." He puffed out his chest. "Besides, I don't have to explain myself to you. Sheriff Carter left me in charge."

Now Zoe was outright staring at him, her mouth open. "What? He so totally did not! My dad has more sense than that!"

"What's that supposed to mean?" He pushed his glasses back up his nose. "You think he put *you* in charge? Anyway, that's not important. What matters right now is that Director Blake has given me a job to do, and I'm not about to let her down." He frowned at Zoe, trying his best to look stern and authoritative. "You keep an eye on things here until I get back."

She saluted. "Aye-aye, Sheriff Captain Fargo, sir!" Then she laughed at him some more.

"I doubt Faramir ever had to put up with things like this," Fargo muttered as he rushed out of Café Diem and headed to where he'd parked Tabitha.

Thirty minutes later, Fargo called Allison. "Hello, Director Blake?" he said once she'd answered. "What was that address again?"

"417 Rosedale," she replied. "I thought you'd be there by now." She sounded perturbed, a tone Fargo was all too familiar with.

He forced himself to press on. "Yes, well, there's a slight problem," he explained. He peered through Tabitha's windshield again, studying the row of houses along the street in front of him. "I've got 415 Rosedale, and 419 Rosedale. But between them—well, I'm pretty sure that's not 417." The big 338 across the front door was a dead giveaway.

Allison sighed. "Great. Just great. It's not there." That last part had been directed at someone else with her, Fargo suspected, because it had been fainter than the rest. A second later she was talking to him again. "I need you to go find out where that house is from, Fargo. As quick as you can."

"Okay." He shut Tabitha off and got out, closing the door behind him. "Um, how exactly do I do that?"

"I don't know, just look around. Find something that gives you its address—and city, if it's not from here. Which, the way things are going, it probably isn't."

"Oh. Okay, sure. Find the address. Got it." Fargo hung up and tucked his PDA away. Then he stared at the neat brick house. How exactly was he supposed to do that? "I'm no detective," he muttered. Then he brightened. "Ah, but I know someone who is!"

Pulling his PDA back out, Fargo dialed a new number, one that had only just been programmed in earlier that morning. It took three rings. "Hello, Sheriff Carter? It's Fargo. I, um, need a little help."

"Here we go—lab number five twenty-seven." Allison stopped in front of a heavy security door, and Zane drew himself up a pace behind her. Some of the labs in the other sections had transparent walls and doors, and others had nice big windows, but Section Five was the most heavily restricted area, where all the top-secret experiments took place, so the walls here were thicker and the doors were reinforced metal and ceramic. And no windows.

Allison tried the security panel beside the door, punching in her access code, but nothing happened. That wasn't supposed to occur—she was the executive director, so she had access to absolutely everything. She tried it again, but still the door didn't budge. Then Zane noticed why.

"Check it out." He pointed to the bottom of the panel, where two small LEDs protruded. The green one was dark, but the red one was flashing steadily.

"Oh, great." Allison slumped against the door. "It's active." A solid red light simply meant the door was locked. A flashing red light meant there was an experiment in progress. Once that security was activated, the entire lab locked down. It couldn't be opened until the experiment ended and the lockdown was lifted. From the inside. "Now what?"

"We could cut power to the corridor," Zane suggested. "No power to the door, no flashing light, no lock." Which wasn't quite true—the door would still be locked, but only mechanically. And that he could get through, no problem. He'd been very good at defeating locks before he'd come to Eureka, back in his "wild" days.

"Good thinking." Allison punched a number into her PDA. "This is Director Blake," she said to whoever answered. "I need you to kill the power to the corridor in front of lab five twenty-seven, immediately. Thank you." She smiled at Zane. "Twenty seconds."

They waited a full minute, just to be on the safe side. The overhead lights winked out after twenty seconds, to be replaced by backup emergency lights along the walls. But the blinking red light remained.

Allison called again and hung up in frustration. "They did cut the power," she reported. "Gunter must have wired the entire lab into whatever alternate power supply he's using. Including the door lock."

"Makes sense, really," Zane muttered, stepping closer and running his hands across the door, checking its surface and its edges. "If you're already running your experiment with it, why not just swap out altogether? Easier to keep everything enclosed, a nice tight circuit, plus you can keep track of all your energy expenditures at once."

"Can you break it down?" Allison shook her head. "Not break it down, of course—we both know better than that." They did indeed—the door's composite material would withstand a direct hit from a small mortar. "Can you crack the lock and get it open?"

Zane grinned at her and pulled a few ever-present tools from his back pocket. "Oh, absolutely," he assured her, kneeling down so he could start unscrewing the access panel. "It just may take a while."

He heard her sigh behind him. "Well, work as fast as you can. I don't know how much time we have left, but I have a feeling it isn't a whole lot."

Zane didn't even bother to reply. He was already studying the maze of wires that controlled the door and mentally mapping the route the locking signal must have taken. He'd never tried cracking a Section Five door before. This was going to be a bit tricky.

Fortunately, he loved a challenge.

"Whaddya need, Fargo?" Carter sounded distracted, which made sense—Fargo was fairly certain he could hear the rush of traffic through the phone. He hated having to ask for help at all, and much less having to bother the sheriff while he was driving. But he knew this couldn't wait.

"Director Blake sent me to Professor Gunter's house," he explained quickly. "Arnold Gunter—she thinks he might be the one responsible. He lives at 417 Rosedale. But I'm here, and he's not. His whole house isn't. There's another house in its place."

"Oh, that's just great. Okay, tell me where that house is from and I'll go get Gunter."

"That's the problem," Fargo replied. "I don't know where it's from. It says 338 on it, but that's all I know."

"Well, have you asked the owners?"

"Um—I hadn't tried that yet." Carter's sigh was a lot like Allison's as Fargo hurried up the front walk. "Hang on."

"I'm not going anywhere."

He rang the doorbell. No one answered, and after a few seconds he rang it again. Then he tried knocking on the door. That led to pounding. "I don't think anybody's home," he reported after a minute.

"That's probably a good thing," Carter pointed out. "One less person or family to worry about wandering loose through Eureka. Okay, you're going to have to get inside and find some of their mail to get the address."

Fargo gulped. "Inside? Isn't that against the law?"

"Fargo, I am the law. And I'm authorizing you to go inside. Besides, we have probable cause—like a house that doesn't even belong in our town!"

"Right, sure, of course." Fargo tried the doorknob. It didn't budge. "Uh, it's locked."

"Yeah, I'd kinda figured that."

"Hang on." Fargo held the PDA off to one side, took two steps back, then leaped forward and slammed shoulder-first into the door. All hundred and sixty pounds of him. The door didn't budge. He, however, fell backward, gasping. "Ow!"

"Fargo, what was that?" he could hear Carter asking, but he thrust out his jaw, took a deep breath, and ran at the door again. Same result. If anything, the second time hurt more. "Fargo? *Fargo!*"

"What?" he finally managed to reply after the third attempt. "I'm sorry, Sheriff. The door's too strong for me. I'm going to have to get help to break it down." Darned door—who needed something that sturdy on their house, anyway? What were they keeping in there, state secrets?

"Fargo, you don't need to break the door down," Carter explained to him, doing that *I'm speaking very slowly so I won't yell* thing he seemed to do a lot. "You just need to find the spare key."

"What spare key?" Had the sheriff been here before?

"Most people keep a spare key just outside their front door, in case they lose their keys or leave them inside and get locked out. Don't you do that?"

"Uh, no—I've got a retinal scanner synched to the door lock. It automatically opens as soon as I pass within range of the infrared beam." He frowned. "Except for that time I had to get my eyes dilated, of course. Fortunately, I have a password backup."

"That's swell. This isn't a Eurekan home, though," Carter reminded him. "Odds are, they'll have a spare key. What does the front of the house look like?"

Fargo squinted at it. "Mostly red. A little brown and orange here and there."

"It's brick?"

"Yep."

"Fine. Can you give me more specifics? Is there a porch or an awning? Does it have an exterior mailbox or a mail slot? Are there potted plants? Is there an external light?"

"Oh." Fargo hadn't even considered all that. He didn't usually pay much attention to architecture unless it was for computer systems. "Um, no porch but there is an awning. Also there are two steps up to the front door. It has a mail slot, and one big potted plant on either side of the front door, and there is a little wall lamp thing next to it as well. On the right side—the right side as I'm facing it, not if you're exiting it." He thought that showed excellent attention to detail.

"Great. Okay, take a look along the inner lip of the awning first. You're looking for a little magnetic box, probably painted the same color as the awning itself."

Fargo checked, stretching on tiptoes to run his fingers along the bottom edge. "Nope, nothing."

"Try the plants next—it'll be the same sort of little box, or it'll be a fake rock with a hidden opening underneath. It won't be buried deeply, just far enough to hide it from view."

The dirt in the pots was slightly moist and clung to Fargo's fingers, getting under his nails. "Nothing here either," he said after checking as thoroughly as he could.

"Okay, try the wall light. The box should be the size of a matchbox, maybe a little bigger, so it'll have to be on a flat spot that has enough room."

Fargo inspected the lamp. It was a squared-lantern style, with several rectangular panes spaced evenly around the bulb and a sloping top and bottom. A curving metal arm connected it to an oblong base mounted on the brick, and Fargo gave a little "A-ha!" as his fingers found the slim box affixed to that base's bottom edge. "Got it!"

"Good job!" Carter congratulated him. "The box should just slide open."

Sure enough, he was able to slide the top to one side and extract a dull metal key from within. The key fit the front door lock, and Fargo gently pushed the door open. Mission accomplished!

"I'm in," he reported.

"Great. Is there a small table right there by the door?"

"No. There's an umbrella stand, though."

"I don't think they'll have their address on the umbrellas," Carter pointed out. "What about a small box mounted to the wall just above the umbrella stand? Maybe one of those things with hooks for keys, and a little mirror?"

Fargo stared. "How did you know that?"

"I've been in a lot of houses. Most people use the box itself to hold their mail until they sort through it. Anything there?"

"Yes!" Fargo carefully extracted the envelopes. "I've got their mail! This is so exciting!" He glanced at the top one, then the next two for confirmation. "The house belongs to a Mark and Debbie Rensen. They live at 338 Ridgemont Drive, Burns, Oregon, 97720."

"Perfect. Thanks, Fargo. Burns is a few hours north—

tell Allison I'll call her as soon as I've got Gunter with me."
Carter hung up.

"Excellent!" Fargo congratulated himself, glancing around. He'd done it! With a little help, admittedly, but still—he'd never had to break into anyone's house before!

Then he realized that was exactly what he'd done. He'd broken into someone's house! Fargo left in a hurry.

CHAPTᵉR 12

"Henry? Hey, time to wake up."

Henry stirred, shifted, and sat up from his previous slouch, blinking a bit. "Oh, sorry about that, Jack—I only meant to doze a little." He glanced around. "Where are we?"

"Burns," Carter replied, his gaze alternating between the road, the speedometer, his rearview and sideview mirrors, and the GPS unit mounted on the dash. "Just turning onto Ridgemont Drive."

"Burns?" Henry rubbed at his eyes and glanced at the GPS display. "I thought we were heading to Lakeview?"

"Change of plans." Carter filled Henry in on the phone call with Fargo. "So we're going to pick Dr. Gunter up, bring him back to Eureka, and hopefully he can shut all this down. Then we can deal with the few places that've already swapped, but at least we won't have any more."

"Sounds good." Henry rubbed a hand over his face. "If

it's still just the ones we know about—now including Gunter's own home—we might be able to leave that end to Jo and Lexi. They'll be heading back toward Eureka anyway."

"Yeah, that could work," Carter agreed. Lexi was in Boise, which meant she had hours of driving ahead of her, so she might welcome the chance to stop a few times on the way. Jo was in Denio, to the south, which meant she could swing west toward Lakeview and then angle northeast to get back to Eureka. Especially since she would be traveling by helicopter. "First things first, though." He grinned. "It's not often I get to make long-distance house calls."

He rounded the corner and slowed the Jeep, studying the buildings on either side. It was a nice residential neighborhood, mostly two-story brick buildings—and that made the wood-and-stucco ranch stand out all the more. "I'm guessing that's where 338 should be," he pointed out, pulling into the driveway. They could clearly make out the number 417 on the front door.

"Great." Henry was already unbuckling his seat belt and opening his door. "Let's grab Arnold and get out of here."

"You know the guy, then?" Carter asked as he followed his friend along the brick path leading from the driveway to the front of the house. It was easy to see where the change had cut off—the walkway ended in a wide concrete step that didn't match at all.

"Sure, he's been in Eureka for years," Henry answered, turning to wait for him to catch up before hitting the doorbell. "Good guy, if maybe a little too focused on his work. But who isn't in Eureka, right? Anyway, I've never worked with Arnold directly but I've certainly seen him enough times, both at GD and around town, and we've spoken enough to be on a first-name basis. He's—"

Henry stopped talking as the door swung open and a man gaped out at them. "Henry!" he gasped, then saw Carter. "Sheriff! Oh, thank God!"

Henry was still staring at the man, who Carter agreed looked vaguely familiar—tall, broad-shouldered bordering on stocky, baldheaded, with close-set blue eyes and a small blond goatee.

"—not Arnold," Henry finally managed. He turned to Carter. "This isn't Arnold Gunter!"

Carter sighed. Of course it wasn't—that would have been too easy. "But this is his house, isn't it?"

"Yes, it is," both Henry and the other man answered together.

"Great," Carter muttered. "A swap within a swap. This is worse than those little Russian dolls!"

"You'd better come in," the other man said, stepping back and opening the door wider.

"Yeah, good idea," Carter said as he followed Henry in and the man shut the door behind them. "We wouldn't want any of the neighbors to wonder what two strange men were doing here, at this house that doesn't even belong in this city!" The man's eyes widened, and Carter held up a hand. "Sorry, it's already been a long day." He held the hand out. "I'm Sheriff Carter—I don't think we've met."

"No, we haven't, though I've seen you around town," their sort-of host agreed. "David Boyd." They shook. "I already know Henry, of course." Henry nodded.

After they'd shaken hands, Carter leaned against one of the entryway's walls. "Okay, Mr. Boyd, why don't you tell us what you're doing in Dr. Gunter's house?"

"I wish I knew, exactly," Boyd admitted. "Come on, we might as well sit down." He led them out of the entryway, up a few steps to the right, and into a nice sitting room.

"You seem to know your way around the place," Carter noticed, watching as Boyd maneuvered past a strange metal sculpture to plop into a comfortable-looking armchair. A matching chair had been placed just on the other side of a small table, and Carter took that one, while Henry planted himself on the couch across from them.

"Oh, sure, Arnold and I are old friends," Boyd agreed. "We used to have a weekly poker game for a while. That fell apart a year or two ago—too many other commitments, couldn't get people to show up on a regular basis—but we still get together every so often."

Carter studied Boyd. The man seemed nervous, or at least jumpy. Not guilty, though, and Carter had a pretty good sense for that sort of thing. Boyd didn't look like he'd caused all their problems, but he did look scared.

Then again, he was sitting in another man's house more than a hundred miles from where it belonged. If that wasn't a good reason to be scared, what was?

"Why don't you walk us through how you wound up here?" Carter asked, crossing his legs and leaning back in the cushy chair. He wanted Boyd to know this wasn't an interrogation. "And don't worry if it sounds crazy—we're here, so we can already guess at some of it."

Boyd nodded and tugged at one ear, which Carter noticed had a small gold hoop earring. "I was getting ready to head to work," he began, "when Arnold called. He said he had something to show me, and asked if I had a minute. I told him sure, if he made it quick, and he laughed. 'Oh, it'll be quick,' he assured me." Boyd shook his head. "Then there was a flash of light, and I felt a little dizzy. When my head cleared, I was standing right there." He gestured at a spot between the chairs and the couch. "I knew Arnold had been working on a way to transport matter—he was on the old SRT project, back in the day, and never quite let it go—so I figured he'd finally gotten everything to work. I thought he was hiding behind the sofa or around the corner, ready to jump out at me, but after a minute he still hadn't shouted 'Boo!' Then there was another flash, bigger this time, and I got dizzy again. After I recovered I looked around and I was still here." He glanced out the window right behind them. "But here wasn't here. If you know what I mean."

"We do indeed," Henry assured him. "David, you're in Burns, several hours north of Eureka."

Carter was surprised to see Boyd nod. "I'd thought as much—I didn't know the exact name, of course, but I could tell the house was several degrees north of its original location." He gave Carter a quick grin. "Spatial coordination is sort of my thing. I'm a mapping expert."

"Got it." Carter leaned forward. "So you didn't know exactly what Gunter was working on, but you knew it had to do with matter transportation?"

"Well—" Boyd glanced down at his hands, which were wringing together. "Something like that. I mean, he was technically assigned to alternate energy sources, and he was working on those. But he never stopped believing in teleportation, and I knew he was still tinkering with that in his spare time."

"It'd have to be a sideline project," Henry agreed. "GD shut down all work on teleportation after the SRT prototype—its range was too short and its power expenditure too high to justify further experimentation, especially with such a high risk factor. Teleportation research is also, technically, illegal."

"I guess he found a way to beat those problems," Carter pointed out. "And probably figured the whole *illegal* thing didn't matter as long as he never got caught. But now it looks like he can't shut the darn thing off." Boyd looked confused, so he explained. "This isn't the only building to go missing from Eureka. And each of them has been replaced by another one, from some other town in the Northwest."

"That can't be good," Boyd commented.

"My words exactly." Carter rose to his feet, and the other two men stood as well. "Where do you live, Mr. Boyd?"

"1210 Albany Court."

"Great. Thank you." Carter glanced at Henry, who nodded.

"If Arnold swapped places with David, he would have appeared in David's living room," Henry said, confirming Carter's own thought. "He could still be there now."

"I'll call Fargo and have him check," Carter said, pulling out his cell phone and punching in his own Eureka cell's number. "Then we'll see about getting you home," he assured Boyd.

"Sounds good," the man agreed, sitting again. He looked a little less worried than he had a minute ago.

"Hey, Fargo?" Carter asked as the researcher answered. "Yeah, it's Carter. Listen, I need you to check another address for me, okay? 1210 Albany Court. David Boyd lives there, but we have reason to believe Arnold Gunter might be there right now instead. Yeah, quick as you can." He rolled his eyes. "Yes, Fargo, this is official police business—you can speed. Call me when you get there."

Next Carter called Allison to update her. After he'd hung up, he glanced over at Boyd. "Any idea where the bathroom is, while we wait? It was a long drive up here."

"I hate this," Fargo muttered to himself as he rang the doorbell. "I really hope someone's here—I don't want to have to break into another home!"

"What was that?" the man asked as he swung the door open. "Did you say something about breaking in?" He glared down at Fargo, and Fargo gulped—this guy was easily twice his size, built like a football player, and dressed like a lumberjack in thick work jeans, heavy boots, a red flannel shirt, and a knit cap. Between that and the heavy black beard covering the lower half of his face, the man looked like he could face down grizzly bears without working up a sweat.

"Oh, no," Fargo said quickly, "I said 'breaking in my new shoes'!" He held up one foot to show off his brown dress shoes, silently whispering thanks for having just bought a new pair last week. "They're still new, and so they pinch my toes."

The big man frowned, but at least he didn't look like he was going to take a swing at him anytime soon. "Whaddya want?"

"I'm with the census," Fargo answered, thinking fast. "We're just gathering basic information—name, address, that sort of thing. Do you live here alone?"

"No, it's me, my girlfriend, and her two kids." The man was still frowning. "I thought they did the census just last year."

"They did, absolutely. This is the pre-census survey— we're gathering preliminary data for the next go-round, so when we actually start the official census we'll be ready." Fargo smiled at him, trying to project confidence and enthusiasm. "So, this is 940 Albany Court, right?" He'd noticed the house number on the mailbox mounted on the screen door.

"Albany Court? This is West Vidalia!"

"Right, of course, sorry about that." Fargo tapped his forehead. "Got the streets mixed up. And your zip is 97635?"

"What?" The guy looked like he wanted to laugh, which was at least better than violence. "97635? Where the hell is that? This is 97031!"

"Oh, yeah, you're right—I forgot." Fargo shook his head. "I think I need to go get something to eat—I'm having trouble focusing. I'll come back later. Thanks for your time." He turned to go, then stopped. "By the way, have you heard about the gas leak?"

* * *

Carter was just returning to the living room when his cell rang. "Hello?" He nodded to Henry and Boyd, who had begun playing chess using a marble-and-onyx set on the coffee table in front of the couch. "Yeah, Fargo, what'd you find?" He sighed. "Great. Okay, where is he from?" He pulled his pen and pad from his front shirt pocket and scribbled down the address. "940 West Vidalia, zip code is 97031, which is where exactly?"

"Hood River," Boyd called out without looking up from the chess match.

"Hood River. Okay, got it." Carter turned his attention back to Fargo. "Good work, Fargo. Let Allison know, would you? Thanks."

"Switched again?" Henry asked, capturing Boyd's queen.

"Yep, for a place up in Hood River, apparently." He looked at Boyd. "Ever been there?" Boyd shook his head. "Well, now your house has."

Henry frowned. "Where is that, exactly?"

Carter was already checking on his cell phone, but Boyd beat him to it. "Right along the Columbia River," he answered, then smiled. "Mapping, remember?"

"Right," Carter confirmed. "Looks like we can take the 20 from here to Bend, then hop the 97 to the 30." He offered Henry an apologetic shrug. "It's going to take a while."

"We don't really have time for that, Jack."

Carter sighed. "I know." He pulled his cell back out and dialed. "Allison?" It took him two tries to force the words out. "It looks like we're going to need that chopper of yours." He gave her their current address. "Yeah, thanks." He hung up. "She said they can be here in ten minutes."

"Right." Henry stood up. "We'd better get ready, then. We can meet them on the front lawn."

That earned him a glare. "Do you have to be so cheerful about it?" Carter grumbled.

Boyd looked confused. "He doesn't like to fly," Henry explained.

"I'm the same way," Boyd admitted. "Can't stand it, actually." He gulped. "Do you want me come with you, though?"

Carter thought about that for a second. "It's probably better if you stay here," he decided. "I don't know how many others we're going to find, and I doubt this copter's going to have a lot of room for passengers." He smiled. "Besides, no point in both of us getting airsick. We will get you back to Eureka, and back to your own house—I promise. But for now it's safest if you just stay here and wait."

Boyd nodded and walked them back to the front door. "I can do that, not a problem." He looked relieved, and Carter could hardly blame him. Still, it had taken guts to make the offer.

"Good." Carter shook hands with him again before stepping outside. "Thanks for your help. Oh, and probably best to stay inside and not answer the door if anyone knocks."

"I won't open it for anyone I don't know," Boyd assured him. He and Henry shook hands as well, and then Boyd closed the door. Carter heard him locking it.

"What're you going to do with your Jeep?" Henry asked as they made their way back toward it.

"I don't know," Carter answered. "Maybe, if Allison sent a second person along, I can ask them to drive it back for me. Or maybe she can send someone along to take care of that later. Worse comes to worst, it'll sit here until I can get back to pick it up." He stroked the roof just above his door. He hated to leave the trusty vehicle behind, especially since doing so put him at the mercy of the GD helicopter. But it didn't look like he had any choice.

A sudden wind kicked up, and Carter glanced skyward, holding up a hand to shield his eyes from the glare of the sun directly overhead. A dark shape was dropping down toward them, and he forced himself not to dive out of the way. The wind was stronger now, shoving him back against his Jeep, but he stood his ground as best he could, blinking back tears as the shape grew larger and resolved into a sleek, angular form the same color as the sky—the only reason he could see it at all was that it was blocking the sun. Then it settled onto the lawn with a faint thump, and a door appeared in its side.

"Sheriff Carter? Dr. Deacon?" someone called out.

"Looks like our ride's here," Henry shouted, leaning into the gale and forcing his way toward the copter step by step. "You ready?"

"No!" Carter shouted back. But he sighed and followed his friend anyway.

He just hoped this one ride would be enough to fix the problem. Find Gunter, bring him back to Eureka, get him to shut it all down. But Carter's stomach was roiling, and he didn't think all of it was anticipation of the hellish flight he was about to endure. There was almost no way the solution would be that easy.

CHAPT^eR 13

"Almost there . . ." Zane connected another wire to his ever-present tablet and activated the connection, watching the displays register the change in current. "Almost there . . ."

"I certainly hope so." Allison's tone wasn't sharp, but it wasn't soft either. He could tell she was starting to get annoyed at the delay. Well, okay, she'd been annoyed about the delay the minute they'd discovered the door was locked.

"I'm working as fast as I can," he assured her, selecting another wire and sliding it back into one of the now-empty slots on the door panel, creating a new loop. "You should be happy it's taking me this long—this security system is almost impossible to beat."

"Under other circumstances, I'd be thrilled," his boss agreed. "Right now, I'd much prefer it was the high-tech equivalent to a knotted cord and a *No Girls Allowed* sign!"

Zane tapped in a command and straightened from his crouch, grimacing as his knees protested. These floors weren't kind. "Well, this should help," he said, and hit the Enter key. Both of them held their breath as the panel's red light blinked on, then off . . .

. . . and stayed off as the green light flickered on instead.

"Yes! Zane, you're a genius!" Allison gave him a quick peck on the cheek even as she reached past him and hit the Open button. She wasn't normally that physical, but he didn't complain. It sure beat a slap on the back!

The doors slid open with a soft *whoosh*, and they stepped into lab 527—and stopped.

Zane found his voice first. "Wow."

Beside him, Allison nodded. "Wow indeed."

The room was amazing. It was huge, one of the larger Section Five laboratories, and clearly on the outskirts, with its far walls roughly chiseled from the surrounding bedrock. The ceiling was equally uneven, metal struts sprouting from it for support and to suspend long banks of fluorescent lights. At least the floor had been leveled before being covered with the standard coin-patterned rubber.

None of that was what had gotten their attention. In fact, they barely noticed the room itself. They were too awestruck by its contents.

Allison was the head of Global Dynamics. Zane was one of its brightest minds. Both of them interfaced with computers and cutting-edge technology on a daily basis.

And the equipment in lab 527 still took their breath away.

There were banks of computers covering every wall. They towered up at least eight feet, blinking lights and small whirring sounds attesting to their constant activity. Cables strung pieces together like a mad scientist's version of Christmas, and readouts flashed from displays all around the room. In many places additional circuitry had been added, sprouting from a computer like a mechanical thorn. There had been no effort to smooth edges or hide elements—everything was geared to functionality rather than appearance.

Allison shuddered to think of the computing power represented by what she saw before her. She suspected that this one system could handle most of GD's computing all on its own, possibly with processing power to spare.

And where was all that light coming from? Because the room was bright, midday-sun-overhead bright, and those fluorescents weren't producing anywhere near that sort of illumination.

"There!" Zane said, pointing off toward one corner. Something reflected the overhead lights there, something tall and curved and shiny, but there was additional light bursting from within it as well. After taking a second to focus, Allison realized she was looking at a tall glass cylinder, fitted with tubes and hoses and impressive metal seals at top and bottom.

A vacuum chamber.

But what was it doing? She squinted, trying to more clearly see its interior against the glare, and gasped as the lights there resolved into flickers and wisps and bubbles of glowing, burning clouds.

"Is that what I think it is?" she whispered, stepping down into the lab proper and crossing slowly toward the vacuum chamber.

"Yeah, I think so," Zane agreed, following her. "He's swapping out gases, replacing them with hydrogen and helium and nitrogen. In other words, he's got a tiny little sun in there, and that's what he's using for a power source." Zane gulped, remembering the last time they'd encountered a miniature sun in Eureka. Zoe's lab partner, Kylee—a genius even for Eureka, at nine years old!—had created a miniature solar system for their lab project. The sun had spun out of control, however, and had transformed from a dwarf star to a red supergiant. Then it had threatened to go supernova. The entire town had nearly become a large puddle of melted goo as a result.

At least this one looked a lot more stable.

"It seems stable," Allison said, echoing his thoughts as she stopped a few feet from the chamber and squinted to make it out more clearly. "He didn't create an entire sun, just a few wisps at a time—just enough to generate the power he needs. It's brilliant!"

"Pretty clever," Zane agreed, shielding his eyes with one hand. Wisps or not, it was bright as a sun. "And that's a whole helluva lot of power he's generating from it, too." He glanced back behind them, toward the center of the room. "But I guess he needs all of it—for that!"

They both stared at the linked monitors arrayed around a computer desk. The connected displays showed a map of the northwest coast, with overlapping close-ups of various locations. Each close-up appeared, zoomed in, then retreated until it was only a little larger than the rest of the map.

A lot like adjusting a camera to make sure you had your subject in perfect focus.

"This's got to be it," Zane said, stepping over to the desk and dropping into the chair set before it. "The MRS. I've gotta say, this Gunter guy is good!"

"One of our brightest," Allison agreed, leaning on the back of the chair so she could study the monitors as well. "The question is, can you figure out what he's got going here, and how it works? And fast?"

Zane twisted slightly to grin up at her. "Are you kidding? He may be one of the brightest, but so am I." He laced his fingers together and cracked his knuckles. "Now let's see what all these bad boys do."

* * *

Half an hour later, Zane slid a component back into place and sauntered back to the desk, perching on its edge. Allison had taken the chair and was scrolling through what activity logs she could access.

"Okay, I've got the basics," he told her. He immediately had her full attention. "We were right, it's the MRS project—Gunter obviously never shut it down, he just set it aside until he could lick the energy problem, then connected the two and started it all back up."

"Why is it swapping out buildings?" Allison asked. "That wasn't part of the original project plan."

"It looks like it's a fail-safe," Zane answered. "From what I can figure, Gunter realized there were fewer and fewer unoccupied spaces in the world. Finding one large enough to hold a transported tank, army, or building would take forever, and could wind up being too far away to be useful—or simply outside the equipment's effective range. So he figured out a way to have the MRS scan the area, find a person or object or structure of similar dimensions, and transport that at the same time. That way it always knows it's got a clear destination, because it just cleared it half a nanosecond before!"

"That makes sense," Allison admitted. "In fact, if he can control it, something like that could make the MRS even more useful. Imagine a hostage situation—you could swap the hostage taker for a cop and end the problem instantly, with nobody hurt. And you could probably arrange it so the criminal winds up in back of a squad car!"

"Absolutely." Zane tapped a finger against one of the monitors. "It looks for the nearest, closest match, which is why it traded one office building for another and a carport for a garage. It must have thought S.A.R.A.H.'s bunker fit the same mold as that little fast-food place, and

the sheriff's office had similar equipment to a gun shop."
And Taggart and I were interchangeable, he thought
but didn't say. I wonder what Jo would have to say about
that? He forced that line of thought back down where he
couldn't hear it, at least for now. "The problem is, it looks
like Gunter activated the program, told the MRS to start
swapping out locations, and then didn't give it any more
specific instructions. So it's got an open-ended command
to exchange everything within range, and it's going to do
exactly that."

Allison sighed. "So it's not done yet?"

"Not by a long shot."

"Okay, can we shut it down?"

"Maybe," Zane admitted. "But I don't think that's a good
idea." She studied him, clearly waiting for an explanation.
"Okay, here's the thing. Yes, I think I can shut it down. I
can disrupt its operating loop, causing a systemwide failure
that'll kill the whole thing in midleap." He rubbed at his
cheek. "That's the problem. It'd be midleap."

Allison nodded. One of the great things about working
at GD was that your boss was a genius, too, so she didn't
need a whole lot of hand-holding. "You'd be interrupting the
program, but you can't guarantee it would be a clean break.
And if it was in the middle of replacing some place—"

"—there's no telling what would happen." Zane
shrugged. "It might just stall out, and neither place would
go anywhere. Or it might have enough computing reserves
and enough power storage to finish the exchange before
shutting down." He shuddered. "Or it might just stop right
where it was, leaving two buildings—and anything and everyone inside—caught halfway." He had horrible images
of the horror movie *The Fly*, but this time with an entire
building full of people being merged together.

"Can't you just hack into the program and tell it to shut
down?" Allison asked him.

"Sure, if I knew all Gunter's protocols, safety measures, and passwords." Zane thought about exactly what he'd need to accomplish that. "I can probably crack his system without those," he pointed out after a second, "but it'll take some time. He's got some seriously heavy-duty encryption going on in here, with redundant security measures and a lot of other stuff. Definitely a little on the paranoid side." He scratched his jaw. "Which makes it even weirder that he didn't program more detailed instructions. Why let the thing run wild like that, especially if you're this much of a control freak?"

"We can worry about the whys later," Allison pointed out. "Right now we just need to stop it. What about just pulling the plug?" She glanced over at the vacuum chamber. "Literally? We could disconnect that chamber from the computer, which would mean the MRS no longer had enough power left to make another swap."

"We could, but there are two potential problems with that." Zane held up his right index finger. "First off, we have no idea if he's got some kind of power storage set up in here. I would if I were him, just to avoid any problems if the power supply ever went down, but it could be anywhere. Unless we disconnect anything like that, cutting the power won't stop the MRS—and it might activate additional countermeasures."

Allison nodded. "What's the other problem?"

"We're talking about a sliver of an artificial mini-sun." Zane looked at the vacuum chamber, and the coruscating lights within it, again. And shuddered. "If we don't disconnect it perfectly, it could blow. And if it did that—"

He didn't have to spell it out for her. If the vacuum chamber blew, it would result in something very much like a tiny, tiny version of a star going supernova. Zane had had several girlfriends "go supernova" on him in the past, usually right when he told them they were now ex-girlfriends.

None of those explosions had threatened an entire town, let along the whole region where that town existed.

"Okay, so we can't touch the power supply," Allison confirmed. "And we can't shut down the substitution program." She sighed. "See what kind of access you can get—maybe we can at least create some new parameters, restrict the process a bit, keep it from grabbing places with a lot of people." She pulled the keyboard toward her and began typing. "Other than that, we wait until Carter finds Dr. Gunter for us. Once we have him, he can explain how everything works and walk us through a nice clean shutdown."

"Well, let's hope he hurries up." Zane pointed at one of the monitors. "Because it apparently considers any building brought into Eureka to now be part of the town as well. Which means it'll start swapping those out for other places as well. If we can't shut this thing down, it'll disperse the entire town to the surrounding cities, and then it'll keep going, over and over again. It won't ever stop as long as there are buildings left, and it'll always have buildings because it brings a new one in for every one it sends out." He looked Allison in the eye.

"This could literally go on forever. And its range is expanding, so it could affect the entire countryside. No one, and no home or building, would be safe."

Allison gave him a reassuring smile. "Carter will find him." She stood and slid the keyboard toward Zane. "But in the meantime, let's see if there isn't anything else we can do to help from here."

CHAPTER 14

"Oh, crap."

The instant the Night Wing touched down, Carter staggered out, then sagged. Henry had jumped out right behind and he pulled Carter back upright. Then they both stared at the house the stealth copter had landed in front of, taking in the details. It was a large, almost sprawling structure, pieced together from irregular chunks of rock with a wide wooden porch and a sagging roof.

Of course, that didn't exactly match the tall, weathered wood buildings that flanked it. Especially since those all had stilts beneath them, whereas this house sat solidly on the ground. Too solidly—from where Carter was, it looked like the building was sinking slightly.

Unfortunately, it didn't match any place he'd seen in Eureka, either. And Henry was shaking his head as well, which meant he also didn't recognize the place.

"I guess we'd better check it out," Henry suggested.

"Yeah, yeah," Carter agreed, shaking himself. At least he was back on solid ground! He felt better just being out of that monstrous contraption—why anyone would ever want to fly, he had no idea. "I swear, this is getting to be like one of those little puzzles you have when you're a kid—you know the ones I mean? They're small flat squares and the pieces slide around inside the frame, and there's one missing so there's room to move the rest? But every time you want to move one you've got to slide three others out of the way first? Those things used to drive me crazy."

"I remember those," Henry agreed as they approached the house. The air here was thick and salty, and smelled heavily of both brine and fish. Which made sense, given that the Columbus River was right behind the row of houses. "I always liked them myself."

"Of course you did."

"There was a trick to them, you know."

"Oh, I know." Carter grinned. "Pull all the pieces out, then rearrange them and put them back in the way they're supposed to go." Henry gave him one of those looks, along with a slight shake of the head. "What? It worked!"

Carter had just raised his hand to knock on the door—a heavy, unpaneled and unvarnished wooden door that looked like it could stop a charging rhino—when it was yanked open from the inside. The next thing he knew, there was a woman in his arms. "Oh, thank God!" came the wail from against his chest.

"Uh, ma'am?" Carter patted her on the back and let her stay there for a few seconds before slowly, gently pulling away. "Ma'am?"

She rubbed at her eyes and brushed long, thick red hair out of her face. "I'm—I'm sorry. I just—" She waved her hand at the scene behind them, and it looked like she was about to break down again. "I can't—"

"I understand," Carter assured her. "Maybe we should

talk inside?" He figured not being able to see her surroundings might help calm the woman down.

"Okay. Yes, of course. I'm sorry. Please, come in." She ushered them through the door, then all but darted in after them and slammed it behind her. She was middle-aged, Carter noticed, and sturdily built, with strong features and weathered skin. Her heavy shirt, thick pants, and hiking boots all looked well worn-in as well. "Won't you sit down?"

"Thank you." Henry took a handsome-looking rocking chair near the fireplace, and Carter settled himself on a stool near it. The fireplace wasn't lit and the room was pleasantly cool, with its thick stone walls and bearskin rugs and the woven tapestries on the walls. It was a cheery place, if rustic.

"I really am sorry," she apologized to Carter again, sitting in the second rocking chair and facing them both. Her fingers were trying to tie themselves in knots, and she visibly forced them to stillness, cupping her knees. "I just—I don't know, I sort of freaked out." She gave them a shy smile.

"Not a problem," Carter told her. "And hell, I don't blame you. If I looked outside and things didn't look right, I'd panic, too."

She leaned forward. "What is going on here, exactly? You're not Gary Baker, and he's the only law we've seen in these parts in three years, ever since Phil Atkins retired."

Phil Atkins? Carter frowned. He knew that name! Then he remembered. Phil had been a federal marshal as well, but less far-ranging than him. A lot of the marshals had loosely defined regions under their jurisdiction, whereas Carter had been the roaming type, assigned to assist wherever there was a problem. And Atkins had been up this way, he recalled, but a little to the east—in the mountains. He'd retired a year or so before Carter had wound up in Eureka, which made the timing just about right.

"My name's Jack Carter," he told her, pulling himself back to the present. "I'm a sheriff from Oregon. This is Henry Deacon. He's a scientist." Henry smiled at her and half raised a hand in greeting.

"A scientist? And a sheriff from Oregon?" She stared at them. "So there *is* something going on here! I knew it! I knew I wasn't just going crazy! I mean, look outside!" She gestured toward the window. "Does that look like the Sawtooths to you?"

Even from where he was sitting, Carter could see the Columbus River flowing past. "No, it definitely doesn't," he agreed. What else was he going to say?

"That's why we're here," Henry added, stepping into the conversation. "There's been a gas leak from a lab in Oregon, and the winds are blowing the chemicals every which way. The gas isn't dangerous in and of itself, but it's been causing hallucinations. We're trying to warn people so no one gets hurt."

"Hallucinations?" The woman buried her face in her hands, shoulders heaving, and at first Carter thought she was crying. Then she lifted her face and he realized she'd been laughing, though there were still tears streaming down her cheeks. "Oh, thank God! I really had thought I was going nuts!"

"No, ma'am, you're perfectly sane," Carter replied, though admittedly he was making a big assumption there. After all, he'd only just met her. "But can I ask you to tell me exactly what happened?"

"Oh, okay, sure." She sat up straighter and brushed her hair back again. "I was washing up after breakfast, right over there at the sink." She pointed, and Carter glanced at the far wall and through the doorway there. He could just make out a sink and stove in the room beyond. "There was a bright flash outside, but I thought it was just the sun glaring off the snowcaps again—it does that a lot up here. I felt a little dizzy and almost dropped my mug, but it passed after a second. Then I looked out the window again and—I think I may have dropped the mug after all. All I know is, one minute I was looking at mountains like always, and the next there was some big old muddy river flowing past, and not a ridge or peak in sight!"

Henry glanced at Carter. "That definitely sounds like it, all right," he said, nodding slightly.

"You said it's not dangerous?"

"Not at all," Carter assured her. "Just confusing. The effects'll pass, though. For now, we're asking that everybody just stay indoors and away from windows. Get some sleep, read a book, just keep yourself busy while we sort this out."

She nodded. "I will. Thank you."

"Not a problem." Carter stood, and Henry did as well. "Oh, one more thing—I didn't catch your name?"

The smile she gave him was almost flirtatious. "Mary. Mary Wallace."

"Well, Mary, thank you for your help, and I'm sorry you had to go through this." Carter made his way toward the door, opened it, and then stopped. "Oh hey, one last thing, actually—I noticed you don't have a street number on your house." He'd half registered that as they'd walked up, but it hadn't fully sunk in until now.

Mary snorted. "Not much need for those in Stanley," she told him, chuckling. "We barely have streets!"

"Fair enough. Well, thanks for your time, and sorry again about the trouble. It should all be sorted out soon."

"Come back anytime!" Mary called after him as Carter let himself out, closed the door after Henry, and headed back to the copter, which was barely visible thanks to its chameleon surface. "I'd love the company!"

"Looks like you've made a friend there, Jack," Henry teased him as they climbed into the Night Wing's rear compartment. The rotors were already beginning to spin lazily.

"Yeah, that's me, making friends all over the country," Carter agreed. He had his phone out and dialed Allison, but it went to her voice mail. So he tried Fargo.

"Fargo, it's Carter," he said once the little scientist answered. "Listen, I need you to check on something for me. I need to find a person's address. Her name is Mary Wallace, and she lives in Stanley, somewhere in or near the mountains. No, I don't know which—wait, hang on, yes I do. She said 'Sawtooths.' She's near the Sawtooth Mountains." He waited while Fargo punched the information into a computer—he'd figured Fargo would have one handy. "Stanley. Got it. Thanks." He started to hang up, then stopped. "No, we don't have him yet. We're working on it. Everything okay there?" He couldn't help rolling his eyes. "Yeah, well, that's why they pay me the big bucks, Fargo. No one said being sheriff was easy. Just keep on top of it, all right? And let Allison know we're still going to be a while. Thanks."

"Trouble?" Henry asked as Carter hung up.

"Not really, it's just Fargo being Fargo." Carter shook his head. "Give him gadgets and wires and computers and he'll try anything. Take him out of his comfort zone, and it's a whole other story."

"That's true of most people," Henry pointed out. "Some of us just have wider comfort zones than others."

"Fair enough. I hope yours includes mountain ranges, because that's where we're going." Carter leaned forward to address the pilot, a heavyset young guy named Sean. "Mary's from Stanley, Idaho, in the middle of the Rocky Mountains."

"Got it." Sean punched in the destination, then pulled back on the stick and revved the copter's engines. The rotors picked up speed, and Carter grabbed frantically at the handle anchored just above the rear door as the Night Wing lifted off the ground. He gulped, feeling his stomach drop, and tried to think about anything but the empty air now separating him from the ground.

Fortunately, Henry distracted him. His friend had entered Mary's address into Carter's GPS unit, which they'd brought from the Jeep, and studied the little monitor as it mapped out their new route. "Jack, that's past Boise, which was the farthest east anything had gone up until now. And it's almost as far north as we are here."

"I know." Carter pounded his other hand into the seat. "It's widening its scope. Which means we could have more homes and buildings leaving Eureka, and it's going to be harder and harder for us to get to them quickly. I'll tell Jo and Lexi."

"Should we ask Lexi to go up to Stanley? She's a lot closer to it than we are."

But Carter shook his head. "She'd have to drive, and this infernal contraption will take a lot less time." His friend grinned at his obvious discomfort, proving that even mild-mannered Henry Deacon had a bit of a sadist in him. "Besides, you're the only one of the four of us who can talk to Gunter, geek to geek," Carter reminded him. "No offense. But I'm going to need you along to translate. Because at this rate, we may not have the luxury of getting him back to Eureka before we try to shut his project down."

Henry nodded. "If he can tell me exactly what he did, I should be able to help." But he was frowning. "There's just one thing that's been bothering me, though."

Carter laughed. "Just one? Because I've got a whole stack of things bothering me!"

"Well, yes, fair enough. But one thing that I'm finding even more puzzling." Henry paused, and glanced out of the copter's small side window. Mary Wallace's house was now just a small light shape against the darker wooden buildings that surrounded it.

"Why did Boyd's house move twice?" Carter supplied. "Yeah, it's bugging me, too. Especially since it means Gunter himself has moved three times—first to Boyd's house, then here to Hood River, and now to Stanley." He shook his head. "I don't know, maybe because he's the center of it all, so he's got the most activity?"

"That's entirely possible," Henry agreed. "He could well be the epicenter. Just in this case he's a mobile one."

"Too mobile." Carter gulped as the copter reached its cruising height and its jet engines kicked in, sending the craft hurtling forward at speeds he really didn't want to consider. "Let's hope we can get to him before he moves again."

CHAPTᵉR 15

Jo pulled the door shut behind her, making sure she heard the lock click securely, and headed for her car. She was still tying her hair into its customary topknot and trying to ignore her stomach's growls. She'd stop off at Café Diem for coffee and a Danish before heading back out, she decided. She could have grabbed something at home, but it wasn't like she had much more than some stale cereal in the cupboard. Why bother when Vincent could—and did—make any food she wanted, on the spot, at a moment's notice?

She'd debated coming back at all, versus staying out in the field. But she'd decided it made more sense to return to Eureka until Carter sent her out again. This way she was on hand if there was a problem, and with GD's stealth copter at her disposal she could reach anywhere on the West Coast in an hour or less. She'd also wanted to be prepared if she wound up having to be away for a few days. Jo kept a jump bag in her car's trunk, of course, with a fresh uniform, a spare outfit, several days' worth of undergarments, water, MREs, ammo, a backup pistol, and so on. Standard military procedure. The problem was, her car had been back outside the office—or where the office had been that morning—and so she'd had nothing on her but what she'd had at the office. Guns aplenty, and ammo, too, but nothing else—no clean clothes, for example. And although Jo could spend—and had spent—days at a time in the same outfit while on ops and stakeouts, she didn't like it. With her bag in hand, she'd be set no matter where Carter needed her, or for how long.

So she'd "hitched a ride" on GD's second stealth copter, which had dropped her off in the small parking lot a block behind the sheriff's office—now Gary's Guns. That had been fantastic! It had been a few years since Jo had gotten to fly in a helicopter, and the Night Wing put even the Blackhawks to shame. Faster, quieter, more maneuverable, visually camouflaged, and completely radar-invisible, it was an impressive piece of work. Jo made a mental note to ask Allison later if she could go back up in one again.

Carter hadn't called to send Jo anywhere else after she'd been to Fields and Lakeview, so she'd checked in with him while airborne, only to find that he was in the other Night Wing on his way to Gunter's current location in the Sawtooth Mountains. She grinned, remembering his voice. He was clearly hating every second of his helicopter ride, which she didn't understand at all but was more than happy to give him grief over. But that meant he was effectively out of the loop until he landed, so Jo was on her own. Once her chopper had lifted off again, she'd retrieved her car from its usual spot, checked in with Fargo and Zoe, and then headed home just to make sure everything here was in order. She'd also taken a quick shower—dealing with

Gary's customers had been a surprising workout. Now, clean and freshly uniformed, she felt ready to face the rest of the day.

Jo was just unlocking her car door—not really necessary in Eureka, but old habits died hard—when a flicker of movement behind her made her stop, spin, and crouch, drawing her pistol in the same motion. Then she stared.

Her house was wavering.

Not waving, wavering. It seemed to be shimmering, its edges blurring and shifting, as if it were a grainy picture going in and out of focus. Then a bright flash of light blinded Jo, causing her hands to rise in front of her face by pure reflex. When she could see again and lowered them, she saw through the spots that her house had changed.

Or rather, it was no longer her house standing there.

"Great." Jo stood up, holstered her pistol, and brushed herself off. "That's just perfect." She sighed. At least she hadn't still been inside—two minutes earlier and she'd have wound up wherever her house had just gone, while her car sat here in the driveway.

Jo shook her head and marched back up toward the front door. As she did, she pulled out her phone—her Eureka PDA rather than the cell she'd commandeered from that one pushy guy back in Denio—and dialed Carter.

"Fargo?" She knew better than to let him get more than an "Uh-huh" in before continuing—she didn't have all day. "It's Jo. There's been another swap. 444 Langston Drive. I'm already there, so I'll check on the new place and deal with anyone inside. I'll call you back when I know if the owners are home, so you can add them to your list—you are keeping a list of all the people who've been transplanted here, aren't you? Good." She sighed. "Yes, Fargo, I can tell you whose house it was. It was mine." She hung up before he could say anything in reply. Whatever it was, she was sure she didn't want to hear it.

* * *

Fargo stared at the PDA, then laughed.

"What's so funny?" Zoe demanded. "Because right now I could really use a good joke."

"Oh, that was Jo," Fargo told her. "She's got another house swap. Her own!"

"What?"

"Her house got swapped, right out from under her!"

"Where is she?"

"Standing outside it." Fargo was clearly enjoying getting to dispense information, and he was dragging this out. Zoe wondered if smacking him with something would speed things up any. "It sounds like she'd just left when it got moved."

"Well, at least she didn't go with it. So she's taking care of whoever's there?"

"Absolutely." Fargo grabbed his laptop, opened it, and began typing something in.

"What are you doing now?" Honestly, Zoe thought, why had her dad insisted she and Fargo work together? Like she couldn't handle this on her own! After all, she was in college now!

"Adding Jo's name and address to the list of places that've been moved," Fargo answered, not even looking up. "I'm keeping a database, so we can track all of them when this is over." Now he did glance her way, clearly smug. "Oh, didn't you think to do that?"

"I don't need to," Zoe retorted, tossing her ponytail back over her shoulder with the head flip she'd practiced years ago specifically for dismissing boys. "I have all of it stored up here." She tapped her forehead.

That got a snort in reply. "Yeah, that's great now, while there're only a handful of exchanges. But what happens if there are dozens more? How many can you remember at once?"

Zoe frowned. "You don't really think there'll be dozens, do you?" She fiddled with her mug—since her dad wasn't here, and since she'd pleaded that she'd need the caffeine to be properly alert, Vincent had caved and given her the double espresso she'd ordered. "Dad'll stop it before it gets that far."

"I certainly hope so," Fargo admitted, pushing his glasses back up on his nose. "But we need to be prepared. Besides, Sheriff Carter can only do so much. A lot's going to depend on him finding Dr. Gunter."

"Oh, he'll find him." Zoe wasn't worried on that score. Back when he'd been a marshal, her dad had prided himself on always getting his man. Or woman. Or runaway teenage daughter. She smirked. She'd given him a run for his money, at least. But catching a geeky scientist? How hard could that be?

Her musings were interrupted by the ring of a PDA. Fargo answered it. "Hey, Jo," he said, and Zoe stifled a laugh at the way his whole posture changed, becoming more laid back and casual and almost sleazy. His voice dropped, too, and she could tell he was doing that deliberately. Poor Fargo—he'd had it bad for Jo as long as Zoe had been here, and probably before that. He also didn't stand a chance. Especially not with Zane around. He was too old for Zoe, of course, but she had to admit Zane was hot. Plus he had that whole "bad boy" thing going for him. And he was a genius, but not smug about it. Jo had definitely found herself a real catch there.

A pair of hands suddenly appeared in front of her, cutting off her vision as they were placed over her eyes. At the same time, Zoe felt the warmth of someone stepping up close behind her. Someone tall, judging from the way she could feel them even to the top of her head. A rush of hot air tickled her left ear, and a deep, soft voice whispered, "Guess who?"

Zoe smiled as she grasped the long fingers with her own smaller ones and turned, raising the joined hands over her head so she pivoted within their grasp. Then she smiled and rose up on tiptoes to give her boyfriend a kiss. Lucas smiled down at her as he returned the kiss, and Zoe felt herself flush slightly.

Yes, she'd caught herself a good one, too.

"Oh, get a room," Fargo muttered from the side, and Zoe glared at him.

"Shut up," she warned. "Lucas came to help. Didn't you?"

"Yeah, of course," her boyfriend agreed. He looked a little concerned, though. "I'm not really sure what I can do, though. What do you need?"

"Nothing yet," Zoe assured him. "We've only had one swap lately that we know of, and Jo took care of it." She didn't bother to explain that it had been Jo's own house that had moved. She could fill him in on that later.

"That was her just now," Fargo informed them, waving the PDA. "She said the transplanted home's owner was still inside, getting ready to head to work for an afternoon shift. A Juliette Morrissey. She bought the gas leak story and is staying safely indoors." He tapped his laptop's screen, where Zoe could see he had a spreadsheet open. "She's from Fort Klamath."

Fort Klamath? Zoe frowned, not sure where that was, and Lucas noticed her expression. "It's a few hours west of here," he explained softly. "Right near Upper Klamath Lake."

Zoe nodded, giving him a big smile as a thank-you. That was one of the things she loved about Lucas—he was smart, but he didn't make a big deal about it. A lot of people—including Fargo—would have rubbed her nose in the fact that she hadn't known the town's exact coordinates instantly. But he'd simply told her where it was. O course, with a lot of things he'd make her figure it out for herself—Lucas was a firm believer in pushing yourself to your limits and challenging your capabilities. She beamed at him again. How had it taken her so long to notice him? And what would she do without him? She'd been thrilled when he'd gotten into MIT early, so they were going to school near each other—at least near enough that they could see each other on weekends. The fact that they both had midwinter break right now, and had both come home to Eureka, was even better.

"If you two are quite done with your little lovefest," Fargo snapped at her, as she and Lucas traded glances, "we should stay alert. There could be an influx of new transplants at any moment."

"Transplants?" Zoe snorted. "What is this, an organ donor meeting? They're not transplants, they're people who've had their homes moved with them stuck inside!"

"Exactly—that's what the word *transplant* means," Fargo replied. "Try to keep up, would you?"

"Keep up? Oh, you—" Zoe grabbed the saltshaker beside her mug and probably would have lobbed it at him and his little smirk if Lucas hadn't taken it out of her hand.

"Come on, there's no need for that," he told them both, his voice soft but firm. "You two fighting isn't going to help anything or anyone. Stay focused."

Zoe nodded. So did Fargo, after a second. They both knew Lucas was right. It was just, oh, Fargo got on her nerves even more now than he had when she'd lived here full-time! "What do you think we should do?" she forced herself to ask him, trying to keep any hostility out of her voice. "To stay ready?"

Fargo thought about that for a second. "I'm not really sure," he admitted finally. "Just make sure we've still got some tables clear, I guess."

Zoe was thinking as well, though. "We should let the

regulars know that they need to keep any inventions out of sight whenever there are people around they don't recognize," she suggested. "And probably warn them not to talk to strangers, or at least to keep any conversation to things like the weather and sports, to avoid revealing anything outsiders shouldn't know." Eureka's very existence was classified, after all.

Fargo nodded. "Right. And I'm adding a line to my database, so we can see at a glance who we've got here and who's still in their homes."

"Good idea." Zoe glanced around. There were a few regulars here already. "I'll start talking to people." She took a deep breath. This could work. She and Fargo had managed to get along okay this morning, though in part that had been because they'd been in separate locations half the time, with her stationed here at Café Diem and Fargo driving to various houses at her dad's or Allison's request. But she could handle this. Lucas gave her a grin that said, *There, see, that wasn't so bad?* and Zoe smiled back.

Yes, she could handle this.

She just hoped it didn't have to go on too long. Because a few hours working with Fargo were enough to try anyone's patience. Any more than that, and even Lucas might not be able to restrain her.

CHAPTᴇR 16

"What is this, nap time?" Allison asked as she kicked Zane's feet off the desk.

Zane looked up at her blearily. His short hair was a mess and he had deep rings under his eyes. He also had his feet up and crossed on the desk and was leaning back in the chair, the computer's wireless keyboard on his lap so he could type in line after line of code. "Sorry, just closed my eyes for a minute," he claimed, stretching. "How long was I out?"

"I have no idea," Allison answered. "You were awake when I went upstairs to make sure there weren't any other fires to put out. You were asleep when I got back just now. That was maybe half an hour ago."

"Is that all?" Zane waved aside her concern. "Barely any time at all." He suddenly noticed the Café Diem bag Allison had placed down on the desk. "Do I smell coffee? And doughnuts?"

She couldn't help laughing. "You do indeed. I asked Vincent to send over a sandwich for me—I figured it was better to stay close in case something else happened—and asked him to include something for you, too. A double latte with vanilla and cinnamon, and three glazed chocolate doughnuts."

"You are, without a doubt, the coolest boss I've ever had," Zane said enthusiastically as he grabbed for the bag. He pulled his coffee and a doughnut from it and immediately stuffed half of the pastry in his mouth, following it with a big gulp of the hot liquid. "Ah!" Allison could practically see the caffeine and sugar hit his system. "So much better!"

"Was your mental break useful, at least?" she asked as she leaned against the desk and sipped her own coffee, which she'd been smart enough to remove from the bag before handing it to Zane. She doubted she'd have been able to get it back from him if she hadn't. "Have you figured out the MRS yet?"

"Not entirely, no," Zane admitted, wiping bits of glaze from his lips and immediately starting in on the second doughnut. "But I've managed to unlock a few features, anyway." He smiled around his breakfast. "Like the activity log."

"Really? Great! Let's take a look." Allison stood and turned to lean over his chair as he called up the log. Together they read through the information the computer had recorded. "Okay, so Gunter had run several tests over the past few days. It looks like he started with plants outside town"— she indicated the log line with her index finger—"and then swapped plants on the edge of town as well. That would be Seth Osbourne's flowers—Carter told me about that."

"Look at this." Zane gestured his last doughnut at the next entry. " 'Target location selected. Designated Target C39A. Warning: Human DNA detected. Designated Target C39A-1. Search for suitable replacement commenced. Search located Target C39A-1. Second location designated Target C39B. Targets relocated. Placement of Target C39A successful. Placement of Target C39B successful.'" He scratched at his head. "What the hell does that mean? How did it find the same target twice?"

"The Baker brothers!" Allison stared at the screen. "It has to be! Carter said he picked up one of the Bakers walking back into town, and he seemed confused—Dr. Baker, not Carter. He apparently seemed surprised that he'd been out walking, because he thought one of his brothers was instead." She shook her head. "Evidently he was right. His brother had been the one out walking, until he happened to be in the MRS's target location. It scanned him, registered his DNA, scanned for a suitable replacement, and found a perfect match elsewhere—the next nearest Baker brother."

Zane thought about that for a second. "Yeah, okay, I'll buy that," he agreed finally. "But look at the next entry: 'Target location selected. Designated Target C40A. Warning: Human DNA detected. Designated Target C40A-1. Search for suitable replacement commenced. Search located second target within approximate area: designated Target C40B-1. Second location designated Target C40B. Targets relocated.'"

"Nora Allen and Karl Worinko," Allison supplied. "They were both out in the woods outside town, and somehow Nora wound up miles farther out than she'd realized, while Karl discovered he was a lot closer to town than he'd thought." She straightened and took a step back, then turned and began pacing behind the chair, thinking. "So it looks like Gunter didn't plan on swapping people, they just kept winding up in his target locations. He was testing his equipment on plants first, and it was just bad luck that those people were there at the right place, the wrong time."

"But then he graduated to inorganics," Zane pointed out. "The next line says, 'Target acquired. Target automotive in nature. Designated Target C41A. Second automotive target located within approximate area: designated Target C41B. Targets relocated.'" He grinned. "That'd be Larry's car, right?" It figured he'd heard about that one!

"Larry's, and Dr. Styvers's." Allison nodded. "Cars are more complex than plants, and closer to buildings in material, so if Dr. Gunter was working his way up to moving buildings as the MRS was designed to do, it makes sense that he'd start with smaller man-made objects." She frowned. "C41? He must have done several hundred smaller tests here in the lab before even starting these. So at least he was following appropriate safety protocols, though he still should have filed beforehand to run his experiments."

"He was probably afraid you'd shut the project down again," Zane pointed out. "Or that the military would take it away from him before he had a chance to perfect it this time." He took a swig of coffee, swallowed, and stretched. "But I still don't get why he's swapping things. That wasn't the original intention for the system. When did he realize that was even possible?"

"I don't know." Allison moved back to her previous spot right behind his chair and motioned toward the monitors. "Scroll up a bit and let's see if we can find anything about it in the log."

Zane tapped a command, and the activity log scrolled back a page.

"There!" Allison pointed. "That one! 'Target selected. Designated Target C09. Target location acquired. Warning: Target location already occupied! Object designated Target C09 redesignated C09A. New object designated C09B. Targets relocated. Placement of Target C09A successful. Relocation of Target C09B to original Target C09A location successful.'"

"Something must have rolled into the spot he'd picked as the end point," Zane suggested. "The MRS detected it, and decided the safest place to put the new object was right where the old object had been, once the old object had been moved." He shook his head. "That's one hell of a subroutine!"

"Gunter must have programmed it for the possibility," Allison decided. "He knew it might happen—it's impossible to guarantee that a location will remain secure and unoccupied, outside laboratory conditions. So he factored that into his protocols. The MRS may have activated that option earlier than he'd planned, but once it had and he saw that it had worked successfully he made that the new primary function."

Zane nodded. "Yeah, he started going after swaps instead of just teleports. First small things here in the lab, then small organics here—probably potted plants or lab mice—and then he stepped up to plants outside." He shook his head. "I'll bet he didn't intend to graduate to people so quickly, not without a whole lot more testing, but when one of the Bakers walked into his target location and the MRS found another brother, it made the switch on its own. And then he knew it could handle people without a problem."

"There must have been other fail-safes," Allison agreed. "Gunter's record is impressive—he doesn't take unnecessary chances." She glanced over at the vacuum chamber, which still shed its glow across the room. "Clearly, since he spent the past several years just developing an energy source that could power his MRS. My guess is the systems would have aborted that first substitution except that the computer scanned Dr. Baker and then found an exact DNA match for him elsewhere. That probably slid just below the fail-safe's cutoff—what could be less dangerous than exchanging something for itself?" She sighed. "And once it had done that, he knew it could handle it, so he disengaged the other safeties."

"And he was right," Zane pointed out. "The MRS really can swap two people without hurting them at all."

"Okay, so we can see the activity log." Allison brought them back to the situation at hand. "Can we stop the program?"

"Not yet." Zane finished his coffee and lobbed the empty cup at the trash can he'd spotted just past the desk. It sailed in perfectly, missing the sides completely and clattering only when it hit the bottom. "Or at least, not without putting anyone currently being transported at risk." He scrolled back down to the most recent entries. "I haven't figured out a pattern or a timetable yet, so I can't risk shutting it down midprocess."

"We can't put anyone at risk," Allison agreed. "Okay, keep trying—see what else you can access. The more control we have, the better our chances of stopping it from moving anyone else, and if we know it's in standby mode we can shut it down safely." She glanced up at the activity log. "In the meantime, that's going to be useful. At least now we won't have to worry that places are switching without our knowledge, and Zoe and Fargo won't have to try figuring out where our own buildings went." She pulled out her PDA. "I'll let them know we've got a complete listing of locations, and that we can keep them apprised of any new exchanges." She hit a key, held the phone up, then pulled it away from her ear and glanced at it.

"Section Five," Zane reminded her.

"Oh. Right." She laughed at herself as she put it away and reached for the landline phone sitting on the desk. "You'd think I'd remember that one." Section Five was shielded against cell phones, wireless computers, and other transmissions, for security reasons.

Zane didn't give her a hard time about the slip. It wasn't like she didn't have a lot on her plate right now. Instead he turned his full attention back to the computer and left the activity log open on one monitor while he began sifting through pages of code on another.

Gunter was thorough, he'd give the man that. The MRS had been well designed and carefully shielded from outside intrusion. Even sitting here at its mainframe, with its own keyboard in hand, Zane hadn't found a way to break into the system while it was active. Yet. But it was just a matter of time. He cracked his fingers and got back to work.

CHAPTER 17

"I hate this," Carter muttered, his teeth clenched so they wouldn't rattle. "I really, really hate this."

"Just relax," Henry advised. He had his head back and his eyes closed—with his arms folded over his chest and his legs out and crossed at the ankles, he looked perfectly capable of napping despite the constant threat of possible, horrible, fiery death. "Try not to think about it."

"Think about what?" Carter demanded. "The fact that we're thousands, maybe tens of thousands, of feet in the air, held up by only a handful of wiring and some metal struts and a few computer chips, all mashed together into an experimental helicopter that's never been fully tested? Is that what I shouldn't think about?"

"Exactly." His friend didn't even open his eyes.

With a sigh, Carter pulled out his cell phone, opened it, and dialed. Anything to take his mind off the harrowing, jarring, jangling flight. He waited through several rings and the outgoing message. "Hey, Allison, it's Jack. Henry and I are on our way to get Gunter now—we should be in Stanley before noon. I'll call you once we're there." He hung up and dialed again. "Lexi? Hey, it's me. . . . Yeah, still alive, thanks—how about you? Everything okay? . . . Great. . . . No, no idea where you should go—have you talked to Zoe yet? She's holding down the fort for me in Eureka. . . . Well, with Fargo's help. She'll know if any new switches have occurred. . . . Yeah, just let me know where she sends you, okay? And—be careful. . . . No, I'm not worried about the Eurekans, though some of them may be pretty scared. Be careful driving. . . . Yeah, you too."

"Where is she?" Henry asked after Carter hung up.

"Just outside Boise. We didn't have any place to send her, but it didn't make sense for her to go all the way back to Eureka when she might have to turn around and drive someplace else immediately afterward. Especially with S.A.R.A.H. not fully functional."

"Makes sense."

Carter jumped slightly as his phone rang in his hand, then shook his head and answered it. He'd gotten used to the ring tone of his Eureka PDA after all this time. "Carter." He could feel the smile stretching across his face. "Hey, Allison. . . . Oh, right, sorry about that—yeah, I should have realized. You're calling from his lab? . . . Great, I've got the number in my phone now. . . . Oh, really? Great, that'll make things a ton easier. . . . Okay, sure. . . . Yeah, we'll get to him as soon as we can. Right."

"What's going on back at GD?" Henry was watching him now, though he was still reclined and clearly relaxed.

"Zane's gotten access to the machine's activity log," Carter answered, dropping his phone back into his pocket so he could return both hands to the handle he'd been gripping the entire flight. "He'll know the second any place gets switched, and exactly where it went, so at least Zoe and Fargo won't have to interrogate people to find out their home addresses. He still can't be sure how to shut the thing down without hurting anybody, though, so we're still gonna need Gunter's help."

"We should be there soon," Henry pointed out.

"I'm counting on it," Carter assured him. "I'm not sure how much more of this I can take." He fumbled for his phone again. "I should give Zoe a call, make sure everything's okay on her end as well."

It didn't escape him that, just two days ago, it had been nice and quiet—and it had driven him nuts. Of course, right now he'd probably welcome a little of that again. He sighed. Some days there was just no pleasing people—himself included.

"G'day, mate! Need a little 'elp?" Taggart had been out for his morning walk and had noticed the man biking up ahead.

It had been the bike that had caught his attention, really—it was one of those portable ones, the kind that folded up so you could carry it into an office or onto a bus. You didn't see that sort of thing in Eureka much—a bike that could wheel itself back home and transform into a desk chair, maybe, but not one that folded up for easier storage.

Then he'd noticed that the biker wasn't moving very fast and kept starting to turn to the left or to the right, like he wasn't sure which way to go.

As he'd drawn closer, Taggart had gotten a better look at the man, and realized he didn't recognize him at all. And he knew most of the other Eureka residents, at least on sight.

The biker startled a little at his voice, and his sudden jerk almost toppled him from his bike, but he recovered in time. "Oh, uh, sure." He was young, late twenties to early thirties, with short red hair, a little goatee, and glasses. Definitely not familiar. "I was just on my way to the grocery store to pick up a few things—we meant to go yesterday but got caught up with some stuff, and then with the whole gas leak thing . . ." Taggart had no idea what the fellow was talking about, but he nodded agreeably because it seemed like the right thing to do. "But the store wasn't where it should have been, and then I did see a store but it was closed, and then I saw somebody inside but he jumped when I knocked on the door, and then he shouted at me but I couldn't hear him through the doors, and then he pulled a shotgun, so I took off, and now . . . now I'm here."

"Right, well, it sounds to me like you're a mite confused," Taggart offered. He held out his hand. "Jim Taggart's the name, big-game tracking's the game."

"Oh. Joe. Joe Merkel." Joe shifted so he could shake hands. "Nice to meet you."

"You too, Joe. So you wanted the store, you say?" Taggart scratched his jaw. "I can take you to the market, if you like. I'm headed that way meself."

"Yeah? That'd be great. Thanks!" Taggart pointed to the left, and Joe swiveled the bike around to follow as he turned in that direction. "So," he asked after a few minutes, "are you new to Lakeview? I don't think I've seen you around before."

"Lakeview?" Taggart chuckled. "Oh, yeah, real new. In fact, I feel like I've not even arrived yet." He laughed, even though it was obvious young Joe Merkel had no idea what he was talking about. "But not to worry. I saw the market earlier, so I know just where it is."

They moved quietly for several more minutes before Joe spoke again.

"Is there still a gas leak? The sheriff said he'd let us know when it was safe to go back outside, but we don't really have much to eat in the house and it looked and smelled fine, so I figured I'd risk it."

"Oh, there's still a gas leak, all right," Taggart agreed. "You'll be okay goin' to the market and back, I think, but after that best if you stay indoors. Sheriff Carter'll be around to tell you when it's safe again."

He wasn't entirely sure what was going on, though he suspected it had to do with that girl who'd somehow been moved in the forest, and to his and Zane's recent experience as well. But if Carter was claiming there was a gas leak and telling people to stay in their homes, he must have a good reason for it. And Taggart had no problem going along with that—provided he wasn't expected to hide in his home as well.

Fargo had set down her dad's PDA when he'd gone to speak to some people, and Zoe beat him to it when it rang. "Hello?" she answered, spinning around as Fargo came rushing back to try grabbing it from her. "Hey, Dad!" She swatted Fargo away. "You're where? Are you kidding?" She wrinkled her nose. "What is that noise? . . . Are you serious? You? I don't believe it!" She struggled to hear him over the background noise. "No, we're managing. Don't worry, we've got everything under control on this end. Good luck! . . . Love you, too. Bye!"

"Was that your dad?" Fargo demanded as soon as she'd hung up, snatching the PDA out of her hand and dropping it into his pocket. "What'd he say? Where is he? Does he have Dr. Gunter yet? And why didn't you give me the phone?"

Zoe rolled her eyes at him. "Yes, it was my dad, obviously. He and Henry are in a helicopter, heading toward a town called Stanley, in the Sawtooth Mountains. That's where Dr. Gunter is—they think." She bit her lip. "Dad must be really worried if he was willing to get in a helicopter—he's terrified of flying." Her look of concern switched to Fargo and became a glare. "And I didn't give you the phone because it was my dad, and I wanted to talk to him, and besides he left us both in charge."

"You told him everything was fine," Fargo accused. "Didn't you? Don't deny it, I heard you—you said everything was fine!" He pushed his glasses up. "Why would you lie to him like that?"

"I didn't lie," Zoe claimed. "And I never said it was fine. I told him we were managing. Which we are. Mostly. Besides, he shouldn't be worrying about things back here right now. He's got to concentrate on getting Dr. Gunter and sorting everything out."

"But it's not fine," Fargo argued, his voice starting to creep higher. "It really isn't!"

No, it wasn't, Zoe agreed privately. They'd managed fine for the first few hours, but around lunchtime all the people they'd brought to Café Diem showed up again, along with a few who had stayed in their homes originally. And all of them were demanding answers. Zoe couldn't really blame them—they'd all been here for several hours, and most of them for the entire morning, and they were tired and scared and confused. They wanted all of this to be over. Plus there hadn't been any further signs of a gas scare, so they were starting to question that story. And if they decided not to believe her and Fargo anymore, there'd be no stopping them from roaming freely through Eureka. Zoe shuddered just thinking about a half dozen strangers loose in the town, blundering into all kinds of things.

They had to do something to keep people calm and distracted, or at least scared and compliant. She just wasn't sure what.

"G'day, Zoe, Fargo. Vincent." She hadn't noticed Taggart's arrival, and the tall Australian startled her as he slid onto the stool next to her. "Havin' quite the little visitors' convention over here, are we? I wish I'd known earlier—I could've brought over the young bloke I just met, instead of takin' him to market and then home again."

Zoe turned and stared at the hunter. "Wait, what? You met one of the visitors? Where?"

"Out on the road," Taggart explained, accepting the tall milk shake Vincent had set in front of him—as with all the regulars, Vincent hadn't even needed to ask to know what Taggart wanted. "He was on a bike, nifty little foldin' thing, and lookin' a bit lost. So I 'elped him out." He took a big swig of his shake and sighed contentedly. "Ah, that 'its the spot! I like this little gas leak story you've got goin'— that's smart thinkin', that is. Your dad come up with that one, then?"

Zoe nodded. "He needed a reason to keep them from wandering through town, and that seemed the best way— because it's gas, the fact that they can't see anything makes sense, and they can blame any strange sights on hallucinations."

"Nice one."

Zoe studied him for a second, thinking fast. Then she smiled. "Taggart?" she said, using her best pretty-girl-needs-a-favor voice. "You could be a huge help to us—and to all of Eureka."

"Oh?" Taggart finished his milk shake, wiped his mouth clean on a napkin, and smiled. "What'd you 'ave in mind?"

Two minutes later, Zoe, Fargo, and Vincent watched from the counter as Taggart spoke to the assembled visitors. ". . . and that's why it's safest for you to stay here in Café Diem, or back in your own homes," he finished. "You want to limit your exposure to the gas as much as possible. We're workin' on gettin' more gas masks, but until then we can only give 'em to key personnel." He held up the one around his neck. "Any questions?"

"Using Taggart was a stroke of genius," Vincent whispered as he wiped down yet another coffee mug.

"It was, right?" Zoe agreed. It really had been a great idea. Taggart was good with people, easygoing and friendly, but he loved to be cryptic and he was very good at not revealing secrets. Plus, with his accent, he could get away with saying things that could have caused a panic if it had been Zoe or Fargo or anyone else—it was so colorful it muffled the blow. And it wasn't like the visitors could use Taggart's accent to pin down Eureka's location, either.

But best of all, Taggart had been carrying a gas mask in his backpack. Zoe had hoped he might be. And it was weathered, a bit beaten up, clearly something that had seen some use. The kind of gas mask that said, *Yes, I really do carry this around and I really have had to use it before, more than once, so believe me when I tell you it's necessary now.*

"I think that's calmed 'em down a bit," Taggart offered as he rejoined them at the counter. "You want me to stick around for a bit, just in case?"

"That'd be great," Zoe told him. "Thanks so much, Taggart." And she meant it. Thanks to his help, everything really was fine for the moment.

Which is exactly when her dad's PDA rang. She and Fargo shared a grimace as he answered it. So much for nice and quiet.

CHAPTᵉR 18

"Glenns Ferry, Idaho. Got it." Lexi sighed. "Yes, Zoe, I'm sure I can handle it. Come on, this is your aunt Lexi you're talking to here. All I have to do is go to"—she glanced at the scrap of paper she'd just scribbled on— "4001 Freemont Street, to where the Freemont Flower Shop was, talk to whoever wound up there from Eureka, and make sure they don't go outside or let anyone else in. Piece of cake." She switched the phone to her other hand and other ear as she put her car in reverse and backed out of the parking space, narrowly missing another car zooming past. Oops. "Yes, I'll be fine. What, are you taking lessons from your father now?" She laughed. "Don't worry, sweetie. I've got it under control. I'll call you when I get there. Love you!"

She hung up and tossed the phone on the seat beside her, switching into drive once both hands were free. Let's see, Glenns Ferry—she could just take the 84 interstate there, if she remembered correctly. She checked the GPS her brother had insisted she install in her car, after the third or fourth time she'd gotten lost driving around Eureka—was it her fault all the streets there curved and jogged and had strange gaps partway through?—and it confirmed that. A nice easy ride down 84.

Perfect.

Lexi was humming to herself as she pulled out of the mall's parking lot and accelerated, cutting off an old pickup truck as she merged into its lane. She held up a hand in apology. *Sorry!*

This was proving to be quite an adventure so far, even for a visit to Eureka. She'd only been planning to pop over to Cafe Diem, grab some breakfast, and then maybe take a walk. Nothing too strenuous. When she'd found herself in a mall in Boise, well, she had to admit she'd panicked. Just a little. But once she'd talked to Jackie she'd calmed down. After all, she was fine. And when was the last time she'd been in Boise?

Fortunately that nice young man had loaned her his phone. She'd still had her old cell phone in her glove compartment—good thing she never threw anything away!—but she'd needed to get it reactivated because it had been inactive for too long. The good news was, she'd wound up at the mall! Her service provider had a store there, and she'd been able to get her phone current again so that she could use it. Her Eureka PDA had taken its place in the glove compartment, at least until all of this was over.

And now she was helping Jackie and Zoe out! How cool was that? Too often when she'd stayed with them she'd felt like a fifth wheel, just idling away the time while her brother did his job and her niece had her schoolwork and her part-time job at the café. And what had she done? Nothing. Oh, she'd helped out a lot during the mayoral campaign, which had been fun—nothing like a little activism to stir the blood!—but afterward she'd gone back to having no job and nothing to do. She'd expected visiting to feel exactly like that again, only shorter.

But not now. Her brother had actually asked for her help! And Lexi was only too happy to provide it.

Too bad it wasn't something a little more challenging. But this would do for now.

"Zoe?" Jo inwardly cursed at the difference between Eureka PDAs and the phones everyone else used—she could barely hear the person on the other end. Still, she'd needed to be back out in the field where she could be the most useful, and taking her Eureka PDA with her hadn't been an option. "Oh. Fargo. Sorry." She couldn't help chuckling at his injured tone—*that* had certainly come through loud and clear! "I just reached Winnemucca. You said 738 Spruce, right?" She peered out through the Night Wing's cockpit window, and then back at the GPS monitor set in its front console. "Yeah, I'll be there in a minute. How's everything on the home front?"

She half listened as she watched the Nevada city grow rapidly beneath her. "Uh-huh. . . . Yeah, that was a good idea, slaving your database to Gunter's activity log. Smart thinking." It was, too—this way every time Gunter's machine transplanted anyone, the information automatically appeared in Fargo's database and alerted him to the addition. That was how he'd been able to tell her about the house in Winnemucca so quickly. He didn't have to wait for Allison and Zane to call.

Jo shook her head at the sudden warmth she felt. Damn it, just thinking of Zane shouldn't do that to her! How was she supposed to do her job if thoughts of him kept intruding?

The copter settled to the ground in front of 738 Freemont

Street, and Jo stared at the modern ranch house sprawled there. The sinking feeling in her stomach drove all other thoughts from her head.

"Fargo? I'm at the house." She was unhooking her safety belts and shoving open the Night Wing's door as she spoke. "I've got a bad feeling about this. No, there's no one else around. But I recognize this house, and if it belongs to who I think it does, we could have a problem. Hang on."

A quick hop had her feet on the ground again, and a dozen quick, long strides took her to the front door. Jo banged on it hard, ignoring the doorbell mounted to the side. It took only a second before the door swung open, and she found herself facing a tall, slender, older man with a bald pate, a sharp nose, and wire-rimmed glasses. Another face popped up in the hallway behind him, looking like a mirror image.

"Yep," she reported to Fargo. "It's the Bakers. I'm going to have to do a head count and get back to you."

"Thank goodness you're here, Deputy," Dr. Baker told her, stepping back and ushering her in. He looked genuinely relieved, as did his brother behind him. "We're so confused! And we can't find our brothers anywhere!"

"First things first," Jo told them as she entered and shut the door firmly behind her. "There was a bright flash of light and a moment of dizziness and then everything outside looked different, right?" They both nodded. "Were all of you in the house at the time?" She was already hitting redial when they shook their heads. "Zoe? Did Fargo tell you—okay, good. Listen, I need you guys to look for the Bakers. . . . Yes, I'm at their house. But I don't think all of them are here, and we need to know how many are unaccounted for. . . . Okay, thanks."

"We can't find them," the second Dr. Baker was telling Jo as she hung up. "Our brothers. It's like . . . it's like they're too far away. It's all hazy."

"They probably are too far away," Jo agreed. "You're in Winnemucca, which is northern central Nevada. We're a good four hours' drive from Eureka, at least. How many are still outside?"

"Six," the first Dr. Baker answered. "Five of them are fuzzy. One is . . . angry."

"One of the five, or the other one?" Her phone rang before he could explain, and she held up a hand. "Hang on. Yeah?" It was Zoe again. "Okay, great. Thanks." She hung up again and returned her attention to the brothers. "Three of your brothers are at Café Diem, and apparently two more are in town and joining them. So that's the five fuzzy ones." She frowned. "Which just leaves the one you said was angry."

"Yes." There were now several Dr. Bakers in front of her, and they all answered in unison. "He is upset. But nearby."

Jo thought fast. She couldn't use the Night Wing to look around the city—it was practically invisible with its stealth coating, but it still ran the risk of getting tangled in the overhead power lines. Plus, depending on where Dr. Baker was, she might not be able to get on the ground fast enough to help him. "Can I borrow your car?" She'd seen the sporty little solar-powered hatchback as she'd approached the front door.

Several identical sets of keys were held out to her.

"I'll find him," Jo promised, grabbing the nearest set. "And I'll bring him back. But the rest of you need to stay put. Understand?"

"Of course," they all agreed, and Jo tried not to shiver as she headed back outside to warn the Night Wing pilot to stay put. It was creepy when they did that!

"Here we go," Lexi said to herself as she pulled up outside a greenhouse. It didn't have any numbers on it, bu

the strip mall on the previous block had been 3001 Freemont, and she could see a Home Depot on the next block
with the number 5001 in big numerals on its side. So this
would have to be 4001, when it was at home.

She parked, shut off her engine, and hopped out. The
drive had been as easy as she'd predicted, without even
a lot of traffic, and she'd passed the time listening to an
old mix CD Duncan had made for her back in Peru. Gor-
geous, brilliant, dedicated, and he had good taste in music!
Lexi smiled to herself. She'd really hit the jackpot with that
one.

Lexi studied the greenhouse as she approached it. She
hadn't seen it back in Eureka, or at least not close up, but
it looked fairly typical—a long, wide single-story building with glass walls and an angled glass roof to allow the
plants inside to get plenty of sunlight. And she could already tell from here that the place was full of plants. Lexi
felt herself perking up. She loved plants, and nature in general. How perfect that the first place she'd been sent to was
a greenhouse!

She reached for the door, and it swung up just before her
fingers touched it, forcing her to hop back a step to avoid
getting smacked.

"Oh, sorry!" the man behind it said. "I didn't see
you there!" He was cradling a large pot filled with rich
brown potting soil and a handful of tiny sprouts. "Are you
okay?"

"Fine, no problem," she assured him. She held the door
open for him so he could concentrate on his plants.

"Thanks," he called over his shoulder as he headed toward an old Acura hatchback. Lexi watched him maneuver
the pot into the backseat and belt it in for safekeeping before turning and heading into the greenhouse herself.

The instant she stepped inside, she sighed. It was warm
and damp in here, perfect for plants, and the air was filled

with the rich, heady scent of soil and greenery. So good! She'd managed to install a few houseplants back in Eureka, but Jackie wasn't exactly the gardening type and when she'd stayed with him she'd been forced to keep her additions to a minimum. Not like this!

"Can I help you?" Lexi turned and saw a woman walking toward her down the wide central aisle. She was wearing gray slacks and a blue button-down shirt, not the sort of attire you'd expect from someone who spent their time digging in dirt, but over that she had a brown canvas jacket, and she was wearing sturdy boots and a set of dirt-stained gardening gloves. As she got closer, Lexi saw that she was a little below average height—shorter than Lexi herself, who was on the tall and gangly side, much to her chagrin— and had light brown hair in a neat bob that framed her face. Pretty, too. And with the rectangular wire-framed glasses she looked smart as well.

In fact, Lexi recognized her.

"You're Dr. Leonardo!" she said as the woman stopped right in front of her.

"That's right." Dr. Leonardo frowned, then nodded, eyes narrowing. "And you're Lexi Carter. The sheriff's sister."

"That's me." Lexi spread her hands. "You don't seem surprised to see me here."

"Should I?" Dr. Leonardo shrugged. "Something moves my greenhouse from South Goddard, on the outskirts of town, to somewhere in Idaho. Obviously, that shouldn't have happened. I figured it was only a matter of time before someone official came to check on me. Excuse me a second." She turned away to speak with a young couple who had been behind her. The woman had her arms wrapped around a pot. "Just make sure you water it well for the first few months," she told them. "And watch out for squirrels— they'll try to eat the tender leaves, so you might need to shoo them away from time to time."

"Thank you so much!" the woman told her. "Really!"

"Yeah," the man agreed. "We've only been in the house a month, and it's great—except for the fact that it doesn't have any shade. We'd been thinking of putting up a porch, but this'll be so much nicer."

"You're welcome," Dr. Leonardo told them, and smiled as the man offered her his hand. Then she watched them walk past her and Lexi and out the front door.

"You're selling trees?" Lexi asked. She remembered that Dr. Leonardo had been involved in the problems with gravity a little while ago, during those few days when Jackie hadn't been sheriff and they'd had the robotic Sheriff Andy instead. Not that she'd been to blame, but it had been her rapid-growth trees that had fallen on several cars and crushed them. Though that hadn't been her fault either, and her trees should have been able to withstand a hurricane without so much as bending.

"Not selling," Dr. Leonardo argued. "I'm giving them away."

Lexi frowned. "Isn't all your research classified?"

"Of course. But I'm not giving away *those* trees," Leonardo answered. "These are just specimens from my control group." She smiled again. "Hey, this is a greenhouse, right? It'd look pretty suspicious if I weren't letting people get plants here, don't you think?"

"But what if something happens with those trees?"

"Nothing's going to happen," the doctor assured her. "They're completely safe. I've got all of my experimental ones locked away, safe and sound. These might be a little healthier than most, and grow a little more quickly, but nothing that'll attract attention." She smiled wider. "Think about it. You're the activist, right?" Lexi nodded. "These trees will provide shelter, shade, and clean air all over this city. They'll make this town—"

"Glenns Ferry," Lexi supplied.

"—Glenns Ferry a more beautiful, more peaceful, more environmentally sound place. How can that possibly be a bad thing?"

Lexi thought about it. She'd been in Africa, in the Amazon, and in other places, fighting to save the world's rain forests. She'd campaigned to make nations rethink their ecological stances and to help educate individuals. And here was Dr. Leonardo, taking advantage of whatever problem had transported her from Eureka to make a difference in a normal community. She could just hear Jackie in her head, warning that it was bound to cause trouble, but she pushed that warning away.

"I'm supposed to make sure you don't leave here," she warned Dr. Leonardo, "and to make sure you don't say anything or do anything that could expose Eureka." Then she smiled. "But no one said anything about not letting you give away plants to people who wanted them."

Behind her, she heard the front door open again, and Lexi glanced back to see an older couple looking around. "What can I do to help?" she asked Dr. Leonardo.

This time the tree doctor's smile was even wider and warmer. "I've got all the trees labeled by species," she explained. "Just ask them what they're looking for and see what would suit them." She held out her hand. "And call me Maria."

Lexi grinned and shook. "A pleasure, Maria." She laughed.

Still, she decided as she went to assist the older couple, probably best not to tell her brother. Just in case.

"Damn!"

Jo had been cruising the neighborhood, searching for Dr. Baker. Fortunately, the Bakers had a penchant for brightly colored Hawaiian shirts, and she knew they always dressed alike, so she was looking for the same emerald-green leaf pattern she'd seen on the Bakers back at their house. And as she'd turned a corner, she'd caught a flash of it—

—being bustled into the back of a police car.

"Great!" she muttered. "That's just what I need! A run-in with local law enforcement!" She was way out of her jurisdiction—not even in the right state!—and had no good reason for being here, much less looking for Dr. Baker.

But she'd better come up with something fast. Because letting him be arrested and locked up wasn't exactly making sure everyone was safe and didn't cause any trouble.

She followed the cops as they drove back to their station, then found a place to park. Somehow she didn't think pulling into one of the spaces marked *Police Use Only* was going to score her any points. Then she checked herself in her rearview mirror, making sure her hair was still pulled back nice and neat and her uniform still looked clean, and got out. There were a few cops milling about and several glanced her way, but none of them stopped her.

"Nice," Jo admitted as she stepped inside. The station wasn't big—she doubted Winnemucca had a whole lot of crime, and most of it was probably the usual juvenile stuff, vandalism and petty theft and the occasional joyride—but the station was new and clean, well lit without being glaring, with plenty of room to move around.

"Can I help you?" a woman asked from behind the desk. She was in uniform, of course, and Jo knew her deputy's tans stood out here among all the city cops' blues.

"Yeah, I'm looking for someone who was just brought in," Jo explained, walking over and smiling. Best to keep this friendly and polite, typical professional courtesy. "I'm Jo Lupo, from Eureka, Oregon. I've been following one of our residents who wandered this way, and I think he was just picked up by one of your squad cars."

The woman studied her badge, then nodded slowly like

she'd decided to give Jo the benefit of the doubt. For now. "Can you describe him?"

"Sure—around six one, skinny, balding, with a beaked nose and wire-rimmed glasses. Oh, and he's wearing a bright green Hawaiian shirt."

That got another nod, this one more confident. "Right, yeah. Danny and Leon just brought him in. Gimme a second." She picked up her phone and dialed an extension. "Danny? It's Maureen. There's a lady deputy here from some town in Oregon, says she knows your drunk and disorderly. . . . Sure. He'll be right out," she told Jo as she hung up.

Jo nodded and forced herself to stay calm and friendly. She wasn't exactly sure what the Bakers did in Eureka, but whatever it was, it was bound to be classified. Which meant the Bakers themselves had all sorts of security clearances— and might show up on a routine ID check. She was hoping to avoid that. But she couldn't force the issue—the only option if the locals didn't want to give him up would be to call General Mansfield, who was in charge of Eureka's military concerns. And she was hoping to avoid that, too.

"You the deputy from Oregon?" The cop who approached her was tall, heavily muscled, and good-looking in a heavy, brooding, cocky sort of way. His badge read *Ortez*.

"That's me." Jo offered her hand. "Jo Lupo. I'm a deputy in Eureka."

"Danny Ortez." His handshake was firm, a little too tight, like he had something to prove. Jo let him squeeze for a second before returning the favor, and was pleased to see him blanch a little, though he didn't react beyond that. He did lose some of his swagger, though. "So what can we do for you?"

"You picked up a guy a little bit ago, over on Dakota," Jo pointed out. She'd noted the street as a matter of course. "Tall, thin, late fifties to early sixties, balding, glasses, bright green Hawaiian shirt." She threw him a smile, the disarming kind rather than the *I'm going to destroy you* one she might have preferred. "I'm here to take him off your hands."

"Yeah, we picked him up," Ortez admitted, hands automatically going to his hips. "Someone called in a disturbance and we found him wandering the street, shouting his head off. Some crap about stealing his town out from under him, kidnapping his brothers." He frowned. "Didn't resist arrest, though. Actually, he seemed surprised to see us, but maybe a bit relieved, too. Asked if we'd come to take him to Sheriff Carter."

Jo nodded. "Sheriff Carter's my boss. Dr. Baker lives in Eureka." She stepped a little closer and lowered her voice, making Ortez lean in toward her. "He's got a few . . . problems, but he's not a bad sort. Completely harmless." She shook her head. "We got a call this morning that he'd been gone awhile, managed to track him to a truck stop outside town, and found out some trucker had given him a ride. I can't imagine what the guy said to him, or what Dr. Baker was thinking, but the sheriff sent me to bring him back before he got himself hurt." She offered him that smile again. "I'm glad you found him before anything bad could happen to him."

Ortez smiled back at her, revealing clean white teeth that must have been the pride of some local orthodontist. "No problem," he told her. "Happy to help a fellow officer." The way his gaze slid over her said clearly that he was hoping she'd be appropriately grateful, and Jo resisted the urge to drop him right then and there. Beating up one of the local cops wouldn't help her get Baker out of here safely.

"That's so great of you," she said instead, continuing to smile. "I need to get him back home ASAP, but maybe after that I can swing back up this way and take you out to dinner or something? As a thank-you."

"I'd like that," he assured her quickly. "I know the perfect place, too." She was waiting for him to say *My place*, but apparently he wasn't quite that stupid. "But you're right, let's take care of your guy first." He turned and indicated the door back into the station proper. "Follow me."

"He was only being charged with disturbing the peace," Ortez explained as he led the way through rows of desks, some of them empty and some of them manned by his fellow cops. "It's only a misdemeanor, and we can waive it for extenuating circumstances. Then I can remand him into your custody."

"Perfect," Jo said. "That'd be perfect."

"Right here," Ortez said, stopping at a desk. The man sitting across from it was watching as they approached, and Jo guessed he was Leon. He was as big as Ortez, maybe bigger, with dark skin, a shaved head, and a small, neat goatee. "My partner, Leon," Ortez offered by way of introduction. "Leon, this is Jo Lupo from Eureka, over in Oregon. She's come for our disorderly."

"I'll go grab him out of lockup," Leon offered, rising from his chair slowly like a whale beaching. "Nice ta meetcha."

"Same here," Jo said to his back.

She endured small talk and low-level smarm from Ortez for another minute before Leon returned, Dr. Baker in tow. Baker brightened noticeably when he saw her.

"Deputy Lupo!" He probably would have reached for her if he hadn't been handcuffed. "Are you here to take me home?"

"That's right, Dr. Baker," Jo assured him. "And don't worry, your brothers are all safe." He looked like he was going to cry.

"Just sign here and initial here," Ortez told her, sliding Baker's arrest sheet in front of her. Jo did so quickly, trying to ignore the fingerprints neatly lined up below his name and mug shot. She hoped they'd been too inefficient to process those yet, but it was unlikely—they'd already had him in lockup, after all.

"He's all yours," Leon said, unlocking the cuffs and sliding them back onto his belt. He gave Baker a small nudge, and Baker stepped toward Jo, rubbing his wrists.

"Thanks," Jo told him, then turned to Ortez. "Really, I appreciate it."

He waved it off. "No problem. Just give me a call the next time you're up this way, okay? And we'll see about that dinner." His grin could have belonged to a lounge singer.

"Absolutely." Jo made a mental note never to pass within twenty miles of Winnemucca, just to be safe. "Come on, Dr. Baker, let's you get you back home." He followed her eagerly, and Jo led him back out of the station and to his own car.

No one stopped them, which was a relief. No one called after them, demanding to know why an apparent crazy had top-secret clearance or higher. No one ran after them, wanting to know why Baker's records came back classified. No one picked up a phone to call the Department of Justice, to ask what was going on.

At least, not yet.

But Jo knew it was only a matter of time.

CHAPTᵉR 19

"This should be it," Henry said as the Night Wing
swung closer to the rocks, revealing a handful of buildings
strung out before them. "Stanley, Idaho."

"I sure as hell hope so." Carter forced the fingers of his
left hand to loosen a bit and flexed them, then repeated the
process with the right. "Because if we have to go any farther I'm getting out and hiring a pair of pack mules."

It had been a tense flight. Not long in terms of miles, but
the pilot had kept them close to the Sawtooths the whole
way up to better avoid detection. Carter had done his best
not to look, but every so often he couldn't help noticing the
cliff faces that had slid by what seemed like mere inches
from his small window. He'd steadfastly refused to face
forward, where the cockpit's wide wraparound front window gave a panoramic view of the mountains they were
constantly in danger of smashing up against.

Carter had kept a death grip on the nearby strap the entire time. His fear of heights wasn't something he had to deal with much back in Eureka. So of course they'd had to go up the side of a mountain!

"I swear, I'll never complain about driving ever again," he muttered as the pilot brought the stealth copter down toward the narrow dirt road, which seemed like the only place they'd have space enough to land. "Or taking a train. Or a bus. Hell, I might even learn to ride a motorcycle just so I can not complain about that, too!"

"Don't get carried away," Henry warned with a smile. But he still had his right hand curled around the handle set above the door on his side, and his left was still straight down and jammed palm-first against his seat. Carter glanced pointedly at them, and his friend chuckled as he, too, relaxed a bit. "Okay, so it was a bad flight. But we're here."

"That we are." Carter studied the town in front of them. "At least, I think we are." He checked his GPS, which Henry had handed back to him at some point during the flight. "This says we're in Stanley, sure enough. But is this really a town? I've seen shopping malls bigger than this!"

"Not up here you haven't," Henry pointed out. "And it's not the size that matters. It's the distance from any other town, and the presence of elected officials."

That was true enough. They'd spotted a few cabins and lodges on the way up, but each one had been separated by at least a half mile of twisting road. People up here in the Sawtooths clearly liked their privacy. Which made this cluster of a few dozen buildings the town center by default.

"Okay," Carter agreed, unhooking his seat belt and shoving open his door. "Let's ask around and find where Mary Wallace lives. Or lived."

Henry had joined him outside—Carter was sure his friend was as eager to get out of the Night Wing after their ascent as he was—and now he tapped Carter on the arm. "I don't think that's going to be necessary." He pointed ahead of them and a little to the left. "Take a look."

Carter followed Henry's arm, and laughed. "Yeah, I guess we won't need any more directions." There, perhaps a quarter mile ahead of them, stood a split-level ranch very similar to Arnold Gunter's house, only this one was painted a warm adobe red with dark brown trim. It stuck out like a sore thumb here with all the rustic cabins and small stone homes around it, much like a city slicker wandering into a frontier town in the Wild West.

Much like they did themselves.

"Can I help you folks?" a voice asked, and Carter glanced back over his shoulder. A man had emerged from the first cabin, just behind the now-camouflaged helicopter, and was ambling toward them. He was short and a little heavyset, and older if the scraggly gray hair peaking from his cap was any indication. He wore thick, sturdy clothing and battered old hiking boots, and Carter stiffened at the sight of the hunting rifle the man carried, but it was held casually with its barrel down toward the ground. That could change quickly, though.

"Howdy," Carter called out, plastering a smile on his face. "I'm Jack Carter, an old friend of Phil Atkins. He heard there was something going on up here, and asked me to stop by and take a look for him."

"Phil sent you?" The man stopped a few yards away and glared at both of them. "That don't sound like him. He always took care of things himself when he was marshal."

"Yeah, he did," Carter agreed, "but you know how it is. He's not as young as he used to be, and that old war wound keeps acting up."

That got a laugh out of the stranger. "War wound? Is that what he told you?"

"No, actually he told me a truck stop waitress outside

McCall stabbed him with her pen when he got a little too fresh," Carter admitted, "but the war wound story is what he gave to most people."

"Heh, served him right, messing around like that!" The stranger closed the distance and held out his hand. "Chuck Walters. Any friend of Phil's is a friend of mine."

"A pleasure." Carter shook, then indicated Henry. "This is Henry Deacon. He's a research scientist."

"Howdy." Chuck's nod to Henry wasn't as warm by a long shot. "So what exactly did Phil send you up here for?" Carter noticed he deliberately avoided looking toward the ranch house behind them.

"That's why," Carter answered, gesturing toward it. "You know as well as I do that it doesn't belong here."

"Nope, it sure doesn't," Chuck agreed. "Should be Mary's place right there, same as it's always been. But this morning, when I headed out to hunt for breakfast, there she was, plain as day. Didn't make a lick of sense."

"Did you see if anyone was home?" Henry asked.

Chuck shook his head. "Nope. Figured if'n it was Mary, she'd pop her head out soon enough. And if it weren't, well, I didn't want to go no closer."

Carter nodded. "Makes sense. Actually, probably the safest thing to do." He puffed his chest out a bit so his badge would catch Chuck's attention. "But we're here to take care of it."

He'd hoped that would be enough to satisfy the local. But of course it wasn't.

"So what's it, exactly?" Chuck asked, following as Carter and Henry turned and started walking toward the house. "And where's Mary? She okay?"

"She's fine," Carter assured him. "A little confused, but completely okay. As far as what's going on . . ." He decided the best thing to do was to stick as close to the truth as possible. "I'm afraid it's classified. But there's no danger, and we should have Mary back home in a few hours. Maybe less." He was hoping for less, but he wasn't counting on it.

"Home?" Chuck gestured at the house. "That ain't her home!"

"No, it's not," Henry agreed. "And that's part of what's going on, but we can't explain any further. I'm sorry. But we should have Mary and her home back where they belong by the end of the day."

"So it's some kinda house swap, like they got on TV?" It took Carter a minute to realize the man meant those "reality" shows about people switching places and living each other's lives for a week or two.

"Something like that," he answered. "I really can't say any more. I'm sorry."

Chuck considered that for a minute, then shrugged. "You know Phil, so I guess I'll trust you. But if Mary ain't back by the end of the week, I'm gonna come looking for you!"

"Fair enough." Carter kept walking, and after a second Chuck stopped and let them continue on without him. He let out a small sigh. "What kind of TV shows do they get up here?" he asked Henry quietly as they walked on.

"I don't know," Henry replied, laughing, "but I'm sure we've got them all beat."

"We certainly have *unscripted* down to a science," Carter agreed.

They walked the rest of the way in silence and didn't see anyone else, though Carter thought he spotted movement behind a few curtained windows here and there. He figured Chuck would have the entire town informed of their names and their purpose here within the hour, but there hadn't been much else he could do about it. At least if Chuck was in touch with Phil Atkins, the former marshal would vouch for him. He hoped.

By the time they'd reached the ranch house's front

steps, Carter was beginning to regret not getting the Night Wing to carry them across the last stretch. Not that he was overheated—quite the opposite. He'd forgotten how cold it could get up in the mountains, even on a nice sunny day, and he'd left his jacket back in his Jeep, back in Burns. He and Henry were both shivering as he rapped three quick beats on the front door.

A few seconds passed and then Carter heard movement on the other side. The door swung open, and he found himself facing a tall, skinny man with a long nose, a weak chin, and a mop of unruly graying black hair. The man looked vaguely familiar, and visibly relieved to see him, an expression that only increased as his gaze swung to Carter's right.

"Sheriff Carter? Henry? Oh, thank God!" Carter was almost getting used to hearing that expression.

"Hello, Arnold," Henry replied, and Carter wanted to shout. Yes! Dr. Gunter at last. "May we come in?"

"Oh, of course, of course." Arnold Gunter stepped aside and let them enter. "Technically it's not my house, of course, but they say possession is nine-tenths of the law, and here I am, and it's not like David's in any position to show up and demand his home back and—"

"Dr. Gunter," Carter interrupted, shutting the door behind him. "Calm down. Take a deep breath. Everything's going to be okay."

Gunter sighed and slouched, losing several inches in height. "Yes. Yes? Yes." He led them into the living room—which also matched his own in shape and size, but had different furnishings and a different, bolder color scheme—and dropped into an armchair. "Thank goodness."

"Arnold, you need to tell us what happened." Henry took the other armchair, which left Carter the couch. He sank down onto it gratefully. The Night Wing's seats were decent enough as military helicopter seats went, but too many hours in any vehicle and your back, legs, neck, and rear began to protest. Spending that time tensed and clutching a safety handle didn't help.

Gunter hesitated, and Carter guessed the reason why. "We already know about the MRS project," he said, and the man gave him a look of both worry and relief. "I'm sure Allison's going to have some harsh words for you when this is all over, seeing as how you weren't even supposed to be working on that anymore, but that's not our concern right now. We need to figure out what went wrong, and how to reverse it. Because houses keep disappearing all over Eureka, and winding up in other cities and even other states."

"I know. It's not good." Gunter pulled a handkerchief from his pocket and wiped his forehead. "Not good at all. Its search pattern is expanding. We have to shut it down before it's too late."

"Too late?" Carter leaned forward. "Too late for what?"

"I think it's caught in a loop," Gunter answered. "It'll start cycling faster and faster, reaching farther and farther to find suitable matches. Eventually it'll overload its own systems, shorting out entirely—and if it does that while performing transfers, whatever it's transporting will be lost forever!"

Carter knuckled his eyes. "Yep, definitely falls under the category of 'not good.' How do we stop it?"

"I don't know."

Carter stared at the tall, gawky scientist. "Tell me you didn't just say that."

"I should be able to control the system through my PDA," Gunter explained. "I slaved it to several remote functions I could key in. That's how I was able to swap David and myself." He shrugged, looking thoroughly miserable. "It performed the switch perfectly. But when I entered the command for it to reverse, something went wrong. Instead of sending me back home and David back to his, it transported me *and* his home to a new location. Someplace by a river."

"Hood River, Oregon," Carter clarified.

"A few hours after that," Gunter continued, "it moved me again. This time to here."

"You're in Stanley, Idaho," Henry told him. "Up in the Sawtooth Mountains."

"Why does it keep moving you?" Carter asked.

"I don't know, exactly. There may have been a faulty line of code in my original instructions, or perhaps there was an energy surge just when I keyed in the return, and that warped the command. Either way, it may well keep moving me until it satisfies some unknown condition, or until it's shut down."

Carter, already rising to his feet, glanced at Henry. "Are you thinking what I'm thinking?"

Henry was standing as well. "We'd better get out of here before it moves all of us to some new location—and leaves our only transportation stranded up here in the mountains."

Gunter leaped to his feet like a drunken marionette. "Absolutely!" His long legs took him across the living room in a few quick strides, and then he was yanking open the door and beckoning them outside. "The transfer could happen at any second—there isn't a moment to lose!"

"Oh, I just love working against a deadline!" Carter muttered as he let Henry go ahead of him and took up the rear, ushering Dr. Gunter to go ahead of him, too.

Gunter was halfway across the threshold when everything around him began to shimmer like the exhaust from a jet engine.

"It's starting!" Gunter glanced back at Carter, eyes wide. 'It's transporting the house—and we're still inside!"

"Come on!" Henry shouted from a few feet ahead of

them, but Gunter had frozen in panic. And the lanky scientist still had one foot past the door frame, and most of one hand and shoulder as well.

Carter wasn't sure what would happen to the man if the house swapped while he was like that, but he wasn't about to find out. He hurled himself forward, shifting his weight so his left shoulder struck Dr. Gunter in the small of the back. His right arm came around the other man's middle as Carter's momentum propelled them both through the doorway and several feet beyond it. They hit the ground with a thud, and Carter bent his knees to absorb some of the impact, though it still shook him as much as the helicopter flight had at its worst. Still, they were both safely out of the house now. Who said watching football never led to anything good?

Behind him, there was a sudden flash of light, and Carter twisted back to stare as David Boyd's house seemed to twist and shrink, its edges and outline blurring and contracting. When Carter was able to see again, blinking away tears, he saw that the red-hued ranch was gone, replaced by a smaller brick building with a bay window and a neat wooden awning over its ironbound front door.

"Thank you," Gunter whispered, sitting up and shaking his head. "I'm sorry I froze. I just wasn't expecting it to happen so soon." He frowned. "One of the fail-safes I programmed in should have prevented the MRS from completing the transfer process as long as anything organic was breaching either target's perimeter. Clearly that one is now deactivated."

Carter gaped at him. "Come again?"

"He means it shouldn't have been able to swap while he was in the doorway," Henry translated. "His being there should have broken the circuit and kept the process from finishing."

"Like a microwave," Carter half asked, remembering

the other morning when he'd tried to reheat his coffee. "If it can't close completely and cleanly, it won't work."

"Exactly. But apparently that's no longer the case here."

"Great." Carter hauled himself to his feet. "Which means we have to worry about people getting cut in half if they're in the doorway when their building moves." He offered Dr. Gunter a hand up. "We need to shut this thing down, and now."

"I agree," the tall scientist assured him as he stood and dusted himself off. "Do you have a way to return to Eureka?" He glanced around, no doubt expecting a car.

"Oh, yeah." Carter gave him a nasty grin. "How do you feel about helicopters?" He shouldn't have enjoyed the scientist's look of horror as much as he did. "It's waiting about a quarter mile that way. I'll catch up in a minute."

Henry and Gunter started walking. Carter, however, shook his head and turned back to the brick home behind him. A new house meant a possible new homeowner, and yet another person he'd have to persuade to stay inside where it was safe. "Here we go again."

CHAPTᵉR 20

"That was lucky," Henry commented as they buckled themselves into the Night Wing's rear seats again. Gunter had meekly taken the middle without a word, though he had turned pale the instant the rotors began spinning.

"Yeah, being transported to who knows where would have definitely put a crimp in my day," Carter retorted, checking to make sure his own belts were tight. "Back to Eureka, as fast as you can," he ordered Sean. The pilot nodded and set the GPS to give him the most direct route back.

"I meant it was lucky that the house was unoccupied," Henry elaborated. "And that it came from Gooding, so Lexi was able to head over there and leave a note for this home's owners. This way they won't panic quite as much when they return from work and find an unfamiliar dwelling awaiting them."

"Oh, yeah. That." Carter glanced sideways at his friend.

"You really are one of those *The glass is half-full* kinda guys, aren't you?"

"It beats the alternative."

"I'd be happy to see it your way," Carter commented, clutching the strap beside him as the copter lifted off again, "if people would just stop stealing the cup." He looked to his left, where Gunter was slouched down as if hiding from curious Stanley residents and curled up into a ball as if that would help in the event the stealth copter crashed. "Don't worry, Dr. Gunter—we're going to get you back to Eureka as soon as possible."

Gunter nodded. "I only hope we're in time."

"See?" Carter insisted to Henry. "Stealing the cup again. 'In time' for what?"

"The MRS is accelerating its pace," Gunter explained. "At least, judging from what you've told me. It could be heading to a terminal overload."

Carter resisted the urge to glare at the gawky scientist. The poor guy was clearly panicked enough as it was. "'Terminal overload' doesn't exactly have a fun ring to it," he muttered.

"It wouldn't be fun at all." Gunter was bobbing his head up and down like one of those toys you affixed to your dash. "If the MRS has decided that Eureka's security has been breached, it will attempt a wholesale replacement of the town's structures as quickly as it can manage. That was part of the original programming, after all, to protect its designated area from incursion."

"Okay, so it's speeding up. Got it." Carter gripped the strap more tightly. "What does that have to do with an overload? Especially a terminal one?"

"The system is using tremendous amounts of energy for each transfer," Gunter replied. "The energy source I created can handle it without a problem, of course—it's essentially an infinitesimal fraction of a sun, and it can just expand as necessary to meet energy demands."

Carter didn't really want to ask, but forced the words out anyway. "That sounds like a good thing, not a bad thing. So where's the problem?"

"It's the energy containment system," Gunter answered. "It can withstand a great deal, but the more energy it has to contain, the greater the stress on its vacuum chamber. After a certain point, it will fracture, and the energy will no longer be contained." The scientist gulped. "The resulting reaction would be akin to a miniature supernova. It would destroy the entire lab in an instant."

"And most of GD and Eureka with it," Henry added. "Plus any structures that were still in transfer at the time. And of course we won't have any way to retrieve the ones it's already relocated."

"Great." Carter gritted his teeth. "We need to let Allison and Zane know—they're in the lab right now, trying to gain access."

"Can you give them your pass codes?" Henry asked Gunter. But the researcher shook his head.

"There's a retinal scan required for full access. I'm sorry. The military insisted on the tightest security possible, and I indulged them."

"Zane's already accessed the activity log," Carter pointed out. "Does that help any?"

"Not really, no," was the disappointing reply. "The activity log is on the outermost level of the system, under only a handful of security measures. It's impressive that your friend managed to unlock that, but the bulk of the systems are still between him and the MRS's core functions."

"So we really have to hurry," Henry added.

"I'm sure we're going as fast as we can!" Carter unclenched his jaw enough to take a deep breath. "Trust me,

I'd love to already be down off this mountain just as much as you would!"

"I'll call Allison and let her know we have Gunter, and the situation," Henry offered, reaching for his PDA. Then he stopped. "Oh, right. Jack, can I borrow your phone?"

Carter barely managed to keep from slamming into the Night Wing's rear door as he shifted to extract his cell phone and toss it to Henry. That was all he needed at this point, to accidentally hit the door release and go plummeting out of the stealth copter while it soared through the mountains.

Then again, he reasoned, if he did fall he wouldn't have to worry about any of this anymore.

And he'd certainly reach the ground a lot faster.

"Well, not the news I was hoping for," Allison said into the phone, "but thanks for letting us know. Zane's still working on cracking those systems, but so far without any luck."

"Hey, I'm doing the best I can!" he protested from the chair beside her, his fingers still flying over the keys.

"I know, I know," Allison assured him. "And I doubt anyone else could have gotten even this far, especially in this short a time. You're doing great." She returned her attention to the phone conversation. "Just get Gunter back here as quickly as you can. Unless Zane works a miracle, I don't think we can access the heart of the program without him." She nodded, despite the fact that Henry couldn't see her. "Call us when you're back in."

"What's going on?" Zane asked as she hung up. "I only caught your end, but it didn't sound good."

"They got Dr. Gunter," Allison explained, stretching. "That's the good news."

"And the bad news?"

"Gunter doesn't think the system can be shut down remotely, and there's a retinal scan and other security measures keeping us out. Oh, and they're currently halfway down a mountainside, so it's not like they can move any faster. Though knowing Carter, he might try telling the pilot to do that anyway." She hesitated for a second. "And there's more."

"More? Let's hear it."

Allison took a deep breath. "Dr. Gunter thinks the MRS has begun to speed up its transfers, due to an internal security protocol. If it continues to increase its speed, eventually it will overload its energy containment system, creating a fault in the vacuum chamber." She glanced at that side of the lab, where the miniature sun continued to cast its blinding light. "The explosion would vaporize most of GD, and a chunk of Eureka along with it."

"This just gets more interesting all the time." Zane studied the monitors and frowned. "Well, I'll keep trying, but I can't guarantee I can hack this. It's some seriously heavy-duty stuff. Gunter should be proud."

"I'm sure he is," Allison replied. "I just hope his genius isn't the one that finally takes us down."

Zane laughed. He actually sounded excited. "Not if this genius has anything to say about it!" And he returned his attention to the monitor and to the keyboard beneath his dancing fingers.

Allison stayed quiet and watched him work. Under most circumstances, in a sheer mental battle she'd bet on Zane every time. But with the inadvertent countdown and the security measures and the switching risks—well, she just hoped his particular brand of quirky brilliance would be enough.

And she really hoped Carter made it safely down that mountain.

* * *

"Yes, I know it's been several hours already," Zoe told the Merkels. "I'm very sorry. We're working as fast as we can—the problem is, we're having trouble isolating the source of the gas leak, and until we're sure we've found it and resealed it, we can't lift the quarantine."

"But I still don't understand," Joe Merkel insisted. "We've lived in Lakeview our whole lives, and we bought our house almost three years ago. I've never seen this diner before. Or any of you people. How does that work? Diners don't just show up overnight!"

"Sure they do," Zoe replied. "You know prefab construction these days—they can build an entire house in two hours, tops." She brushed her braid back over her shoulder. "We needed a base of operations, some place we could bring people safely while we handled the problem. And food is very comforting, so we thought a diner would be the right choice—it's pleasant, relaxing, and calm."

"—and if I have to tell you again, I'll seal all your windows and doors and unleash a rapid-consumption viral acid cloud in there!" Fargo shouted. "Your walls will be stripped bare in minutes! They'll eat the couch right out from under you! Now sit down, shut up, and enjoy your chicken marsala!"

He stomped away from the corner booth, slowing and straightening when he realized Zoe and the Merkels—and many of the diner's other patrons—were staring at him. "What?" he asked as he approached the counter. "They need to understand who's in charge here."

"Whatever." Zoe ignored him and focused on the Merkels again. "Look, I know this hasn't been easy for you, and we really do appreciate your patience. I promise you, we are doing everything possible to return you to your homes and your lives. The minute we're sure it's safe, we'll take you straight back."

The couple stared at her for a second, then glanced at

Fargo, then back at her. "I guess we're better safe than sorry," Joe said after a few seconds' pause. His wife nodded. She couldn't take her eyes off Fargo, and she wore the exact same expression Zoe knew she sometimes wore herself—especially when Fargo was around. It was a combination of terror, contempt, and horrified fascination.

"Exactly!" Zoe told him. "Now if you'll just have a seat again, what can I get you?"

She let out a sigh as the Merkels moved back to their table, and then she turned to pass Vincent their order.

"You've been so great," she told Vincent after he nodded and handed her a full tray of drinks and appetizers in return. "Really. I don't know what we would've done without you."

"Oh, happy to help," the rounded chef answered. "You know me—the more to feed, the merrier. Besides, what you said to those people was true. Diners are a natural place to gather in a crisis. There's a reason they call it *comfort food*."

Zoe nodded and turned to scan the room again as Vincent bustled back to the kitchen. Café Diem had been a godsend, and convincing Taggart to help had been one as well.

Even so, she wasn't sure how much longer they could handle it all.

The transplanted outsiders were becoming more and more restless. Not that Zoe blamed them. But the longer this went on, the more agitated those people became, and the more they hated being cooped up. All they needed was for a handful to decide they wanted to stretch their legs, and how was Zoe going to explain that one? As it was, they'd already had a few close calls when a Eureka resident had brought a current project into the café and caught the attention of the newcomers.

Fortunately, Fargo had stepped in each time. Zoe hated

to admit it, but he was doing a great job keeping everything together. He could alternately threaten and whine,
beg and bargain, and everyone in Eureka knew him. Not
all of them liked him, but they all knew him. And they all
knew he was completely capable of following through on
his threats.

With Fargo handling the locals, keeping as much tech
out of the café as possible, she and Taggart got the transplants. Right now Taggart was out making sure none of
those strangers were wandering the town unescorted, so
Zoe was left dealing with the ones here in the café

So far, plying them with food and drink was keeping
them calm

But they could only eat so much.

A nearby beep startled her out of her gloomy thoughts,
and she half jumped, turning to find the sound's source. It
had come from Fargo's laptop, she realized after a second.
And when she swiveled the machine around, she spotted a
small alert bouncing up and down along the screen's bottom edge.

It was the icon for the database.

Already guessing and dreading what that alert meant,
Zoe pulled up the database window. She read the information there, read it a second time to make sure, then sighed
and picked up her dad's PDA. He was going to love this.

CHAPTeR 21

"Tell me you're kidding."

Jo listened, then sighed. "No, Carter, I know you wouldn't kid about something like this. It was just wishful thinking." She tilted her head, trapping her phone between shoulder and cheek, and gestured to Davey, her pilot. Then she input their new destination into the GPS. He studied the resulting directions, nodded, and yanked hard on the stick, sending the Night Wing on a sharp tilt as it angled into a hard turn. "Don't worry, I'm on my way."

She was about to hang up when she thought of something. "Henry's with you, right? Ask him if there's anything I need to know." She listened. "Uh-huh, Mr. Meesey's car, busted driver's-side window. Dr. Banash's car, no rebreathers. Got it." Then she clicked the phone shut and dropped it into her lap. "Time to make up some distance," she told Davey. He grinned and gunned the Night Wing's twin jet engines, slamming both of them back into their seats as the stealth copter shot forward.

The good news was that Adin, California, wasn't that far away, at least not by air—it was almost directly west of Winnemucca, and she'd just left the Bakers when Carter had called with the latest assignment. If she'd been driving, she would have had a problem, because there was no way to strike out due west from Winnemucca. Not unless you had a real off-road vehicle. That would have meant heading back north on 95, then northwest on 140, then back south on 395 before splitting off on 139. Up here, they didn't have to worry about any of that.

Jo frowned and studied the GPS, which was mapping their progress in real time. Time was definitely of the essence here. There was no telling what would happen if Adin locals got there before she did.

After all, Henry wasn't exactly careful about putting stuff away in his garage. And he usually left the door wide open, too.

Less than twenty minutes later, the Night Wing roared down over Adin. Jo was in a good mood, and she knew she probably had a huge grin on her face. She couldn't help it. She loved to go fast. And flying a top-secret, experimental stealth helicopter at full speed across the country? Even better. They'd spent the whole time jammed back in their seats, shaken up by the vibrations from the engines, watching the scenery blur past below.

It had been awesome.

Now they were in Adin, and Davey slowed the copter down while Jo checked the GPS for directions to the specific address. According to Carter, Henry's garage had been replaced by a standard mechanic's garage, so she figured it was going to be on the outskirts of town, or at least in one of the more industrial neighborhoods. No one wanted to live right next to a bunch of broken-down cars and a handful of gas tanks.

"Better set me down here," Jo instructed a few minutes later, a block or so away. She could see Henry's garage straight ahead of her, but all around it were used-car lots and warehouses—the vacant lot here was the only place she could see for them to land, barring the street itself.

"Not a problem." Davey, a narrow little guy with a bright orange Mohawk, set the Night Wing down so smoothly there was barely a bump. "I'll keep it running."

Jo waved back at him as she hopped down and strode toward Henry's. This shouldn't take too long. And at least from here it didn't look like anyone had disturbed the place.

She was almost to the garage when a car burst from its open door and blew past her, hightailing it in the opposite direction. And "hightailing" was definitely accurate—it was one of those big old cars, the long, lean kind with the fins in back and the taillights jutting out from them like fangs. It was a beautiful machine, and she could hear the heavy, throaty growl of its engine as it sped on by her.

"Perfect," she muttered. She thought fast. She could tell Davey to get in the car's way, but there was a good chance it wouldn't stop in time, especially since she wasn't sure he could turn off the Night Wing's camouflage. That would leave them stranded here, and would get her some harsh words from Allison for destroying a top-secret prototype. Or—she spotted the vehicle still sitting in the garage and grinned, breaking into a sprint.

Or she could catch them herself.

Fortunately, Mr. Meesey had brought his car in to have his broken driver's-side window replaced. Which meant she didn't have to worry about the car being locked, or even about opening the door. Instead Jo grabbed the door frame and threw herself feetfirst through the missing window, sliding in behind the driver's seat as if she'd practiced that move a hundred times. Which of course she had. And her mother had hated her watching *The Dukes of Hazzard*!

Henry had left the keys in the ignition, and Jo twisted them and gunned the engine. She slammed the car into drive and hit the gas, hurtling out of the garage and racing after the stolen car.

After all, it wasn't like Dr. Banash had come all the way out to Adin to collect it.

The car thieves had a good thirty-second head start, and Banash's car boasted a four-hundred-cubic-inch V-8. There was no way Jo could catch up to it, not in Meesey's battered little Honda Accord, especially not with that much of a gap. But Jo grinned to herself and fumbled for a small device in one of the pouches on her belt. She didn't have to catch them. She just had to get close.

She'd hoped seeing a car coming after him might scare the thief into stopping, but of course she'd known her pursuit could have the opposite effect. Which it did, apparently, because the other car sped up instead.

"Great, make me chase you," Jo muttered, leaning forward as if that could lend her more speed. "That'll just make things worse for you when I do finally catch you."

The gap had increased slightly, and Jo worried that she'd lose them entirely—until she saw that the road ended in a T about three blocks past the stolen vehicle. Thinking fast, she yanked her wheel hard to the right, the tires protesting again as the car rose briefly on two tires and whipped into a tight turn. She had almost missed the cross street, and her left wheels would have bumped the sidewalk if they'd stayed on the ground. As it was, she had to steer frantically to avoid both a fire hydrant and a lamppost, but then she was past the danger.

A quick tug brought her left wheels back to the ground

with a sharp jolt, and then she was braking and hauling the wheel hand-over-hand in the other direction. She hurtled onto the next street, accelerating again as soon as she was facing more or less straight.

Now she was racing down the street one block over from the car thieves. There were two blocks before this street T'ed as well. She'd had to pick left or right, and had gone with right on instinct.

She hoped she'd picked correctly.

"Yes!" Jo whooped as, a second later, a long, lean, dark shape hurtled past her down the next cross street. They'd gone right! She had a chance!

She was almost to the cross street herself and swung the Honda wide to the left so she could take the turn without having to do a three-pointer—the cross streets were narrow, only wide enough for a single car to pass, and she couldn't afford to lose the time it would take to back up and adjust. Whoever was driving Banash's car clearly wasn't as experienced as she was, and they must have slowed a good deal to make the turn before, because she was only a few hundred feet behind them once she'd pulled onto the same cross road. And she was starting to close the distance.

They obviously saw her coming and put on another little burst of speed, but they'd lost their lead. Jo closed the gap, little by little, hoping Meesey's car didn't overheat before she got within range. She kept a close eye on the other vehicle and raised the gadget she'd extracted from her belt, gauging the distance between them.

Two hundred eighty feet, she judged.

Two seventy.

Two sixty.

Two fifty.

"Almost," she muttered. She wanted to get a little closer, just to be sure.

Two forty.

"Gotcha!" Jo pushed the gadget's single large gray button. The entire device was the size and shape of a garage door opener. The letters stamped across it read *Speed Governor.*

Ahead of her, the stolen car began to slow. Jo braked herself, pulling back so she wouldn't slam into them. That wasn't exactly the chase-ender she had in mind.

Instead she watched closely as the other car slowed further and finally pulled to a stop right in the middle of the road. She couldn't help laughing as she imagined the look on the driver's face.

The speed governor was a little gizmo Henry had worked up for her. It emitted some kind of magnetic field, he'd explained, that affected the carburetor of any vehicle within 250 feet. She hadn't really followed the technical details, but the upshot was easy enough—it slowed them down, eventually to a full stop. Every time.

She wondered yet again if she should tell Carter about it. Or about the fact that there was one in his Jeep's glove compartment.

Nah.

Not yet, anyway.

Pulling up right behind the stolen car, Jo returned the gadget to its belt pouch and cut her engine. Then she kicked open her door, climbed out, hitched up her belt, and strode toward them in her best menacing manner.

One thing she never really got to do in Eureka was highway stops.

She was going to enjoy this.

The windows were tinted, but she could make out several figures as she stepped up beside the driver's-side window. So it was car thieves, plural. That was fine—she had plenty of handcuffs and hand-ties to go around.

"Step out of the car," she barked, rapping hard on the window.

The figures didn't move. Or at least, they didn't open the door—one of them was gesturing, but Jo couldn't make it out clearly.

"Step out of the car," she repeated, tapping the window again.

This time the door rattled, but it still didn't open.

"I won't ask you a third time," she warned, her hand going for her gun. Then she remembered what Carter had relayed from Henry.

This was Dr. Banash's car.

The rebreathers.

"Oh, crap." She grabbed the door handle and jammed the release button down, yanking hard at the same time. The door flew open with an audible pop, and a slight figure tumbled to the ground to land gasping across her feet.

The two others in the front seat weren't moving.

"You're lucky I caught you," Jo told them under her breath as she leaned in and hauled first one and then the other out onto the street. She could see their chests rising and falling, so they weren't dead, just passed out.

That wouldn't have been the case in another few minutes.

Dr. Banash was a marine biologist. Henry had modified his car to double as a bathysphere so the good doctor could drive into the lake or the river and take samples. The doors had vacuum seals on them, and the car had rebreathers to cycle air through and draw oxygen from the water when submerged.

Unfortunately, Henry had been working on the rebreathers right before he'd left town. Which was why they weren't in the car.

These three kids—because Jo could see now that they were teens, probably fifteen or sixteen—had almost suffocated in their stolen car.

"Would have served you right," Jo said, nudging one

in the side with the tip of her boot. He groaned and rolled over, which she took as a good sign. She didn't actually want to see them dead.

Too much paperwork involved.

Jo dragged the first kid—the driver, who'd apparently gotten off easiest as far as the oxygen deprivation went—onto his feet, then tied his hands and shackled him to a nearby fence post. Then she crouched down in front of him so they were eye to eye. "Talk to me," she commanded once he was conscious enough to stare at her. "How'd you get the car?"

He just blinked at her.

"We can do this the easy way or the hard way," she warned him. "And trust me, this is the easy way." He gulped. "How did you get the car?"

"It was just sitting there!" he answered finally, his voice somewhere between a shout and a sob. "It had the keys in it and everything!"

Of course it did, Jo thought. After all, Henry had been working on it, and he'd probably needed to turn the engine over to get certain systems online. It was just like him to leave the keys in there, even when he went out, but who in Eureka was going to steal it? Especially from inside his garage? After all, Meesey's car had had the keys in the ignition as well.

"Did you touch anything else?" she demanded.

The kid stared at her. "What, like all those broken-down old computers that were everywhere? No way, lady! I've already got a MacBook Pro at home—why would I want any of that old junk?"

Jo breathed a little easier. Good thing Henry cared more about function than form—his homegrown supercomputer put most of GD's systems to shame, but it did look like a crazed computer geek had used old computer innards to redecorate. That had been her biggest concern, that they'd activated any of the software Henry had running. Some of those programs could probably call down nuclear strikes if you typed a command in wrong.

Moans and curses behind her told Jo that the other two were also starting to wake. She quickly dragged first one and then the other to the same fence and hand-tied them as well. She was careful to keep them out of each other's reach.

"Wait here," she told them, rising to her feet again.

"What, are you kidding?" one of them asked. Jo ignored him.

First she pulled Meesey's Accord over to the side and parked it properly. Then she started Dr. Banash's car up and drove it back to Henry's garage. She couldn't get it started without the doors being closed, but as soon as the engine turned over she cracked the driver's-side door again and left it that way, holding it by the handle to keep it from flying open as she drove. She was feeling a little light-headed by the time she guided the car back inside, but that passed as soon as she stepped out again.

The rest of Henry's garage looked about as she remembered, though she wasn't sure she'd know if anything had changed. It was a bewildering array of tools and computers and wires and tires and other car parts. At least she didn't see anything obviously out of place, and his computers were all off or running screen savers or internal diagnostics.

The boys were still only semiconscious when Jo trekked back over to them. She didn't bother talking to them as she hopped in the Accord and drove it back to its previous position in the garage. At least she didn't have to worry about running out of air in this one!

Henry's garage had a lockdown mode just like the sheriff's office, so once Jo had made sure nothing obvious was missing or altered it was a simple matter of stepping back outside, closing the door firmly behind her, and entering the code into the concealed security panel just to the side of the door frame. There was a faint click as the door locked, and a series of clicks and soft thuds as bars slid into the door from all sides, securing it fully. The panel's tiny LED went from green to red, showing that the garage was fully sealed, and Jo nodded. Another job well done.

Then she headed back toward the waiting Night Wing. She'd let Carter know she had this situation under control and find out where he wanted her next.

Jo was whistling as she climbed into the stealth copter and nodded to Davey. He spun the rotors back up to full speed and was lifting off even as she buckled in.

The shouts and cries from the three boys still hand-cuffed to the fence faded into the distance as the Night Wing flew away.

CHAPTᵉR 22

"Okay, everybody," Zoe called out. **"Just settle down,** please. We'll have your food out in just a minute, okay? Fargo's getting the screen set up, and we'll give you a little time to get settled, then we'll start the movie. After that, we'll give you rides back home, so you can just relax, eat, and enjoy."

She let out a sigh as she stepped down from the little stage at the far end and trudged back to the main counter. A few people called out questions as she passed, and she answered them as best she could, but honestly she wasn't entirely sure what she was saying at this point. It was all a big blur.

"Nicely handled," Vincent told her when she reached the counter and slid onto a stool. "And I think showing a movie was a brilliant idea."

"That was Fargo's," Zoe admitted, and Fargo puffed up a bit where he was fiddling with the projector. "But thanks,

Vincent. And, really, thanks again for letting us use your diner as our refugee camp. I don't know what we would have done without you."

"Oh, pshaw," he told her, waving off the compliment. "You know I'm happy to help. And it's been sort of fun, actually." He leaned over the counter and lowered his voice a little. "You want to know the truth? It can get a little boring making the same thing every day. White bean and truffle soup, chicken marsala, bouillabaisse, gazpacho, Ethiopian kitfo, Moroccan tajine, Guatemalan *pepián* blackened trout with hollandaise—I felt like I was in a rut. Now I get to play with orders I never get, for everything from grilled chicken and tomato soup to country-fried steak to tossed lentil salad to a New York pastrami on rye! I'm having a blast!"

Zoe laughed. "As long as you're enjoying yourself." She was glad; Vincent was one of the nicest guys in Eureka, and it was a rare treat to see him so giddy.

Taggart ambled back over from a cluster of tables and leaned on the bar between her and Vincent. "So, how much longer d'we reckon this is gonna go on, then?" he asked, though he kept his voice pitched low. "'Cause folks're gettin' restless—and I don't just mean the newcomers."

Zoe looked where he'd nodded and saw a handful of Eureka residents she recognized. They were all casting wary glances at the Merkels and some of the other visitors. She couldn't blame them. It wasn't easy watching everything you said and not being able to use your computer, your PDA, or any other devices you had. But they couldn't risk it—all they needed was one outsider seeing some program or gadget that wasn't even supposed to exist yet and Zoe would never hear the end of it. Plus her dad would be majorly disappointed. And she wasn't about to let him down.

Her PDA rang—hers, not her dad's—and Zoe glanced at it, then quickly answered. Speak of the devil! "Dad?"

"Hey, sweetie!" he replied. "How're you doing? You still at Café Diem? Everything okay there?"

"I'm good, thanks," she told him. "Well, a little frazzled, and completely exhausted, but otherwise fine. Yeah, I'm here—so're Vincent and Fargo and Taggart. We're getting ready to show a movie—that romantic comedy that came out last month. We thought it'd help calm people down."

"Great idea!" He sounded impressed, and Zoe decided not to tell him whose idea the movie had been. At least, not yet. "Well, Henry and I found Dr. Gunter and we're on our way back—we're actually almost to town now, so we should be touching down at the café in a few minutes. I'll see you soon. Love you!"

"Love you, too," she replied before he hung up. Then she turned to share the good news with the others. "They found Dr. Gunter! And they'll be here in a few minutes!"

"Oh, thank God!" Vincent responded, visibly relaxing. "Because if I have to make one more turkey burger on multigrain I might scream!" He was smiling, though, and Zoe laughed with him. Still, she felt the same relief he did, and she could tell Fargo and Taggart did as well. Her dad would put everything right. He always did.

"I think I'm gonna go out and meet him," she decided out loud, and headed for the door. "You guys are good, right?"

"We've got it covered," Taggart assured her with a surprisingly gentle smile, and Fargo nodded. "Go on." It was times like this that she could see why Jo had dated the lanky Australian. The rest of the time, she wanted to scrub the image from her head with steel wool.

Zoe stepped outside and took a deep breath. There was a pleasant breeze, and the sun was high, casting its radiance across the clear blue sky. And with her dad back, everything would be okay. She hoped.

She saw a dark shape overhead and felt the wind pick up at the same time that she heard a beeping from back inside the café. A beeping she'd come to know all too well.

"Oh, not again!" Zoe wailed. She glanced up at the growing shape, then back over her shoulder toward the café door, torn. Should she go see what was going on? Or wait until her dad had landed first?

"Zoe!" Fargo called from inside. "We've got another alert! There's a switch happening! It's—oh, crap! It's—"

His words cut off, and Zoe had to cover her eyes, turning away as a blinding flash of light erupted just in front of her. There was a loud thud, and she tried to look around, but all she could see were spots.

"Zoe? Zoe!" That was her dad, calling from somewhere close by.

"Dad?"

Zoe was still blinking furiously when she felt someone step up beside her. Then strong arms wrapped around her in a fierce hug. She rested her head on her dad's chest, breathing in the familiar smell of his cologne, and hugged him back. He was home!

"Are you okay?"

"I'm fine," she replied after a second. "I just—whatever that flare was, it messed with my eyes. They're starting to recover." The spots were fading, and shapes were beginning to blur back into view again. She glanced back behind her, toward the source of the light—

—and stiffened.

"Oh. Oh, wow."

Now she knew why Fargo had cursed—and why his words had cut off so abruptly.

Café Diem was gone.

In its place stood a diner. The sign over the front door read *Elkhorn Café*, and she could see several very surprised-looking people staring at her through the windows.

There had been another switch, all right. One of the worst ones imaginable.

Zoe pulled back from her dad slightly, glanced up at him, and offered a weak smile. "Guess it's a good thing I came out to meet you, huh?"

"What just happened?" Vincent whispered as the lights flickered and then came back on. "Was that what I think it was?"

Fargo gulped and nodded. "We just got translocated," he agreed. "We've been switched with a diner in Elka, Nevada."

"Lights're still working," Taggart noted. He didn't look too concerned.

"I've got a backup generator," Vincent explained. "With the way things keep knocking out the power grid around here, I decided it was a good idea."

"How long will it last?" Fargo asked him.

"It's a portable nuclear fusion plant," Vincent replied proudly. "It draws oxygen and water molecules from the air and splits them to provide power. It'll run indefinitely."

"Great." Fargo was busy typing on his laptop. "I lost the signal when we moved, but I'm relocating it. I tapped in on a secure wavelength, so I should be able to reconnect without a problem, and we're still well within range. We'll need to let Sheriff Carter know where we are."

"He was just arriving when we moved," Taggart said. "I'm sure he's guessed what happened by now."

"Yes, but he doesn't know where we are, exactly," Fargo reminded him. "And I don't know what he wants us to do next."

"I say we go ahead as planned." Vincent straightened and swiped a dishrag across the counter. "I'll serve food, we'll watch a movie—maybe two—and then we'll let people know that the gas leak has gotten worse and we've had to quarantine the café. I've got a whole closet full of emergency supplies, including pillows and blankets, so if it goes that long we'll all just bed down here for the night. Hopefully everything will be back to normal in the morning."

"And if it's not?"

"Then we can panic." Vincent glanced at his watch. "Now if you'll excuse me, I don't want the burgers to burn."

"He's got the right idea," Taggart commented as Vincent headed back into the kitchen. "We stay calm, they all stay calm. Otherwise, we'll have pandemonium."

"And for good reason," Fargo retorted. "We've just been moved a good two hundred miles southeast of our previous location! We were disassembled, shunted through the atmosphere, and then reassembled at the other end! We could have wound up with our heads on backward! Or with our legs where our ears should be! Or with each other's left arms! Or—"

Taggart reached out with one long arm and slapped Fargo across the face. "Pull yourself together, man!" he warned quietly. "There's people 'ere countin' on you!"

The sharp sting had done the trick, and Fargo blinked rapidly but when he spoke his voice was calm again. "Yes, you're right. Thank you. We need to stay calm and keep focused." He lifted Carter's PDA from where it rested on the counter, then set it back down. "That's not going to do us any good now—we're not in Eureka any longer." Instead he tapped a command into his laptop, setting up a Skype account and dialing in Carter's number.

"There is one good thing about all this," he commented as he waited for the computer to connect. Taggart eyed him quizzically. "At least now we don't have to worry about these particular strangers wandering loose through our town!"

"Thanks, Fargo," Carter said after listening. **"Yeah,** Vincent's right—the best thing is just to go ahead with what you'd planned, then let everyone know they need to remain in the café for safety reasons. I'm heading over to GD with Dr. Gunter now, and we'll get everything back where it belongs as soon as possible. I'll keep you posted."

"How's he doing?" Zoe asked. They had taken her car— Carter's was still in Burns, unless Allison had brought it back already—with Zoe graciously yielding control to her dad, and it was all Carter could do not to keep holding her hand while he drove. Part of the reason he'd gripped her so tight when he'd hugged her was so that she wouldn't notice how badly he was shaking. Sure, plenty of people had been relocated by the MRS, and all of them were fine, but the thought of his little girl being sent to some other city right in front of him, as if going away to college weren't already bad enough—Carter forced the thought away, though he knew it would come back to haunt him the next time he slept.

"He's managing," he replied when he had his voice under control again. "A little panicked, but it wouldn't be Fargo if he wasn't. Vincent and Taggart will keep him under control, though."

"He really did handle himself fine," Zoe offered grudgingly. "I couldn't have kept everyone calm and contained without him."

"You guys did great," Carter assured her. "You both did. I'm proud of you, sweetie." The smile that lit up her face woke an answering smile in him, and Carter marveled again at how things had changed. Two years ago he'd felt like he barely knew his daughter. Now she was his entire world, and he felt like they had an amazing bond. All thanks to this crazy little town.

"Should we send people to go get them?" Henry asked from the backseat, and Carter glanced at his friend in the rearview mirror.

"I don't know," he admitted. "Let's get to GD and confer with Allison and Zane first, see where we are with getting the MRS shut down and everything restored." His gaze slid to the other man in the backseat, but Dr. Gunter shook his head.

"I won't know until I can examine the logs and the code," he explained. "I hope it's an easy fix, but I won't guarantee it."

"Fair enough." Carter considered the possibilities. "If it doesn't look like we can get them within the next hour or two," he decided, "I'll call Fargo and tell him to make his way back, along with any other residents who were transported with them. Vincent and Taggart can keep an eye on the rest, especially since I'll ask Vincent to lock the doors behind Fargo and not open them again until they're safely back home." He frowned. "We'll need to find another place to bring any transplanted visitors, but I think having Fargo on hand, especially with that laptop connection to the MRS activity log, is worth asking him to make the drive. I might even be able to send the Night Wing to pick him up." The fact that Carter himself wouldn't be able to use it if it was already out on an errand was an added bonus.

"Definitely," Zoe agreed. He must have made a face at her, because she laughed. "What? Okay, sure, he annoys me sometimes—well, most of the time. But he really was a big help. And if you've got to head back out again, I don't want to wrangle strangers all on my own."

"I might," he admitted. "It depends on what we find at

the lab, and what Dr. Gunter can do there." He glanced over at her. "Do you want me to drop you off somewhere? Pilar's, maybe?"

But his daughter shook her head. "I'll head over there later, but I'd like to actually see what's been causing all this mess, if that's okay. And hear what can be done about it."

Carter couldn't argue with that, so he focused on the road again and sped toward GD. And, hopefully, some answers.

CHAPTᵉR 23

"Dr. Gunter! So good of you to join us!"

Allison strode across the lab, hand out, and the startled researcher couldn't do anything but shake it. It was obvious he was trying to read the GD director's tone and expression, trying to gauge if her words had been sincere or sarcastic, to get an idea of just how much trouble he was in. Allison was an expert, however, and looked like she was deliberately sending mixed signals, from the warmth of her smile to the cutting edge of her voice. Carter almost felt a little bad for the guy.

Almost.

"Thanks, Carter." No mixed signals there, he was relieved to see—when she turned to him her voice softened, and her smile widened. As usual, he found himself smiling back.

"Yeah, well, no problem," he assured her, waving his hands. "It was just a matter of—well, okay, yes, it was a problem. But we got him. So now he can set everything right. Right?" He directed that last question toward Gunter himself, adding a bite to it, and was pleased to see the tall scientist flinch. Allison wasn't the only one around here who could intimidate people.

He didn't get why she rolled her eyes at him, though. What had he done this time?

"Yes, yes, of course," Gunter assured him, twisting back a little to look at him before turning to give Allison his full attention again. "Director Blake, I just want to say, I am so very sorry about all this. I had no intention of any of this happening. I just wanted—"

"You just wanted to continue working on a classified project that had already been canceled," Allison cut in, and there wasn't any masking her irritation this time. "You siphoned time, money, and resources from your stated assignment to work on the MRS instead, in secret. You've violated at least a dozen protocols, not to mention several security issues. There will be a full inquiry when all this is over; don't for a second think there won't." She frowned. "But your work on the energy field is extremely impressive, so that will probably work in your favor. And what you did accomplish with the MRS is brilliant—despite the problems it's created."

"Yeah, it's brilliant, all right," Zane offered from the desk. He hadn't even turned around, though he had waved a hand in their general direction. "I'm still trying to figure my way through the lines of code."

"Oh, I can parse it for you," Gunter offered, and—with a quick glance at Allison, who granted permission with a nod—he scurried around her and down into the lab proper, sinking into the second desk chair even as he swung it beside Zane. The two immediately began conferring in rapid, hushed whispers.

"Do you think he'll be able to fix it?" Carter asked Allison, watching the two scientists get to work.

"I don't know," she admitted. "Zane's made some progress, but this thing has a whole nest of protocols and procedural structures he's having trouble following. Gunter should be able to explain all of those—he built and programmed the whole thing, so he should know every line of it—but once they're in there's still a question of what can be done." She shook her head. "Even if he knows how to shut it all down, we have to be sure it'll be safe to do so. We can't risk losing anybody, either by permanently stranding them elsewhere—or worse."

"Anything we can do to help?"

The question earned him another smile, this one a tired one. "No, but thanks. You did the most important thing, which was getting him back here. Now we've just got to give him time to sort out the problem and find a solution."

Carter nodded. "Well, in that case I'm going to head back into town, check on everyone who's left, and make sure there haven't been any new swaps we don't know about. I don't suppose you've got my Jeep stashed here somewhere?"

"It's sitting in the parking lot, right next to my car," Allison informed him. "Now go before you cause a crisis just by standing here."

"What, like I'm some sort of trouble magnet?" he protested, though he was grinning as he said it. "Come on, I'm like the one sane person in this town!" Behind him, Zoe cleared her throat loudly, and he threw her a glance. "Yeah, that goes for you, too—you're as crazy as the rest of them! And you're only here on break, anyway!"

"I get the crazy from you," she replied, laughing. They continued to bicker playfully as they waved good-bye to Allison and Zane and Dr. Gunter—the latter two not even acknowledging their departure—and headed out the door.

* * *

"It's no good." Gunter shoved back from the desk and stood, pacing anxiously in front of the desk. "It just won't work. We're no closer to solving this. And we need to be! We do not have much time left!" They'd been going over the computer's systems, trying to find a way in, for what felt like hours, though it might have been minutes. Neither of them had glanced at a clock lately. There was simply too much to do.

"I know, I know," Zane agreed. "Terminal overload. It'd help if we had a countdown or something, so we could get an idea of just how much time we had left!"

"I wish there were," Gunter said. "But I never anticipated this being a problem—under normal circumstances the system would never be swapping locations so rapidly, and so the energy expenditure and the vacuum chamber's capacity would never become an issue."

"But now it's got no fail-safes to slow it down, and it's accelerating out of control," Zane grumbled, rubbing at his eyes. "I know. But there's got to be some way to see the progression. Even if we can't get a countdown, we should be able to see the energy expenditures—hang on." He lunged for the keyboard and began frantically keying in commands.

Gunter stepped over behind him and hovered over his chair. "What are you doing?"

"I've got access to the activity log," Zane reminded him, still typing, "and thanks to your pass codes and retinal scan, we've got complete access there instead of the limited view I was able to call up before. Using the log, we can find out when the energy began cycling up, because it'll be the first transfer that occurred this morning. Then we should be able to look at the energy expenditures for each transfer—"

"And I've got the calculations for the vacuum chamber's capacity limits already!" Gunter slid into his own chair, grabbed the second keyboard, and began entering codes of his own. "We can extrapolate the system's speed, graph the energy increases, and pinpoint where that will intersect with the chamber's containment limits. Brilliant!"

Zane shrugged. "Yeah, well—okay, it is." He grinned. All weariness was forgotten as he concentrated anew on the task at hand. At least they were getting somewhere! Because if they knew how long they had, they could get a better handle on how much time they had to stop things from reaching that point. They might even be able to throw off the increased transfer speeds completely, which would stop the process and allow them to disconnect the system. He wasn't going to hope for that just yet, but this was a big first step.

He just wished he had another cup of coffee to make sure his mind stayed sharp the whole way through.

"Okay, we've got something," Zane told Allison, Henry, and Carter as they all sat or leaned around the desk, munching on doughnuts and swigging coffee. It wasn't up to their usual food standards, but that was all the Elkhorn Café had been able to offer in the way of quick nourishment. And at least it was caffeine and sugar and carbs. "Actually, several somethings—none of them particularly good."

"Of course," Carter groaned. "Why change now?" Allison swatted him on the arm, and not for the first time Zane wondered if there was something going on between the two of them. Now wasn't the time to think about it, however. They had far more pressing concerns. "Okay, hit us with the bad news."

"Well, first off"—Zane glanced at Dr. Gunter, who nodded—"we can't shut it down."

"I was afraid you were going to say that," Carter muttered. "Why not?"

"It's my fault," Gunter offered, gulping as everyone

turned to stare at him. "When I swapped David and myself, just as a fun little test, the MRS didn't want to cooperate at first. What I was asking for violated several protocols, including sending a part of itself—the PDA I'd slaved to it to act as a sort of remote terminal—to a different location. But I really wanted to show off—David's one of my closest friends here, and one of the only people with clearance high enough to even know about the MRS project, and I was too proud not to tell someone." He looked down at his hands, which were tapping anxiously on the desktop. "So I disengaged a few of the safety protocols until the system accepted the targeting information." He shrugged. "It was stupid, I know, but I wasn't thinking at the time."

"Unfortunately, he wound up disconnecting more than a few protocols," Zane said, picking up the explanation. "He overrode most of the system's fail-safes. And once it completed that first transfer, the MRS began running several more almost immediately. It took the others as part of the same ongoing transfer, which means the fail-safes are still inactive. We've managed to pull a few back to active status, but not all of them. And we can't restore the rest until the transfer finally ends. Whenever that is."

"So we can't shut it off because all the safeties were removed," Carter repeated, "and we can't put most of them back in place until we shut it off."

"Exactly." Zane polished off another doughnut and followed it with a big swig of coffee. He could already feel the caffeine washing through him, making him buzz again. Foul stuff, this coffee, but effective. "But that's not the worst part."

"No, of course it isn't." Carter shook his head. "Fine, I'll bite—what's the worst part?"

"The terminal overload."

Both Carter and Henry nodded. "Gunter warned us that was a possibility," Henry pointed out.

"Oh, it's more than a possibility," Zane corrected. "It's happening. And we managed to figure out when."

The others waited quietly. For all of three seconds. Then Allison glared at him. "Well?"

"The first in this string of transfers began at eight fifty-eight A.M. Pacific time, this morning, when Dr. Gunter swapped himself for David Boyd," Zane explained. He took a deep breath. "And at its current rate of increase the vacuum chamber will pass its containment limit after four hundred minutes of continuous activity."

"Four hundred minutes?" Carter was gaping at him. "That's, what, six and a half hours?" He worked out the time. "That's just a little after three thirty!"

"Exactly."

"So we've only got"—Carter glanced at his watch—"an hour and a half to shut this thing down before it blows up, taking all of GD and most of Eureka with it?"

"Yup." There wasn't much else to say.

"And you can't stop it."

"Well, we can't just end the program," Zane qualified. "We're still working on ways to overload the system, or confuse it, or trick it—anything that'll make it finish out whatever transfers it's already got in the queue and then shut down. Even if it only pauses, as long as we know it's not running we could try to disconnect it."

"Okay, so you're going to keep trying to shut it down," Carter commented, rising to his feet. "Meanwhile, it's going to keep swapping people and places." He sighed. "I guess I'd better be ready to go after them." He wasn't looking forward to getting back in that stealth copter, but speed was definitely of the essence now, so he'd swallow his pride and hold on like hell.

"Do you want me to go with you again?" Henry asked.

Carter thought about it for a second. "You told us earlier that it was speeding up," he reminded Dr. Gunter. "Is that definitely true?" The scientist nodded quickly. "In that case, Henry, I think I'm going to need you to work on your own. We'll cover twice as much ground that way. I just hope between the two of us, Lexi, and Jo, we can reach everyone."

"I'll certainly do what I can." Henry stood up and tossed his coffee cup in the trash. "I'll go get ready." He thought about it. "You know, we've only got the two Night Wings."

Carter grimaced. "Yeah, and believe it or not, right now I wish we had at least two more."

His friend clapped him on the back. "But since we don't, you should assign one to Jo—she's already out there, and she's more familiar with helicopters than any of us. I can take the other one. We'll cover the far-reaching stuff, and you can handle anything that's within driving distance, plus coordinate everyone."

"That . . . makes sense." Carter tried not to show how relieved he felt. "Thanks, Henry." His friend shrugged, but the little half smile he offered made it clear he knew how much Carter appreciated the suggestion.

"Carter, it's time to bring in my security team," Allison pointed out. "They can help, they know the area and most of the people involved, and right now you can use all the help you can get."

He nodded. He still worried that General Mansfield would hear about the problem and decide to step in, but right now keeping things under control was more important than keeping it quiet. "Okay, thanks. I'll set them to patrolling the town." Then he thought of something else. "Actually, maybe we should start by getting everyone who's left off the streets and to some place safe."

"My thoughts exactly. We'll take them to the bunkers."

"Right." Carter frowned. "If your security guys can help evacuate the remaining residents, that would be great.

I'll need Zoe and maybe Taggart to help keep an eye on the transplants, but everyone else can go, which means fewer people we have to worry about being transported out of here."

"Done," Allison agreed. "Henry and I will issue a general evacuation, and I'll have my team report to you for specific orders." She asked another question as Carter turned to go. "What about Fargo? He's already out there, with Vincent and the others. Maybe he can help on that end?"

"I'd rather have him back here," Carter replied. "He did a great job rounding up strangers with Zoe, and I'm going to need them both working at full capacity once things start moving again. Besides"—he grinned—"letting Fargo loose out there? Probably not the best idea."

"No, he'd probably break something," Allison agreed. "Or reconfigure it. Or both." She nodded. "I can send the second Night Wing to get him and anybody else from Café Diem—then when it gets back Jo can take it."

"Perfect—I'll let them both know," Carter called back as he headed for the door. "Keep me posted if anything changes. And the second you know where a place has gone, let me know."

"Will do," Zane promised, waving as the sheriff hit the door panel, darted through while the door was still sliding open, and disappeared down the hall. Henry had left just ahead of him, so only Allison and Dr. Gunter remained.

"Okay," Allison said, finishing her own coffee. "Time to get back to work, boys. The clock's ticking."

CHAPTᵉR 24

"Aw, you're kidding me!" Carter griped, waving at Henry to hold up as he listened. "Where? . . . Great. Yeah, I'm on it. Did you call Zoe yet? . . . Okay, I'll do it. Thanks."

"Something new?" Henry asked as he waited for Carter to catch up. "Or the same old thing?"

"Same old thing," Carter agreed, "but with a new wrinkle. Hang on." He unlocked the Jeep with one hand and dialed with the other. "Hey, sweetie, it's me," he said as Zoe answered. "Listen, we've got another one. 558 South Claremont. Fargo's not back yet, so can you take care of it by yourself? . . . Thanks. Yeah, I'm heading out as soon as I can. Allison will keep you updated on any new switches, and we already told Fargo to call you when he gets in so the two of you can coordinate. You'll have to find a new base camp, but—I know, I know. You've got it under control." He laughed—if only he sounded that confident! "Okay. Bye."

Henry was already buckled in and waiting impatiently.

"Why don't we take care of the house on Claremont ourselves?"

"Because we—or at least one of us—has to get to the house it replaced," Carter pointed out. He started the Jeep and reversed it, pulling out of the GD parking space and heading back into town. "And that's going to take a while." He frowned. "Probably too long, in fact."

"Where is it?"

"San Bernardino."

"San Bernardino?" Henry stared at him. "But that's Southern California! It could take a whole day to get down there! Even with the Night Wing it'd probably take an hour or two—and we don't have that kind of time!"

"Trust me, I'm well aware of the drive involved," Carter assured him. "Remember, I used to drive all over this whole region when I was a marshal. I actually know San Bernardino pretty well, and L.A. even better—in fact, I've still got at least one buddy down there. He's——"

Carter hit the brakes just shy of the hologram that both protected and shielded Global Dynamics.

"What's wrong?"

"Nothing, nothing's wrong." Carter had his phone out again—good thing he was using his old cell phone still, and not the Eureka-based one! "Something might actually be right for a change. I could have sworn I still had—yes!" Henry clearly wanted to ask more questions, but Carter held up a hand as the phone dialed and then rang. *Please pick up,* he thought. *Please pick up. Please*— "Brad?" He almost shouted from sheer relief. "Hey, bud, it's Jack Carter—how are you? . . . Yeah, I'm good, thanks. . . . I know, it has been a while. Listen, are you still in L.A.? . . . You are? Great! Could you do me a huge favor?"

Carter glanced over at Henry, thinking fast. "Yeah, here's the thing—I'm a sheriff now. . . . I know, me either! It's good, though. A lot less travel, so I get to see my daughter every day, which is great. . . . The town?" Henry raised an eyebrow. "It's . . . interesting. Not what you'd expect. Definitely keeps me on my toes." That got a nod and a chuckle.

"Anyway, listen, I've got this . . . situation. We had an incident up here a little while back, I can't go into the details but there's a big court case coming up. And our star witness just took off. I finally tracked him down, but he's in San Bernardino. Can you sit on him for me?"

Henry was holding his breath. So was Carter.

It only took a second for Brad to reply. "Excellent! He's at 1320 East Marquess," Carter recited from memory. "His name's—" He looked at Henry expectantly.

"Oh, right." Henry frowned, concentrating. "558 South Claremont? That's Ted Mosley's place."

"—Ted Mosley," Carter finished.

"He's about my height, stocky, with thick black hair and a bushy beard," Henry added, and Carter repeated all that over the phone. "Oh, and he lives alone except for Janey, his mountain lion."

This time Carter was the one staring. "He's got a pet cat," he said after a second. "A big one. Named Janey. Careful of her. It should be just the two of them, though. Yeah, if you can hold on to him for a day or two, nobody in or out, I'll swing by to collect him or send my deputy down. Great. Yeah, if I can I'll come down myself and we can grab a drink. Sounds good, Brad. Thanks."

Carter hung up and let out a sigh. "Taken care of," he explained as he put the Jeep in motion again and rolled through the force field.

"So who is this guy?" Henry wanted to know.

"Who, Brad? Brad Voelker—FBI, stationed out of L.A. We met a few years back on a kidnapping case. Hit it off pretty well, worked together a few more times after that. I knew I could count on him to help us out. He'll keep Mosley inside—and that mountain lion of his, too—and won't let anybody near them until we can either reverse all this or go get him."

"Nicely handled," Henry agreed. "And a good thing, too. Los Angeles to San Bernardino—he can be there in a heartbeat."

"Exactly." Carter glanced over at his friend. "Where do you want me to drop you, anyway? Aren't you taking the Night Wing?"

"Once it's needed, absolutely. In the meantime, I can help you cover the new houses here."

"I won't turn down help, that's for sure," Carter told him. "But where to? Your garage isn't there anymore."

"No, but I'll bet my fire engine still is."

"Your what?" Carter shook his head. "You were going to take that thing?"

"Sure, why not? It's an official Eureka vehicle."

"Henry, it's a fire engine!"

"Is that a problem?"

"Yes, it's a problem." Carter ticked off reasons on one hand, keeping the other on the wheel. "First off, it looks ridiculous. Second, its top speed is what, forty? Third, where would you put people if you had to drive them back? On the ladder? Fourth, it looks ridiculous."

"You said that already."

"Well, it's worth repeating! Seriously, you can't take that. Not if you want anyone to listen to you at all."

"All right, fine." Henry harrumphed and crossed his arms. "Swing back by my place, then. I'll take my car."

"Do you even have a car?"

"Of course I have a car!" Henry looked slightly insulted. "I just don't drive it much. I like the fire engine better."

"What are you, five?"

"Easy for you to say," his friend pointed out. "You drive a police car."

Carter started to reply to that, stopped, started again, and stopped again. "Jeep," he corrected finally, though it was almost under his breath. "It's a police Jeep. And I almost never get to run the lights."

"Whatever you say, Jack."

They drove the rest of the way to Henry's house in silence.

"Well, well," Zoe called out as the Night Wing landed and a small, slight figure stepped out of the rear door. "If it isn't Acting Sheriff Douglas Fargo, back to show off his quality."

"Ha-ha," Fargo replied as he approached. "Very funny. I see you needed my help again." The Night Wing lifted off behind him, presumably heading back to GD or out to another city again.

"Don't flatter yourself," she warned him. "My dad thought you should come back, that's all. I can handle it fine on my own."

"Sure, yeah, of course." Fargo glanced around. "Lost the café, though, didn't you?"

"*I* lost it?" Zoe's hands went to her hips. "*You* were the one inside at the time!"

Fargo matched her glare for glare. "Which means I couldn't have lost it, could I? I was still there!"

"So I didn't lose it at all, then! You stole it!"

"I stole it?"

"Yes! You disappeared with it, which means you took it, which means you stole it!" Zoe crossed her arms over her chest. "You're a café thief!"

"What? Well, you, you—" Fargo pushed his glasses back up his nose, trying to think of a suitable retort. But nothing came to mind. After a moment he slumped a bit. "I got nothing."

"Don't worry," Zoe assured him, patting him on the shoulder. "I'm sure it'll come to you." She smiled. "Welcome back."

"Thanks." Fargo glanced around. "So, the bookstore? Good choice."

Zoe grinned. "Thanks! I figured it had seats, drinks, and familiar surroundings. Plus if anyone sees a book they don't recognize, they'll just assume it's boring and ignore it."

"Smart." Fargo patted the laptop he was carrying. "So where can I set up?"

"Come on, I'll show you."

Together, the two of them headed inside to get ready for what they both knew could be another long and busy day.

After dropping Henry off to get his car—which turned out to be a sleek silvery gray sedan—Carter got ready to head out again himself. But he stopped before he'd reached the edge of town.

Calling Brad had been a brilliant idea—even Henry had thought so. And the "escaped witness" story was perfect.

Why couldn't he use that again?

Flipping his phone open, Carter scrolled through the numbers in his Contacts list. Then he called one.

"Marsha? Hey, it's Jack Carter," he said after a second. "Yeah, I'm good, thanks. . . . Too long, absolutely. Listen, are you still with the Frisco PD? . . . You are? Great! Do you think you could do me a favor? See, I've got this witness in an upcoming court case, and he might be heading your way. . . ."

Fifteen minutes later, Carter hung up, leaned back, and smiled. This just might work!

He'd called all of the old friends who were still in law enforcement in this part of the country. And there were a lot of them—after all, half of his job as a federal marshal had been liaising with other agencies. FBI, local PD, Highway Patrol, Homeland Security, not to mention several buddies who were still marshals themselves or worked elsewhere in the Department of Justice system. Hell, he knew people in the Coast Guard, but he hadn't thought they'd be able to help much.

The rest, though—he'd given all of them the same story, that there was a big criminal case coming up in his town and several of their witnesses had skipped town, and now all of his old buddies were on the lookout. If a house or office swapped anywhere in their area, he could call them up and send them over there, and they'd sit on whoever was inside. Assuming anyone was there—once the evacuation was complete, most of the swapped houses would be empty anyway. Still, it was better to be prepared for any Eurekans refusing to leave their homes.

That took a lot of pressure off him—he'd coordinate them all, and keep track of everyone, but all he had to handle now were the swaps within Eureka. And he had Henry, Jo, and Lexi to help as well.

All he had to do was keep everyone working together.

Piece of cake.

He put his Jeep back into drive and hit the gas, accelerating as he headed toward the outskirts of town. He figured he'd simply make a full circuit until Allison called him with details on any new swaps.

The thing was, he realized as he drove, coordinating all those different officers and agents really wasn't a problem for him. It was something he was good at. Hell, back in his marshal days it had been something he was known for. Some marshals were amazing at tracking fugitives. Others were experts at hostage negotiation. Still others excelled at witness protection. A few were renowned for their marksmanship, their tactical expertise, and their combat training.

But him?

What had Jack Carter been known for?

His people skills.

He'd been one of the department's top coordinators. He'd worked with every other agency: Homeland Security, the NSA, Firearms and Tobacco, local sheriffs, the CIA (on loan as consultants only, since they couldn't officially operate on U.S. soil), the Coast Guard, forest rangers. Often he'd had several of those agencies on the same case and had kept everyone balanced and focused and under control.

And what's more, he'd enjoyed it.

He liked talking to people. He liked helping people. And he liked persuading people to get along and work together.

Who did he coordinate with now?

He worked with Allison, of course, but that wasn't the same thing—in a very real way he worked for GD as much as for the town in general. Getting the various scientists and researchers and technicians to cooperate sometimes took some doing, but that was a few individuals rather than an agency. He'd had to deal with the military once or twice, when General Mansfield had gotten worked up over something and sent in troops or brought them in personally. And of course there had been Eva Thorne, the corporate "fixer" Mansfield had dispatched to bring GD back in line after all the issues with the Artifact and everything else that'd happened.

But under normal circumstances there weren't any other law enforcement agencies in Eureka. It was just him and Jo.

Hell, even the Eureka Fire Department consisted of Henry and his beloved fire truck!

It wasn't quite the same.

Carter switched on some music, but it wasn't enough to distract him. He was too busy thinking about the past, about what he used to do. About what he'd given up.

He'd made the decision to stay in Eureka. Twice.

But was this really where he belonged?

It was a fascinating town, no question about that, and he really liked some of the people here. Plus there was Allison, though he still didn't really know what was between them, if anything. And Tess, but she was in Australia for the foreseeable future. And Eureka was so isolated! He almost never left, and they almost never had visitors—for very good reasons. But that meant he only interacted with the locals, and he and Jo were the only officers around.

And although being sheriff here certainly kept him busy, it wasn't quite the same as traveling all over the country. Not to mention coordinating a multi-agency manhunt.

He couldn't help wondering, was he really in the right place anymore?

And if so, for how much longer?

Zoe was in college now, which meant she was only here for a week or two at a time, and perhaps a month or so over the summer. And she had plenty of friends she could stay with when she visited. He didn't need to stay in Eureka for her. The question was, did he want to stay here for himself? Or did he want to strike out for greener pastures?

And if he did leave, where would he go? He'd been offered a job with Homeland Security a little while back, but he'd turned it down. He wasn't sure they'd offer one again. What if he'd missed his window of opportunity? What if, by the time he was ready to leave Eureka, he wasn't fit to work anywhere else?

What if that had already happened? What if he'd gotten so rusty he couldn't do his old job anymore? Perhaps it was a good thing this crisis had come up, in a way. It called on all those old skills, the ones he barely used anymore. Were they still sharp, or had they faded through neglect?

Carter adjusted his rearview mirror, checked his speed, tugged on his seat belt, and sighed.

It looked like he was about to find out.

CHAPTER 25

Allison had just made it back to her office—for what seemed like the first time in days—when her PDA rang. A single shrill beep sounded through the room, and then again. And again.

She cringed. She'd programmed that particular ring because it was the loudest, the most obnoxious, the most annoying one she had in the system. And she wanted the ring to reflect its caller.

But it wasn't like she could avoid answering. Not him.

With a sigh, she dropped into her chair and scooped up the gadget. "Good morning, General Mansfield," she said as brightly as she could. "How are you today? And what can I do for you?"

Then she had to hold the PDA away from her ear. Even with several inches between them, she could hear him loud and clear:

". . . hell is going on down there?" he was bellowing.

". . . reports of rapid-growth trees from the Amazon project all over some town in Idaho!"

"I'm sure that's an exaggeration," Allison offered, but the general wasn't done yet and swept right past her claim.

". . . security flagged a background check on the Bakers—from a police station! In Nevada!"

"Probably some kind of glitch," she tried again, though she doubted it would do any good. "Maybe they put in the name incorrectly—there are a lot of Bakers in the world, after all."

"With the exact same fingerprints?"

Allison took a deep breath. "Okay, listen," she started. "No, listen! You want to know what's going on? Fine." It wasn't like he wouldn't find out eventually anyway—he was the military's overseer for all of Eureka, and her direct boss. She'd have to file a report about everything once the situation had been dealt with, and he was the person who would read it, so no sense putting off the inevitable. "Do you remember the MRS project? . . . That's right. Well"— she drummed her fingers on her desk—"it seems Dr. Gunter wasn't as willing to close it down as you were."

She explained the situation as best she could, trying to minimize the risks—both security and actual—as much as possible. But Mansfield had been appointed to Eureka for a reason. He was paranoid about the town's security, and even more so about GD's. His biggest fear was that the scientists there would find some way to destroy themselves and large portions of the country, and either would do so or would somehow lose that secret to a foreign power. And he was determined to keep either of those scenarios from happening—by any means necessary.

"Eureka is now under martial law," he informed Allison crisply as soon as she'd finished speaking. It was a wonder he'd waited that long. "I will be dispatching Major Holmes to serve as my eyes and ears there—you will report to him, and do everything he says, the instant he says it. All of GD's security personnel will answer directly to him. I'm issuing a full evacuation of all nonessential personnel, effective immediately. Anyone not crucial to containing or solving this problem is to head to the bunkers. Is that clear?"

"Yes, sir." What else was there to say to that? She had been about to issue the evacuation notice herself, though hers would have been a bit less insistent. She was relieved herself, knowing that Kevin and Jenna would be safe in the bunkers with their nanny until all of this was over.

She would be staying where she was, however. As would Zane and Gunter. Everyone else could go.

"I expect a complete list of the buildings and homes already translocated, along with the people inside them."

"I can have that for you in a few minutes."

"I want it a few minutes ago!"

"Well, the time machine is still on the fritz, so it'll have to be a few minutes from now, instead." Not surprisingly, he didn't laugh. "Fargo's mirrored the activity log to his laptop," she said, pulling her own keyboard to her and typing a quick message. "I'll ask him to link that to your computer as well, so you've got the complete list. And it'll update every time the machine relocates anything."

"Fine."

A few seconds passed, and then a reply pinged in Allison's inbox. "It should be on your screen now," she told the general.

"Hang on." She could hear him fiddling with something, pushing some keys, and muttering to himself, and bit back a smile. Why would anyone assign a nonscientist to oversee Eureka? Typical military thinking. But it meant that half the time their explanations went right over Mansfield's head. Still, he had advisers on staff for things like that. She wouldn't be surprised if one of them was helping him with the laptop right now.

"Got it," he confirmed finally. "Hm. All right, it looks like nothing vital has been moved yet, so that's something, anyway." Allison wanted to protest—Café Diem was the unofficial center of the town! And Henry's garage was a mainstay. But she decided it was best to keep quiet. Let the general think the matter was less severe than it was. That was fine. She especially didn't want him to realize just how many experiments Henry had lying about his garage half the time.

"Who's dealing with the translocations?" was the general's next question.

"Carter. He has Jo, Henry, and Lexi helping him."

"Henry Deacon? The man we arrested not all that long ago for putting the entire town at risk to avenge his dead girlfriend and save one little boy's life? And who the hell is Lexi?"

Allison couldn't help bristling. "Henry is the town's mayor, and thus our highest elected official," she reminded the general crisply. "And that little boy happens to be my son!" It was hard to maintain her indignation, however, especially when she answered his second question. "Lexi Carter is Jack's sister."

"A civilian? He has a civilian helping him on a matter of high security?"

"She was one of the first to be translocated, and she's familiar with the world outside Eureka, which most of our residents are not," Allison pointed out. "He's making use of her."

The silence on the other end meant the general couldn't find fault with that. At least, not right away.

"Well, it's out of his hands," was his final decision. "This is a military matter now. I'll be dispatching troops to each location to cordon off the areas and quarantine the buildings. No one in or out."

"We have the matter well in hand, General. Sending troops will only exacerbate the situation."

"Not your call, Dr. Blake," he reminded her firmly. "Where is the MRS itself?"

"Section Five, lab five twenty-seven."

She could almost hear the grinding gears in his head. "How likely is it that this thing will try to relocate part of GD?"

Allison had been dreading that question, especially since she knew she couldn't fake the answer. "It hasn't touched Global yet," she said. "Probably because it's located here itself, so it doesn't want to manipulate its own surroundings. But we can't be sure it won't begin to target portions of the building." Especially since the process was speeding up, she thought but deliberately didn't say. Time enough for that later. She hoped. If General Mansfield knew about the impending deadline, he would take more drastic action and would probably eliminate any chance of Zane and Dr. Gunter fixing the problem. And they had only a little over an hour left!

"If it transports any part of GD," Mansfield warned, "I will take immediate steps to correct the problem. Do you understand?"

Allison gulped. "Yes, sir," she managed despite the tightening in her throat. She knew from past experience—including several times when he had come very close to ordering "thermal cleansing," which would reduce the entire town to ash in a matter of minutes—that Mansfield never made idle threats.

She couldn't entirely blame him, Allison thought as she hung up. If the MRS did relocate part of GD, it would be putting cutting-edge technology in the hands of normal people. Technology that in most cases had not been thoroughly tested yet. Technology that could be deadly even in the hands of the men and women who had created it. Tossing such devices and viruses and animals and software and other projects out into the world, where anyone could wander across them and activate or use or free them?

It could spell the end of the world. There were at least three projects in Section Five that she knew were capable of such devastation. And that wasn't even counting the miniature sun Gunter had powering the MRS itself.

Allison leaned back and closed her eyes for just a second. Then she sat forward again and picked up her PDA.

She needed to warn Carter that he was about to have company.

"I'm on my way back," Carter assured her. Then he dropped the PDA back into his pocket, braked, and spun the wheel, spinning his Jeep around so it was pointing back toward GD.

Damn Mansfield! Ordering a townwide evacuation was likely to cause a full-scale panic anyway, and bringing in troops wouldn't exactly calm any nerves. Carter could understand the general's reasoning, but he didn't agree with it. Still, there was nothing he could do to stop it. He'd have to make the best of matters and try to keep the military from getting out of hand and the residents from getting too worked up.

Dark shapes appeared in his rearview mirror, and Carter glanced back, squinting. Unless he was mistaken, those were military transport helicopters on the horizon. Mansfield hadn't wasted any time. He'd have troops cordoning off the town in a matter of minutes, and marching through the street soon after. Carter frowned and stepped on the gas. He wanted to be there when this Major Holmes touched down.

* * *

David Boyd was just coming out of the bathroom, still rubbing a towel over his head to remove the last drops of water, when he heard something shatter downstairs.

"Hello?" He raced down the stairs, ignoring the fact that he was wearing only a towel around his waist—he didn't mind using Arnold's shower or linens, but drew the line at borrowing his friend's bathrobe.

"Don't move!" A trio of black-clad figures burst onto the landing just as he reached it, rifles in hand. All pointing directly at him. "Get your hands in the air!"

David's hands shot up.

"Identify yourself!" the foremost figure demanded. He was dressed in full military gear, David noticed. Complete with helmet and gas mask. Had they heard the gas leak story?

"David Boyd," he answered.

"Boyd, David," the man in the rear said after a second. "You live at 1210 Albany Court in Eureka." It wasn't a question, but David nodded anyway.

"This isn't your house," the leader pointed out. He hadn't lowered the rifle, but somehow his posture had relaxed slightly.

"No, sir," David confirmed. "It's Arnold Gunter's. We swapped places right before the house moved." He figured, since they knew who he was, they weren't here for a supposed gas leak. The nods they gave each other confirmed that suspicion.

"Have you spoken to anyone since you arrived?" was the next question.

"Only Sheriff Carter and Henry Deacon. They found me shortly after the switch. The sheriff told me to stay inside and not speak to anyone else, so I haven't."

That got another nod, and—finally!—the rifles lowered. "Good." The leader glanced around. "The perimeter's secure. We're here to babysit you until the situation's resolved."

"Great." David relaxed a little. "Thank you. Would you like some coffee?"

The soldier considered for a second, then gave a slower nod. "That'd be great, sir. Thanks."

"I've got a pot on in the kitchen," David told him. "And there's some croissants in the oven." He often cooked when he was stressed, and he hadn't figured Arnold would mind. "Why don't you help yourselves?" He turned to go back upstairs.

"Wait—where are you going? Sir."

David glanced back. "Sorry, but I don't usually entertain guests wearing nothing but a towel." One of the soldiers actually laughed, and David relaxed still further as he hurried up to get dressed. He felt more secure than he had since this whole thing had started.

He just hoped he had enough food to feed however many soldiers had been sent to guard him.

"Dr. Leonardo?"

Maria Leonardo glanced up, surprised. She hadn't heard anyone approaching. Then again, she'd been engrossed in examining one of her new hybrids, and considering that she sometimes forgot to eat when she was working, it made sense that she might miss the sound of footsteps behind her as well.

Her brain was still registering the fact that whoever'd arrived had called her by name—she'd told her recent "customers" to call her Maria in order to preserve at least a hint of anonymity and security—at the same time that she noticed the newcomer's attire.

Black.

All black.

Black camo pants. Black camo jacket. Black gloves. Black boots. Black helmet. Black face mask.

Black assault rifle.

She was staring at a soldier. In full assault gear.

"Be careful with that thing," was the first thing she thought to say, pushing the rifle barrel down farther with one hand. "These plants are in a delicate stage. Brushing that against them could result in system shock."

"Dr. Leonardo?" the soldier—she realized it was a woman—asked again. "I'm Corporal Salis. I'm here to secure the facility. Come with me."

"Give me a minute." Dr. Leonardo turned her back on the soldier, noticing as she did that there were several more behind her, and others fanning out through the aisles, to place the small protective dome back over the tiny sapling. It wasn't ready to handle unfiltered air or direct sunlight for very long yet.

Corporal Salis waited impatiently until she'd straightened up again. "Okay, I'm ready." Dr. Leonardo wiped her hands on her jeans—she was glad she kept a spare set of clothes in the back office—and followed the soldier toward that same office. Other soldiers moved into position behind her, boxing her in.

She tried not to let them see how frightened she was. She'd known there was a chance the military would hear of what she'd done today. And even though she'd given away only unaltered specimens, her experiments were classified, and giving away any materials involved in those experiments could land her in some pretty hot water.

She hoped Lexi wouldn't get in trouble for helping her, though. She'd like the sheriff's sister. And it was rare to find someone else in Eureka—or at least from there—who felt as strongly as she did about saving the environment.

Dr. Leonardo smiled as she stepped into the small office. Her trees were going to provide shade and comfort and fresh air all over Glenns Ferry for decades, even centuries to come. Whatever her punishment, that was worth it.

One of the Bakers answered the door—and found himself staring down a rifle barrel.

"Hello," he said. "Are you looking for the people who live at this address? Because we're only visiting."

"Dr. Baker?" The soldier holding the gun asked. "Are all of your brothers here with you?"

"All of us who were relocated, yes," Baker replied. "The rest are still back in Eureka."

"Fine. Has anyone contacted you or spoken to you?"

"Deputy Lupo was here," Baker told him. His brothers had joined him now. "And my brother had an unfortunate encounter with the local constabulary. But the deputy sorted all that out."

"We've already wiped those records," the soldier told him. "No one else has come to your door?"

"No," Baker answered, then amended his statement as one of his brothers nudged him. "Well, the mailman did, but he simply slid some mail through the slot." He lifted the sheaf of envelopes from the side table. "Here they are. They don't belong to us."

"That's fine." The soldier glanced around. "You're under quarantine. We'll place a guard outside to make sure it's enforced. Please close the door behind me."

He backed away, slinging the rifle over his shoulder as he did, and Dr. Baker waited only a few seconds before closing the door as instructed. He locked it for good measure.

"Well," one of his brothers said as they all returned to the sitting room. "That was expected."

"Yes," another agreed. "And oddly comforting."

"We should warn the others," Dr. Baker pointed out. His brothers nodded as they all sank down onto chairs around the room. Then they all focused on their missing siblings. The range was extreme, but they were all together in this. And this was important.

CHAPT^eR 26

"Hello? Dr. Todd?" Jo knocked on the cabin door.
She was in Superior, Montana, and tracking down this place
had actually been trickier than most of the switches she'd
dealt with so far. That was because the former force field researcher's small, rustic cabin blended perfectly with the other
homes in this town. And they were far enough apart, and few
enough in number, that they didn't appear to have house numbers. Just names on the mailboxes. She'd had to call Fargo
back to get the name of the person who'd been swapped, just
so she could make sure she'd found the right house.

And she still wasn't completely convinced, because no
one was answering.

"Hello?" She tried the door, and it wasn't locked. "Dr.
Todd?" She'd met him once before, when one of his old
experiments had wound up in Fargo's pocket and had put
the wiry little scientist at risk. Seriously at risk. So much so
that the only way to save him had been to shoot him.

Jo had enjoyed that part immensely.

"Anybody home?" She pushed open the door and stepped inside. "Dr. Todd? It's Deputy Lupo, are you here? If so, I really need to speak with you!" The former researcher hadn't been thrilled to have his privacy disturbed the last time, and Jo doubted he'd gotten more sociable since then. But she had to be sure he was here—and if not here, she had to find him. She couldn't risk another Dr. Baker.

She started down the hall, the unfinished floorboards creaking under her feet—and froze.

The creaking continued for half a second before stopping also.

Jo had her gun out by the time the cabin fell silent again.

That hadn't been her footstep.

Could something have happened to Dr. Todd? She'd announced herself clearly, and the cabin wasn't that big—if he was in here, he should have heard her. And although he didn't like visitors, he hadn't struck her as the kind of man who'd actively hide from an official visitor. Or try to sneak up on one.

Which meant someone else was in the house.

He'd left his door open. Pretty common in Eureka, where people were more interested in quadratic equations than stealing TVs. But it could get you in trouble elsewhere. Not that Superior had struck her as a hotbed of villainy, but she'd only seen it from the road so far. Maybe there were teen hoodlums around, like the ones who'd stolen that car from Henry's garage.

And maybe they weren't just looking for a quick joyride.

Moving carefully, she edged down the hall, gun up near her face, both hands firm on its grip, her head swiveling from side to side, looking for any movement, listening for any sound.

There.

A faint whisper on the other side of the wall to her left. Someone had shifted their weight. They knew she was here, and they were waiting for her.

But how many?

She'd heard only the one creak. Did that mean there was only one intruder, or was it just that only one had moved?

Jo inched toward the door to her left as silently as she could.

Then she heard another creak.

This one from farther along the hall, and to her right.

Damn!

Abandoning stealth for speed, she lunged forward and threw herself through the door, tucking her right shoulder in and rolling as she entered the room beyond. In a second she was up again, one foot flat on the floor and the other knee down, gun held straight out in front of her in one hand, the other palm steadying it, as she locked eyes with her target.

Who had his own gun already trained on her.

He had an assault rifle.

She had a pistol.

That didn't worry Jo. It wasn't always about bigger, as she'd proved time and again to soldiers twice her size.

No, what worried her was the way he held his weapon. Calm, focused, steady. Trained. Possibly as well as she was.

They faced off for a second. She couldn't see his features behind the gas mask and helmet.

Then that mask shook slightly. And a sound echoed forth from it.

Laughter.

Laughter?

Then he spoke.

"Not bad, Lupo. Good to see you haven't lost your edge."

Jo stared. She knew that voice. "Tango?"

When he laughed again, she knew she was right.

"Tango, what the hell are you doing here?" She stood and holstered her pistol, and Tad "Tango" Nelson slung his rifle back over his shoulder. "What's going on? Where's Dr. Todd?"

"We've got Todd," her old squadmate assured her. "Safe and sound. We were just about to evac when we heard the door." He pulled off his gas mask and helmet and grinned at her, white teeth a sharp contrast to his dark skin. His hair was as buzz-cut as ever, but she noticed some gray mixed in with the black now. "Good to see you, Jo."

"You too." She stepped up and gave him a tight hug. "I guess Mansfield's involved now, hm?"

"Yep. Mobilized us and sent us out, along with a half dozen other teams. Evac when possible, isolate when not. Nobody in or out without clearance." His grin widened. "I guess I'll make an exception for you."

"Hey!" She put her hands on her hips. "I am the deputy sheriff of Eureka," she pointed out. "Dr. Todd is a Eurekan resident. That makes him my jurisdiction. And you know I have clearance."

"I do now." He put up his hands as she swung at him. "Hey, hey! Come on! I was kidding!"

Just then his shoulder mike crackled. "Corporal Nelson, report."

"Nelson here," Tango replied. "Dr. Todd located. Prepping for evac now. Deputy Lupo also on scene. Request permission to coordinate with her."

There was a pause.

"Acknowledged," came the eventual reply. "Deputy Lupo cleared for this op. Proceed."

"Well, looks like we're working together again," Tango

said to Jo as he stepped past her and back into the hall. He gave a sharp whistle and four more men appeared from various rooms. One of them had Dr. Todd with him. The researcher looked annoyed, and maybe a little puzzled, but not too concerned. Most of GD's top personnel had been dealing with military officers for far too long to let a little thing like a commando squad home invasion worry them.

"Good," Jo replied, following Tango and his squad. "It means I can save your ass again."

"That was a fluke," her old teammate protested.

"Which time?" she shot back. A helicopter was settling on the front lawn, and Tango began hustling his team toward it.

"Care to join us?" he asked. "Faster than driving."

She laughed and shook her head. "Who says I drove?" She waved at what appeared to be an empty patch of lawn, and Tango gaped as a door appeared in thin air. Davey waved back, then pulled the door shut again.

"What the hell was that?" her old squadmate demanded.

Jo gave him a wicked grin. "Sorry, Corporal, you're not cleared for that information." She punched him in the shoulder—but not too hard. "I'll meet you at the next spot. Radio me when you've got intel." He gave her a thumbs-up, and Jo watched as the squad secured Dr. Todd and then climbed into the helicopter after him. It was already lifting off by the time Tango had hoisted himself up into the cabin.

With a sigh, Jo walked around the concealed Night Wing, pulled open the passenger door, and clambered back into her seat. The military was involved. Great. That was going to complicate matters.

And she knew that at least part of it was her fault. She should have gotten to Baker sooner.

Damn it! She banged a hand against the door, then

shook her head and gestured for Davey to get them airborne. Well, nothing she could do about it now.

She wondered if Carter knew yet.

"Sorry, ma'am, no access beyond this point."

The soldier speaking to her was very young, very polite, and very cute in that clean-cut military sort of way. Lexi gave him her best smile.

"Look, I know you've got a job to do," she told him, "but I really need to make sure my friend's okay. She hasn't been feeling well lately, and didn't meet me for lunch today, so I'm really worried about her."

She could see him starting to relent.

"Where does she live?" he asked, glanced over his shoulder and past the barricade.

"Right over there." Lexi rolled her window down the rest of the way and stuck out her arm, pointing at a two-story stucco building painted an improbable dusty orange. "936 Del Monte."

The instant she said the address, the soldier stiffened. When he faced her again, all friendliness was gone. "I need to see some identification, ma'am."

"What?" Lexi shrank back a little.

"Step out of the car, please." His hands tightened visibly on the rifle he was carrying, though he still held it across his chest. That was something, anyway. "Now, ma'am."

"Okay, okay." Lexi put the car in park, shut off the ignition, and stepped out. She left the keys in. "Is something wrong?"

"Identification, please." His eyes, such a pretty shade of green, had gone flat.

"Fine." She dug in her purse and pulled out her wallet, extracted her driver's license, and handed it to him. "Really, I don't know—"

But the soldier was speaking into the mike clipped to his collar. "Lieutenant, I've got Lexi Carter here. Sir, yes, sir!"

It sounded like they knew who she was. Lexi shivered. That couldn't be good.

A minute later, a second soldier approached from behind the barricade. He was wearing the same black gear as the first one but carried himself differently. He walked with more authority. This had to be the lieutenant the first one had called.

"Hi," Lexi said brightly, holding out her hand. "I'm Lexi Carter."

"Lieutenant Brill," he replied, though he didn't accept her handshake. "Ms. Carter, I'm going to have to ask you to leave. This is a military operation, and you are not cleared for it."

"Oh?" Lexi accepted her ID back from the first soldier. "A military op?" She leaned in a little and lowered her voice. "There isn't really a gas leak, you know."

He didn't even acknowledge the statement. "Ma'am, you will need to leave at once."

Lexi considered the two men. She knew guys, and these two had the whole *We're not budging an inch* stance going on. They were serious. She was not going to be able to wheedle her way past that barricade. Besides, they were obviously here for the same reason she was—to make sure Tracey Stilson didn't get herself in any trouble here in Willows, California.

So, mission accomplished.

Sort of.

"Okay, then!" She gave them both another smile. "I guess I'll just head back home. Thanks! You both have a really good day, okay?" The younger one smiled slightly, though the expression vanished when his lieutenant glanced his way. They both watched without a word as she hopped back into her car, started it back up, and put it in reverse.

"Sorry, Jackie," Lexi whispered as she drove away. "I guess I'm out of the house-swapping business." She turned left, heading for the highway. She doubted there was much she could do to help back in Eureka, but it was clear she wasn't going to be able to get anything done outside it anymore. And at least she'd be back with Zoe and everybody else.

Or maybe, she thought, she should just head home to Duncan.

That cheered her up, and she was singing along with the radio as she pulled onto the interstate and sped up.

"I'm sorry, Dr. Deacon, I can't let you through."

Henry glared at the tall young woman blocking his way. "Soldier, you clearly know who I am," he said, carefully reining in his temper. It didn't do to lose your cool, especially with someone who had several inches and more than a few pounds of muscle on you. And carried a really big gun.

"Yes, sir."

"Which means you know my clearance rating. And that I am a duly elected official of Eureka." He gestured toward the building on the far side of the street. "And that is the Eureka Lanes, an establishment from my town. That makes it my responsibility."

The soldier frowned slightly. "All due respect, sir," she replied, "but it's General Mansfield's responsibility until he says otherwise. And he said no civilians were allowed through in either direction."

"I'm not a civilian," Henry pointed out. "I'm the mayor. And I'm a GD scientist with Section Five clearance. Do you have any other scientific advisers on-site?"

That made her scowl, though not at him. "No, sir, we do not."

"Then how, exactly, were you planning to disconnect the building's gravitic conversion fields?" he asked her.

The blank look he got back was reply enough.

"Talk to your commanding officer," he instructed. "Tell him that if I can't get in there and reroute the power around those fields within the next half hour or so, the resulting interference could generate a low-level gravitic pulse that will fry every electrical circuit for two miles around and produce miniature gravity wells that flatten anything in their range."

It took her only six seconds to start talking rapidly into her mike. Henry counted them.

Less than eight seconds later (he was still counting), her commander gave her the okay to let Henry through.

"Thank you," he told her as she saluted and stepped aside.

"My pleasure, sir." She leaned down a little. "Will you be able to shut off that thing you mentioned in time?"

"The gravitic conversion fields?" Henry made a point of glancing at his watch, then nodded. "Yes, thanks to you."

She didn't ask him anything else, just stood and watched as he jogged across the street to the bowling alley.

"Henry?" Bill Severin, the alley's owner, opened the door as he approached. "Is that really you?"

"It sure is, Bill," Henry responded, quickening his pace. "Got anybody else in there with you?"

"Sally and Jeff. And Mr. Thompson. He was getting in an early practice set." Mike Thompson was on the Eureka Dynamos bowling team.

"Great. Get them all away from the lanes, okay? I need to shut down the gravitic conversion fields before we have a problem."

"The—?" Bill had always been fast on his feet; you had to be to run a popular business in Eureka. It didn't hurt that he actually had degrees in applied engineering, quantum physics, robotics, and a few other fields. "Oh, right. I'm on it."

He held the door wider, and Henry slipped past him into the bowling alley.

"Had to talk them into letting you past, eh?" Bill said quietly once the door had shut behind them.

Henry slapped him on the back. "Exactly."

"So where are we, anyway?"

"Tremonton, Utah." Henry shook his head. "It's a long story. You guys doing okay?"

"Oh, sure, we're fine." Bill grinned. "Wanna bowl a few frames?"

"I can't, but thanks. I need to be back out there for whoever gets relocated next." Bill held out his hand, and Henry shook it. "Just keep Sally and Jeff and Mr. Thompson in here, okay? The military will stay outside, and they'll keep anyone else away. Hopefully we'll have this sorted out soon."

"What if we don't?" Bill asked as Henry headed back outside.

"Then I guess you'll have to open a satellite branch," Henry replied over his shoulder. He could see the same soldier watching him intently, and waved at her, giving her a big thumbs-up to make sure she didn't get too nervous.

He just hoped the next soldiers he encountered would be as accommodating.

Or as gullible.

"Okay, where is he?" Carter demanded, stepping into Gunter's lab. Allison glanced up but Gunter and Zane continued working, not even acknowledging his presence.

"I assume you mean Major Holmes?" Allison asked. "I have no idea. I thought he'd check in here first, but I haven't seen him yet."

"Have you spoken to him?" Carter stopped beside the desk and folded his arms across his chest.

"Several times. But he hasn't asked me to meet with him in person, and he hasn't said anything about coming out here." She gestured toward the door. "He must be the type who prefers to be in the thick of things." She raised an eyebrow at Carter. "Not unlike a certain sheriff I know."

He harrumphed, then changed topics. "Where are Kevin and Jenna?"

"Safely in the bunkers with their nanny." She smiled—leave it to Carter to remember to worry about her kids, even at a time like this. "What about Zoe?"

"Won't budge." He grimaced, but she could see pride warring with anger and parental concern. "I told her it was an order and she laughed at me."

"Gee, your daughter, stubborn?" Allison teased him. "Where could she get that from?"

This time pride won out. "Yeah." He beamed. "Nobody's gonna push my little girl around." He switched gears again, and the frown returned. "But this Major Holmes—we need to talk. You don't know where he is?"

"I'm assuming he's somewhere in town, but as to anything more specific, your guess is as good as mine."

"Great." Carter's scowl deepened. "This guy comes to our town and takes control, but can't even take the time to meet us face to face? That doesn't bode well."

"Mansfield wouldn't have sent him if he couldn't do that job," Allison pointed out. "I think we just have to put any hurt feelings aside and let him do it. It's not like we have a choice."

"You don't, maybe," Carter corrected. "You work for Mansfield. I don't—I work for the town." He launched himself toward the door again, taking quick, hard strides. A second later he was gone.

Allison sighed. Carter was good at his job—very good—but he had some real problems with higher authorities, and especially with the military. She just hoped he didn't say or do anything to get himself in trouble. Because right now, they really needed him.

CHAPTeR 27

"What exactly do you think you're doing?"

Zoe turned, startled, and almost dropped the tray of coffee mugs, teacups, water glasses, and sodas she was carrying. If she had, it certainly wouldn't have been her fault, either—the man who'd just barked that question was standing so close the tray grazed his chest.

His military-grade-camo-clad chest.

"I'm serving drinks," she replied after a second, glad that growing up with her dad meant uniforms and ranks didn't impress her much. Judging by the oak leaves at his collar, he had plenty of rank to spare. "Why, would you like anything?"

"There's a full evacuation," he told her crisply. "All nonessential personnel are to report to the bunkers immediately."

Zoe frowned. "This is essential." She didn't let on that she'd already heard about the evacuation order—she'd just finished arguing with her father about why she wouldn't be obeying it. Now she suspected she was about to have the same debate all over again.

But the officer barely heard her reply, because he'd just noticed the other people around. "All of these people are transplants!" He scanned the room, though mirrored sunglasses hid his eyes. "They don't belong here!"

"That would be the meaning of *transplant*, yes," Zoe agreed. "If they did belong here, they wouldn't be transplants. Is there a point to all this?" It amused her to see the same little throbbing vein at his temple as her dad got when she did this to him. Authority figures were so predictable.

She'd already guessed what Mr. Military's response would be. "I meant that they do not belong in this Eureka establishment! They have no clearance and should be sequestered in their own homes immediately!"

"Some of them were at work when they were switched," she informed him. "Their homes are hours away from here. Did you want me to just put them on a bus?"

Whatever Mr. Military had been about to say in reply was cut off as Fargo came rushing over. "Major Holmes! What a pleasant surprise! It's been a while." He held out his hand, which the apparent major stared at. "Fargo. Douglas Fargo. We met on General Mansfield's last inspection tour."

"Oh. Yes. Of course." Major Holmes accepted the handshake. "Good to see you again, Dr. Fargo."

"You too. Now, what can we do for you?"

The major puffed out his chest, almost upsetting Zoe's tray again. "General Mansfield has placed Eureka under martial law and ordered a full evacuation. He sent me to see that his wishes were carried out."

"Of course. I can patch you directly into everyone's PDAs, if you'd like."

"Yes. Please. Thank you." Major Holmes looked like he didn't know what to do with such unexpected cooperation.

Fargo pulled out his PDA, hit a button, then passed it to the major. "There you go. Just speak into it. Everyone in town will hear you."

"Ah. Yes." Major Holmes cleared his throat. "Residents of Eureka, and visitors. My name is Major Holmes. I will be in charge of Eureka until the current situation has been resolved. I am placing the town and its environs under martial law. There will be no departures and no arrivals without my express approval. Weapons of any kind are restricted entirely to myself and my men. I am also ordering a full evacuation of all residents not directly involved in containing or solving the current situation. Please make your way toward the nearest bunker with all due speed but proceed in an orderly fashion. That is all." He closed the PDA and handed it back to Fargo.

"Thank you," he said. "Now please clear these people out."

"I already told you," Zoe said, "some of them have nowhere else to go. And besides, what's wrong with having them here? Are you afraid they're going to share stories? 'I was home watching TV when my entire home transported itself to Nevada—with me still inside!' 'Oh, I know what you mean—I was minding my own business the other morning and then—wham! I'm in Montana!' How exactly is this a problem?" She was getting angry now, and letting her temper talk, but she didn't stop. Instead, she got right up in Major Holmes's face. "You're clearing everyone else out, so there's nobody left to tell—and even if there were, nobody in Eureka would be surprised one bit. And the more you keep them comfortable and happy, the less they'll think about the situation at all. By the end of the day they'll head back home thinking this was an amazing opening of a new bookstore, and dwelling on that rather than the fact that they and their house are as much as two states away from their listed address."

"She's right," Fargo chimed in, much to her surprise. "Keeping them here, together, where we can speak to any of them easily and also keep an eye on them all at the same time? It's perfect. If we send them back home, we'll have to worry that one or more might slip past your soldiers. And they'll be tenser, ready to attack or flee at the slightest provocation. But as long as they can sit here and order muffins and cookies and drinks, they'll stay all day and all night. It's a safe, familiar setting, and it puts them more at ease. Which makes your job easier—and ours."

Major Holmes thought about that a second. "All right," he agreed, "but I'm holding the two of you personally responsible for each and every transplant that walks through those doors. Understood?"

"Sir, yes, sir," Zoe replied, throwing him as crisp a salute as she could manage. He ignored her again, nodded to Fargo, and marched back down the stairs and out.

"What the hell was that?" Fargo asked as soon as the major had left.

"My dad called a minute ago to warn me—the general somehow learned about the building swaps," Zoe told him. "He's worried about the same thing that had my dad worried—what if any one person from here goes for a walk down their new location's Main Street, using a nanocloud recorder and a miniature controlled sunburst? He wants to keep everything from blowing up super huge."

Fargo was staring at her. " 'Super huge'?"

She shrugged. "It fits."

"That wasn't what I meant, though," he insisted. "I know why he's here, and about General Mansfield's concerns. Which are totally valid, by the way. Eureka's very existence is classified, so these people are already breaching military security just by being here." He adjusted his glasses. "What I meant was, what was that all about, getting all up in Major Holmes's grill?"

Zoe laughed. Fargo trying to use "street talk" was both ridiculous and entertaining at the same time. Still, he had stood up for her, and that meant he deserved an answer. "I don't know," she admitted. "Oh, he ticked me off with his 'I'm in charge' attitude, sure. And these people are people, not cattle—they deserve better than being locked in their homes, especially for something that isn't their fault. But I don't know why I went off on him." She shrugged. "I guess in a way these people remind me of me when I first got here. I was kind of a transplant, too, except that I had papers allowing me to be here. But I didn't fit in." She adjusted a few of the items on her tray. "I guess I'd just like to know that somebody would have stood up for me the same way, if it had been the other way around."

"Zoe Carter, Champion of the Confused Visitor," Fargo teased her, but there was no bite to it. "They're lucky to have you." He looked as shocked at the compliment as she did. "Of course," he added a second later, grinning, "I'm not so lucky. You could have landed me in the brig for insubordination!"

"Oh, yeah, like you don't deserve that a thousand times over," Zoe replied.

"Hey, I'm not the one who started my time in Eureka in jail!"

"No? Maybe you should have—it might have done you some good!"

Still bickering good-naturedly, they split up to finish their tasks—Zoe to deliver drinks and Fargo to reset the Eureka community desktop and basic functions so any visitor with Wi-Fi could access a few basic sites and nothing else. That way it would be safe for visitors to surf the Web while in Eureka, and the town wouldn't have to worry about the transplants accidentally seeing details for some project they shouldn't. Or even accidentally broadcasting their location.

As long as they could offer free Wi-Fi, free cable, and free drinks, the transplants weren't going anywhere for a while.

Zoe just hoped they resolved things before Major Holmes started to question how many people they could cram into the bookshop all at once.

"Look, guys, I appreciate that you're doing your jobs," Carter said. "But I'm doing mine. So I'd appreciate it if you'd let me through." He could see the house beyond them, and also the lightning flashes that were erupting from the half-open door. Delia Apnell lived there—she was an expert in electromagnetism, particularly applied and focused electrical bursts.

Lightning strikes.

And right now, it looked like she was using her miniaturized lightning bolts to keep the soldiers from forcing her to leave her home.

"No can do, sir," one of the soldiers blocking his way insisted. "Orders."

"What orders, exactly?"

"No civilians in or out," was the answer. "No exception."

Carter rubbed a hand over his face. "I'm not a civilian! I'm the sheriff of Eureka! I've got clearance!"

The soldiers didn't reply.

"Oh, this is ridiculous!" He tried to push past them, and suddenly had two rifles in his face. Barrel first.

"Whoa, whoa!" He backed up a step, raising his hands. "Let's table the testosterone, okay? We're all men here—no need to try to prove it."

"A-hem."

The throat-clearing had come from behind the two guards, and Carter looked past them to see a slightly shorter soldier. Despite the heavy black assault gear, she was clearly, undeniably female. And, judging by the lack of a rifle, probably the commanding officer here.

Whom he had just inadvertently insulted.

"Way to go, Jack," he muttered to himself. "At last, a level head," he said more loudly. Then he extended his hand. "Sheriff Jack Carter, Eureka."

She shouldered the guards aside and shook his hand. Her grasp reminded him of Jo's—firm to the point of crushing. "Captain Barbara Yang, United States Army." Now that she was closer, he could see there was a slightly Asian cast to her large, dark eyes, high cheekbones, and smooth olive skin. Pretty, too, in a stern sort of way. More reminders of Jo.

"I need to get in there," Carter told her. "I can help."

"We've got the situation under control."

"I'm sure you do, but that's not the point. You're here to contain the situation, right?" She nodded sharply. "That's great—it's actually a huge weight off my shoulders. But I still need to make sure my people are okay. Which could be a good thing for you, too. Let me talk to her, and I may be able to get her out of there without anyone getting fried to a crisp."

Captain Yang just looked at him.

"Look," he tried again, "we're on the same side here. We want the same thing. Let me help."

"Not my call," she answered.

He sighed. He'd been hoping to avoid this, even though he'd known that probably wouldn't happen. "Fine. Let me talk to General Mansfield." He could have asked to speak to Major Holmes, but the man still hadn't bothered to locate Carter, and so Carter decided he'd just take things to the top right from the start. And if that annoyed Holmes for going over his head? So be it.

A few minutes later, Carter was sitting in the army

unit's mobile command center, staring at a monitor—and at Mansfield's craggy features.

"Carter," the general said by way of greeting. "Why am I not surprised?"

"General, nice to see you again, too." Carter didn't point out that the last time they'd spoken, it had been when Mansfield had fired him. He figured there was no point in bringing that up, especially since it had later turned out that Mansfield lacked the authority to do so. The meeting was a sore point for both of them.

"The situation is now under military control, Sheriff," Mansfield was saying. "Your help is no longer required. Evacuate to the nearest bunker along with everyone else."

"With all due respect, sir, I think I'm of more use out here." Carter had spent the time while waiting for Mansfield marshaling his arguments. "I know these people, and they know me. I can calm them down a lot more than a bunch of soldiers, especially ones who break into their homes." He glanced at Yang over his shoulder. "No offense."

"We don't need them calm, Carter," the general replied. "We just need them contained."

"That's not actually true, though, is it?" Carter leaned in a little toward the monitor. "You know what these people are capable of. What if one of them panics? Do you want to count on the fact that your troops can handle whatever gadgets or chemicals they might have hidden away for home defense? Think about it." He could tell Mansfield was doing exactly that. "Let me work with your troops. I can go in and talk to them directly, make sure they know the best thing to do is cooperate and wait patiently. That way your people don't have any problems, I've made sure my people are safe, and everybody's happy."

One thing he did like about Mansfield was that the man knew how to make decisions on the fly. "All right," he agreed almost the instant Carter stopped talking. "I'll let my troops know that you're to be granted access and given full cooperation." He grimaced for just a second. "Deputy Lupo's already working with one unit, and Dr. Deacon has bypassed another. I'll grant them access as well."

"And my sister?"

"Don't push your luck."

Carter leaned back. "Fair enough." He thought of something else. "Oh, your troops might encounter local law enforcement at a few locations, or FBI. They're with me."

Now Mansfield looked definitely displeased. "You brought the feds in on this?"

"I asked a few buddies to help keep tabs on escaped witnesses to an ongoing criminal case," Carter corrected. "That's all they know."

The general nodded. "Not bad, Carter," he conceded. "All right, I'll let my commanders know to play along." He signed off without another word.

"Nice talking to you, too," Carter muttered as he stood up. Yang was waiting. "So, can I go inside now?"

She didn't say anything, but she swiveled slightly so he could pass.

CHAPTᴇR 28

"Uh-oh."

"Hm?" Zoe lifted her head and looked around. She'd been napping—keeping up with all these out-of-towners was exhausting! Of course she had unlimited access to coffee, and her dad wasn't here to tell her no, but after the fourth cup she felt like she was going to vibrate right through the floor, so she'd switched to Vitaminwater. Which was great for hydration but not so good on keeping you awake.

The worry in Fargo's voice, however, had cut through her semisleep. He was sitting nearby, his ever-present laptop precariously balanced on the chair arm, the screen reflected on his glasses.

"What, uh-oh?" she asked, levering herself up a little and brushing her hair back out of her face. Honestly, sometimes she just wanted to chop it all off! Then she thought about how much Lucas liked her long hair, and smiled. Maybe not.

Fargo's reply snapped her back to the present and the crisis at hand. "There's been another switch. A big one."

"Where?" Her chest felt tight. "GD?"

But her partner in crime shook his head. "No, that's still safe. But this one could pose some problems anyway." He glanced up at her. "Tesla High."

Zoe stared at him. "They took the high school?" A part of her wanted to cheer—yes, no more applied cybernetics with Ms. Kassbaum!—but the rest of her was already waking up and clicking into damage-control mode.

"Yeah. Swapped it with a school in Roseburg, Oregon."

"Great." Zoe forced herself up out of the chair and began pacing, trying to get the blood flowing again. Preferably to her brain. Her head still felt foggy. "Well, Tesla's been closed since this morning, so it's practically empty. There might be a janitor or two around, and maybe an overzealous teacher—like Ms. Kassbaum!—but definitely no students." Even in Eureka, teenagers knew to take advantage of a day off.

"Which is great," Fargo replied, "but what about the other school?"

"Oh."

"Exactly. Oh. As in, oh, it's a Friday afternoon, and that place is crawling with high school students! What happens when the school day ends? Several hundred teenagers get unleashed on Eureka!" He pushed his glasses back up. "Assuming the military doesn't arrest them all first."

Zoe froze. "Yeah, wouldn't that go over well," she muttered. "If Major Annoying gets there first, he'll storm in and throw everybody in the brig. Good luck keeping that one quiet!" And the last she'd heard from her dad, he was still trying to keep Delia Apnell from electrocuting everyone who approached her front door—him included. Zoe grabbed her jacket. "Come on!"

Fargo clutched at his laptop and half rose. "What? Where are we going?"

"We've got to get there and contain the situation before he does." Zoe was already heading for the door, leaving Fargo no choice but to follow her.

Zoe drove like a madwoman and skidded to a stop in front of the high school just as the first military Jeep was pulling up. Major Stay-in-Your-Holmes was riding shotgun, and Zoe headed straight for him.

"Back off," she warned. "We've got this."

It was clear the man didn't have daughters—hell, he probably didn't have children at all, or any other redeeming relationship beyond maybe a potted plant—because his look was one of clear disbelief.

"Excuse me?" he managed after a second. "Young lady, need I remind you—"

"Yeah yeah, you're a big high military guy and the town's under martial law and that makes you in charge, yada-yada-yada," Zoe said, cutting him off. "I got it the first time. But you need to back off now, Mr. Military Commander, and let us handle this situation."

"And why is that?" He didn't look amused.

"Because otherwise it could ignite a major incident." That was Fargo, breathless from having raced to catch up with her. Zoe shook her head. How was it that he had so much nervous energy and such a narrow build, yet he was so out of shape?

But at least he'd gotten the major's attention. "Explain." He crossed his arms over his chest and tapped his foot, making it clear that this had better be both short and good.

"That school contains twelve hundred fifty-three students, thirty-nine teachers, a principal and vice principal, six cafeteria workers, two security guards, and five custodial engineers." He noticed Zoe's expression. "I pulled up their records on the way over. The point being"—he returned his attention to the major—"this is the largest group of outsiders to enter Eureka. Ever."

"I had already guessed that," Major Holmes informed him. "Which is why we're going to cordon off the entire building at once." He started to gesture to his men, who had by now pulled up all around them.

"You can't," Fargo told him. "Or at least, you shouldn't," he amended quickly. "Sir."

"And why not?"

"Picture this," Zoe cut in. "A normal school day in"—she glanced behind her—"Ellen Witte High School, in Roseburg, Oregon. Everybody's just going about their business. When all of a sudden, armed soldiers burst into the building! They wave guns at everyone and order them all to stay seated and not move! So what do you think everyone's going to do?"

"Stay seated and not move?" It was clear the major wasn't getting it.

"No! I mean, yes, probably—you guys are scary and have big guns! But they're also going to talk about it. A lot. And once this is all over and they return home, they're going to talk about it even more. To each other. To their friends. To their parents." She gave him a sharp glance. "On the Internet."

That did the trick. The major paled. "It's a public relations nightmare," he whispered.

"Never mind the public relations," Fargo added, "think about the security issues. Over thirteen hundred people, all asking questions about what happened to them and where they were? Somebody's bound to figure it out. Which means good-bye to Eureka's classified location!"

Major Holmes glared at them like they were the ones who had caused this problem. Which they hadn't—though in Fargo's case, it was usually a fair assumption. "All right, so how do you propose to fix this?"

"Let us keep everyone contained," Zoe answered. "You can establish a safe perimeter, just out of sight, in case any kids wander off too far. But if we're the ones actually talking to people, they won't realize just what's going on. We'll keep them safely inside and away from the windows. When this is all over, they'll just go home and never even realize what happened." She hoped.

The major considered for a second, then gave them a brusque nod. "All right. You two take the lead. But if I see kids come pouring out of that building, I'm going to capture first and ask questions later. Got it?"

"Yes, sir!" Zoe saluted and he returned the gesture, either not realizing or not caring that she was mocking him. Again.

"Okay," she asked Fargo as the major moved away to issue orders to his men, "now what?"

"Simple," he replied. He led her back over to her car and propped his laptop on the roof. "I just hack into the school's public address system and call in a bomb threat." He was already typing in commands.

"What?" Zoe yanked the laptop away from him midkeystroke. "No! You can't!"

"Why not?" Fargo adjusted his glasses again. "It's perfect! They'll lower the blast doors and hunker down, and when it's all over we'll just call off the bomb scare and they can raise their shields and go home. Problem solved." He grinned, looking very pleased with himself, and reached for his computer again.

But Zoe twisted out of reach, holding it over her head. "Are you insane?" she asked. "Blast doors? Shields?" Then she realized something. "Oh my God, you grew up here, didn't you?"

"Absolutely." Fargo strutted slightly. "I'm a third-generation Eurekan. My grandfather, Pierre Fargo, first—"

"Yeah yeah, I know," Zoe interrupted. She remembered the whole big deal a while back when Fargo's grandfather, whom everyone had thought long since dead, had turned up in cryogenic suspension. After they thawed him out, they'd discovered that he'd actually come up with some of the scientific breakthroughs that had first put Eureka on the map. "But my point is, you never went to a regular high school."

Fargo grinned at her. "Tesla High, Class of Two Thousand."

"Right." Her arms were getting tired, so she lowered the laptop and rested it on her car again, but was careful to put herself between it and Fargo. "Okay, let me explain something—most schools do not have blast doors."

"They don't? What about radiation shielding?" Zoe shook her head. "Then what do they do during meteor showers, or gamma bursts, or EM pulse misfires?"

"That sort of thing doesn't happen outside Eureka," Zoe pointed out. "Most schools have a lock on the doors, and maybe a chain for after hours, and that's about it."

"Oh." Fargo scratched his head. "So how do they respond to bomb threats?"

"They send everyone outside, and marshal them in the schoolyard or across the street."

Fargo winced. "Guess that wouldn't do much for keeping them inside, then."

"Not a lot, no." Zoe relaxed a little. "We need something that'll keep them quiet and out of the way, not drive them all into a panic. Got any ideas?"

Fargo frowned. "I could create a sleep ray of some sort, zap them all with theta waves and knock them all unconscious."

"And explain later how they all fell asleep at the same time, in the middle of the day?" She rolled her eyes. "No thanks. This isn't some cheesy sci-fi movie—it's real life. Real non-Eureka life. It's got to be something that could happen in Roseburg, Oregon."

"Cattle stampede?" he offered. Zoe glared at him until he shook his head. "No, maybe not."

They both thought quietly for several minutes—if "quietly" meant Fargo occasionally throwing out ridiculous notions and Zoe vetoing them. Finally she sighed.

"We're just gonna have to go with the gas leak story," she said. "It's the best we've got. And at least it's consistent."

Fargo nodded. "Okay. How do you want to play this?"

Zoe grinned. At least she'd get to have a little fun.

"Yes, ma'am," she explained fifteen minutes later. "We're currently investigating the source of the leak, and we think we have it all under control, but if you could keep your students and staff within the building until we give the all-clear, that would be much appreciated."

"I certainly will," Principal Atchley replied. "Thank you." She frowned. "If you don't mind my saying so, Ms. Carter, you seem awfully young for a federal marshal."

Zoe laughed. "I get that a lot." She smiled. "They fast-tracked me through training, and I caught a big break on my first case, which led to an early promotion. Would you believe I'm twenty-nine?" That was the age she'd had Fargo put on the fake ID he'd made for her while she was running home to change into her college interview suit. Thank God Dad had insisted on a conservative look for it, and she'd given in but had disliked the suit enough to leave it behind when she'd left for school! And thank God he had kept his old marshal's badge. The security guard had taken one look and escorted her straight to the principal's office—the first time that had happened and been a good thing.

"Should I let the students know, do you think?" Principal Atchley asked as they both stood—Zoe was amused to realize that the principal was actually an inch or two shorter than she was, though clearly a decade or more older than even her supposed age. "Our power's out, but I can go door to door and speak to the teachers."

"I think that's a good idea," Zoe agreed. "Better to squash any rumors before they start. Just assure them that you're not at any risk as long as you keep the windows closed and the blinds down and stay well away from any exits." She smoothed the front of her suit. "They may not be able to access the Internet or use their phones, I'm afraid—some of our equipment produces a counterfrequency that can interfere with such devices."

The principal cracked a smile. "I'm hardly going to complain about students not being able to text their friends or Twitter during classes."

"Of course." Zoe smiled back. "And I apologize about the power and the phones. Standard protocol—we want to prevent any risk of stray sparks, in case the gas in question is combustible."

"Oh. Yes, good thinking." The principal had recoiled slightly at that thought. "Well, thank you again, Ms. Carter, for coming to speak to me. I admit I was beginning to wonder what had happened."

"Happy to put your mind at ease," Zoe assured her. She shook hands with the woman and headed back out, instructing the security guard as she passed to close the doors behind her and then keep well away from them.

"How'd it go?" Fargo asked as she approached.

"Perfect." She grinned at him and released her hair from the tight bun she'd coiled it into—she'd borrowed Jo's look, figuring it would make her seem older and more professional. Evidently it had worked. "Did you jam their signal?"

"Of course." Fargo was grinning as well. "No cell

phone signals in or out and no Internet access. Completely cut off."

"Great." Zoe sighed. "We should let Major Holmes know it's taken care of." And hope her dad and the others fixed the problem before it got too late in the day, she added silently. It was one thing to keep a high school full of students during normal class hours, but if they were still here this evening, things could get awfully tricky.

CHAPTᵉR 29

"**Zoe and Fargo are doing a great job of keeping Ma-jor Holmes out of everyone's hair,**" Allison assured Carter over the phone after he'd called to let her know that Delia Apnell was finally heading to the bunker with the rest of Eureka's residents. "Really, they've worked miracles. But things aren't getting any better. The high school—"

Carter interrupted her. "Wait, high school?"

Allison frowned. "Yeah, I thought you knew. Tesla High got swapped with a school from some place in Oregon."

"Roseburg, Oregon," Zane filled in without looking up from where he and Dr. Gunter were examining the wiring in one of the MRS data banks.

"Right, Roseburg. Tesla's been closed all day, of course, so the only people there were the custodians and a few teachers trying to get a jump on their lesson plans. No problem on that end. But on this side—" She sighed.

"It's three something in the afternoon and those kids are

going to be nearing the end of the school day any minute, an hour tops." Of course Carter knew about high school schedules—he was a good dad that way.

"Exactly. We're not entirely sure how we're going to keep them occupied if we haven't sorted everything out by then."

"School assembly."

"What?"

He repeated himself. "School assembly. Have the principal call one, make it mandatory—give some vague talk about the dangers of today's society, how important it is to be prepared, so on and so forth. I know Tesla doesn't have 'em, but Zoe's old school used to do 'em all the time. Drove her nuts. 'An hour of my life wasted,' she always said."

"Carter, that's perfect!" Allison straightened. "If they call the assembly right now and it lasts an hour, that'll bring them to a little after four. By which point—"

"Either they get sent home or they find themselves sitting on the surface of a new sun."

"Something like that, yes."

"How's it going with Zane and Gunter?" Carter asked. "Are they any closer to shutting this whole thing down?"

Allison glanced at the two scientists. "They're working as fast as they can, but disengaging those fail-safes really played havoc with the system's core programming. It actually activated several subroutines just to remain functional, and that's been part of the problem—they've got to trace the exact logic path the MRS followed in order to go back along it and reverse each step. If they do it properly, they can shut it down."

"And if they don't?"

"Then I get to work on my tan. All at once."

"So you need more time?" Allison could tell by his tone that Carter had something in mind. She usually regretted that tone.

Still, she didn't see any reason to lie. "Yes, we need more time."

"They reactivated some of those fail-safes, right?"

"A few of them, yes. They think."

"They think? Great."

"What are you thinking, Carter?"

"I'm going to buy you some more time," he told her. "And hopefully throw enough of a wrench into things that the computer gasps for air."

"That would help," Allison admitted. "It's an amazing system, but it's only got so much processing power—if it had to struggle with something, that would probably draw computing power from a few other areas, and Zane could use that to break through."

"Right." There was a brief pause. "The activity log—how fast does it show a target location?"

"As soon as the MRS selects it."

"Uh-huh. And how much time between selection and being sent halfway across the country?"

"A few seconds, maybe. Why?" Allison didn't like where this conversation was heading.

"Any way to stretch that out?"

"I don't know." She glanced back at the two scientists. "Is there any way to slow the process," she asked them, "so there's a lag between target selection and transfer?"

Gunter thought about that for a second. "Yes!" he announced finally, brightening. "I can order the system to run a full target verification subroutine! It'll rescan the entire target location, then compare that to maps and databases to confirm that it has the correct target. That should take it several minutes, at least."

Allison relayed that information to Carter. "I hope it's enough," he muttered. "Okay, tell them to do it the next time a target comes up. Call me the instant you have an address. Oh, and ask Gunter to double-check that he restored that one fail-safe—he'll know which one I mean."

Allison gripped the phone more tightly. "Carter, what are you going to do?"

"Something incredibly stupid," he replied. "But hopefully exactly what they need to take care of this thing once and for all." He hung up before she could ask any more questions, leaving Allison holding the phone and with a growing sense of unease. Carter often did incredibly stupid, incredibly brave things. They usually saved the day, and everyone around. But every time he put himself at risk she felt her heart lurch. It was starting to lurch now.

Still, there wasn't much she could do about it from here. And she suspected if she didn't go along with his plan, things would be a lot worse for everyone. She just had to trust him. Again. Fortunately, Carter hadn't let her down yet.

"This is crazy," Carter admitted to himself as he climbed back into his Jeep and started the engine. "Am I really going to do this?"

But yes—yes, he was. Because it might be the only thing that saved them all. And he was willing to take that risk. Again.

His phone rang, as he'd known it would. "Where?" he demanded as he answered. He was already putting the Jeep in motion. As an afterthought, he hit the lights and the sirens.

"92 West Edison," Allison replied. "Carter—"

"Did they activate that subroutine?" he said, cutting her off. He spun the wheel and took a sharp right. Fortunately 92 West Edison was near the center of town, and so was he. If it had been on the opposite side of Eureka, he doubted he'd have time to even try this.

"Yes. Listen, Carter—"

"Whose house is it?"

"Dr. Herrera's."

Carter nodded. Dr. Paulo Herrera was Eureka's cloud scientist. They'd met before. "Good, I need you to call him."

"Call him? Carter, we evacuated everyone, remember?"

"And plenty of people refused to leave their homes," he reminded her. "Herrera might have been one of them. He's certainly clever enough to stay behind if he thinks it would win him some points with someone. Call him. If he answers, tell him to open his front door. Wide open. And then to step way back."

"Carter, you can't—"

He hung up and tossed his PDA onto the passenger seat beside him so he could concentrate. The good thing about martial law and mandatory evacuation was that the streets were empty.

He pulled up at 92 West Edison in record time and had the door open before he'd shut off the engine. Then he was racing for the front of the pleasant little two-story stucco. He'd obviously been right about Herrera, because the paneled, white front door was wide open.

And the whole house was beginning to develop an odd shimmer.

Swell, Carter thought. No time for second thoughts. Which was probably for the best.

He took three running steps, covering most of Herrera's lawn, and then threw himself forward with all his might. Carter sailed into the air, arms outstretched, straining to cover the distance. It was a perfect flying tackle—and his target was the empty doorway.

Whoomph! Carter grunted as he hit the ground and the doorjamb slammed into his side, driving all the air from his lungs. Oof! But he was halfway in the house, exactly as planned. The shimmer was all around him.

"Sheriff?"

Carter glanced up. Dr. Herrera was standing just beyond the entryway. As always, the scientist looked less like a typical researcher and more like a politician, with his sharp suit, close-cropped hair, dark good looks, and winning smile. "Hey, Doc," Carter replied, still gasping for breath. "Thanks for opening the door." He didn't try to get up.

"Can I help you up?"

"No, thanks." Carter straightened his legs behind him. "This should all be over in a minute."

One way or another.

"It's completed the subroutine!" Gunter shouted, even though Zane and Allison were standing right beside him staring at the same computer screen. A new line had appeared on the monitor: "Target C64A verified. Searching for second target location. Second target located: designated Target C64B. Preparing for target relocation."

Allison had the lab's phone in her hand. She quickly dialed Carter again, but he didn't answer. "What the hell is he doing?" she demanded of the empty receiver before slamming it back down again.

"Look!" Zane pointed at the monitor and all three read the new text together:

"WARNING: living entity detected across target perimeter. Fail-safes activated. Relocation paused."

"Yes!" Zane and Gunter were out of their chairs in an instant and racing for the data banks. "He's jammed up the system! If he's tied up enough processing power, we can cut through the rest of the subroutines and security protocols!"

Allison was still staring at the screen. "Does that mean what I think it means?" she muttered.

"If you think it means he's probably standing in the

open doorway," Zane commented over his shoulder, "yeah, I'd say that's exactly what he's doing."

"That man is insane!" Allison shuddered just thinking about what would have happened if the fail-safe hadn't been restored properly.

"Probably," Gunter agreed from amid a pile of wiring and chipsets. "But he may have saved us all."

Allison sighed. Yes, that was Carter to a T.

"Got it!" Zane yelled after a few seconds. "We've got access!"

"Excellent!" Gunter glanced up at Allison. "Tell the sheriff to kindly step aside."

"What?"

"He needs to move out of the doorway," the lanky scientist repeated. "Right now the entire system is paused. But we can't stop the loop until it's in motion again."

"Oh. Right." Allison started to dial Carter again, then thought better of it. Instead, she called Dr. Herrera's PDA. "Hello, Doctor," she said once the cloud scientist answered. "Could you hand the phone to Sheriff Carter, please? Thank you." She took a deep breath and tried to stay calm. Not that calm ever lasted long with Carter around.

"Are you completely insane?" Allison yelled the second Carter accepted the PDA from Dr. Herrera. "Do you realize what would have happened if you'd been wrong?"

"I'd be half the man I used to be?" Carter asked. He could hear her groan. "I gather it worked, though?"

"Yes, it worked," she acknowledged grudgingly. "Now you need to move aside."

"What?" Carter sat up, being careful to stay in the doorway. "What are you talking about? We put it on pause, right? As long as I'm here, it can't transport this house—or move on to the next target."

"Absolutely," she agreed. "But apparently we need the program back in motion before we can shut it down. They've got the access they need now—they think. So if you could let it run again, we can move on to the next step."

"Fine." Carter stood up, dusted himself off, and stepped back out of the house. The instant he did, the shimmering intensified. Then the entire building wavered, flickered— and vanished. Another structure had appeared behind and through it, like a pair of overlapping ghost images, and now that one solidified. Its own shimmer faded, and Carter found his nose almost pressed against the dark-lacquered oak door of a handsome red brick home.

"Okay, it's gone," he told Allison, turning back toward his Jeep. "What happens now?"

"I don't actually know," Allison admitted. She'd relaxed a little once she knew Carter was safe. Being transported elsewhere was one thing, but cut in half? She shuddered.

"You don't know? You said we were moving on to the next step!" he pointed out over the phone.

"Yes, but I don't know what that is." She glanced over to where Zane and Gunter were still digging through the MRS's guts. "I suspect we have to let it transport a few more while we get set up for whatever it is we're doing next."

"This is ridiculous!" She could tell that Carter was nearing the end of his rope. So was she, actually. "Can't we just have the darned thing send itself somewhere and be done with it?"

"That'd never work," she replied. "It'd shut itself down before it could—" She broke off midsentence and jumped off the desk where she'd been perching. "Zane!"

"What?" He bolted upright so fast he conked his head on the open data bank panel. "Ow! What?"

Carter was saying something into the phone, but Allison ignored him. "If we tell the MRS to send itself someplace, what would happen?"

Zane considered. So did Gunter, who stood up a bit more cautiously than the younger man had. "It wouldn't be able to," Zane said after a minute. "It'd hit a logic loop. The whole program would grind to a halt."

He and Gunter exchanged a glance.

"Yes," the MRS creator agreed. "I think that just might do it!"

"Carter, you're a genius!" Allison told him quickly. "I'll call you back in a bit." She hung up and set the phone back on its cradle, then turned to the two men standing before her. "All right, gentlemen, let's bring this thing crashing down!"

"We need to disconnect the automatic congruence comparison circuits," Gunter warned, racing to another data bank near the far wall and yanking off its front panel. "That's what lets the MRS decide which locations are a good match for its target site. With these offline, it won't be able to compare locations properly, which means it won't be able to confirm that any location is appropriate for the target to relocate there."

"I'm hacking into the coding on its selection array," Zane announced, fingers flying over the keyboard as windows appeared and disappeared in a flash and lines of code raced across a corner of the screen. "After your first switch with David Boyd, the MRS swapped you again. Then it decided you were no longer a viable subject for transference, but at the same time it needed to complete the process and effect a perfect replacement. So it began selecting its own targets. If I can just work my way into that section of the program"—one of the windows onscreen began to flash, throwing up names and locations only to have them disappear as fast as they formed—"then I should be able to"—the

last name vanished, to be replaced by a blinking cursor—
"Yes! Force it to accept external target selection!"

He stood up and gestured Allison toward the chair with
a bow. "Care to do the honors?"

"Why, thank you." Allison seated herself and slid the
keyboard in front of her. Then she began to type. "Target:
Laboratory number five twenty-seven, Section Five, Global
Dynamics, Eureka, Oregon." She hit Enter and sat back as
the MRS attempted to relocate—itself.

Zane and Gunter stepped up behind her, and all three of
them watched the system's progress on the activity log:

"Target selected. Designated Target C65A. Searching
for target location."

"We need to disable its self-authorization protocols!"
Gunter exclaimed, bounding back toward one of the lab's
other sections. "Zane, can you scramble its access to those
circuits for a few minutes, until I can rig a physical bypass?"

"I'm on it," Zane replied over his shoulder. "'Scuse me,
boss." Allison slid aside as Zane leaned over to take control
of the keyboard. She watched as he called up another portion of the MRS's labyrinthine programming. "Got it." Then
he pulled a tiny thumb drive from his pocket and waved it at
the monitor, just barely brushing the large screen.

"What was that?" Allison demanded.

"Oh, nothing," he told her, grinning as he began typing
again. "Just a little computer virus I carry in case of emergencies. Around here, you never know when something's
going to go haywire and need to be utterly corrupted."

She laughed—she couldn't help it. "Why didn't you use
that in the first place?"

"Not powerful enough to crash the whole system," he
explained. "It can only corrupt a small program, or a small
piece of a larger one. But all I needed it for right now was
to mess with the self-authorization protocols and keep
those locked up. That's well within its reach."

"You didn't even plug it in anywhere," she pointed out.

"I don't have to." Zane looked far too smug, as was often the case. "It's an optical virus, made up of light emitters that pulse a particular pattern directly into any computer through any optical interface—including a mostly passive one like a monitor. I just aim it at the appropriate lines of code on a screen, activate it, and presto! It bombards the code with conflicting information, overwriting data on the fly." He gestured toward the window, where gibberish was now spewing forth. "Total chaos."

"Done!" Gunter announced, jogging back over to them. He held up a pair of short interface cables. "I rerouted the protocol chips and shunted their data arrays into a remote storage device. The MRS can't access that directly."

"Perfect." The three of them turned to study the screen again just as new words appeared:

"Target location C65B selected. Awaiting authorization for location confirmation."

A set of coordinates appeared below that line, along with an address in La Pine.

"Reject it," Zane urged, but Allison had already reclaimed the seat and was doing exactly that.

"Location rejected," she typed, and hit Enter.

"Target location C65B rejected," the system responded a second later. "Seeking alternate location, designated C65C. Alternate location selected. Awaiting authorization for location confirmation."

New coordinates appeared, this time in Nyssa.

Allison rejected that location as well.

"How long can we keep refusing its choices?" she asked as the MRS began searching for a C65D.

"As long as it takes," Zane answered. Gunter nodded beside him.

"Let's hope it doesn't take long," Allison replied. "We've only a few minutes left."

* * *

By the time the computer had reached C65Z1, Allison suspected it was getting desperate.

"It's going farther and farther away," she pointed out as she rejected the new location, this one in Delta, Utah. "What sort of range does this thing have, anyway?"

"I'm not really sure," Gunter answered. "Theoretically, the entire United States, possibly all of North America, but of course I hadn't tested it for range yet."

"Great. We could still be sitting here doing this when its countdown hits zero and the whole place melts down," Allison muttered. She sat up and paid attention, however, as the computer displayed something new:

"Alternate location, designated C65Z2, required. Please select suitable location."

The line was followed by a blinking cursor.

"Yes!" Zane slapped Gunter on the back, almost sending the gawky scientist staggering across the room. "That's what we've been waiting for!"

"I'm on it," Allison assured him. She was already entering the information:

"Alternate location C65Z2 selected: Laboratory number five twenty-seven, Section Five, Global Dynamics, Eureka, Oregon."

She hit Enter, and the three of them held their breath as they waited for the MRS to try swapping itself—with itself.

The cursor continued to blink, taunting them, and Allison found her eyes watering from staring at that one spot so fixedly. "Shouldn't it have shut down by now?" she whispered. As if the computer would hear her!

"It's processing," Zane assured her. "This thing's immense and has all kinds of protocols and secondary systems and subroutines. It needs to run the calculation through all of those before it can decide what to do."

Gunter nodded. "Exactly right. It's considering its options right now, modeling the transfer to check for feasibility. It should be done soon."

Several more seconds stretched on, but finally the cursor blinked and winked out, replaced with new text. But as Allison read it, rather than relief she felt her stomach sink:

"Location C65Z2 rejected. Selected location deemed unsafe. Searching for more secure location within operational parameters."

"No, no, NO!" Zane banged a fist down on the desk, then stepped back and began pacing. "Rejected? How could it reject it? We took its selection system offline!"

But Gunter sighed. "We forgot its security protocols subarray," he pointed out. "If the MRS determines itself to be at risk, it can activate those protocols and make them its primary programming system instead."

"But why would it consider itself at risk?" Allison asked. "We told it to put itself right back here where it belongs!"

"I don't think it was the location itself that was the problem," Zane answered. He leaned on the desk and rubbed his face with one hand. "I think it was us."

"Us?"

"Everything we did to gain that kind of access," he explained. "Pulling open panels, removing wiring, rerouting chips. All of that. It registered it as unapproved access, which meant its systems had been breached." He gave her a rueful smile. "My little virus probably didn't help matters much."

"Okay, so what now?" she demanded. "We try again?"

Both of the men shook their heads. "We still have access," Zane pointed out, "but not as much control as we did a minute ago. Its security protocols are hard-coded into the base system, and that's packed in tight next to the vacuum chamber. I'm betting we can't touch anything there without releasing some kind of security countermeasure."

Gunter nodded. "It would vent a tiny portion of gas from the chamber into this room." He clutched the desk for support. "It would be like a miniaturized solar flare. The entire room would heat to several million kelvins in seconds."

Zane whistled. "I like it toasty, but that's a bit much."

"Is there some way to use that?" Allison asked. "Maybe rig something to interfere with those portions of the MRS via remote, so that the entire lab does melt down but without anyone inside it?"

"We don't have the time to put anything like that together," Zane reminded her. "I mean, sure, if Henry were here he could probably whip something up in a few hours, even with all the signal shielding. But he's not here, and it would take me a lot longer than that." He shook his head, and then offered the obvious in a low voice. "One of us could do it, while the other two got out."

Gunter straightened up. "I'll do it." He was pale, his skin waxy, and sweat was rolling down his face as he gulped, but he didn't waver. "This is all my fault, so it's only fair I'm the one to fix it."

"Are you absolutely sure you could make the system react in that way?" Allison asked him.

"Not one hundred percent, no," he admitted. "It's one of the security measures it has programmed in, but there's an entire list of factors it'd use to determine which measure was necessary for any given incident."

"Which means you might try to sacrifice yourself, and get hurt or killed anyway, but without the MRS destroying itself."

"It's entirely possible, yes."

"And if that happened," Allison continued, "Zane and I

would have to return to the lab from whatever safe distance we'd removed ourselves to, having lost valuable time, and would have to attempt to stop it anyway, but now without your expert guidance."

Gunter surprised her by giving her a smile. "If you don't want me to kill myself, just say so."

She laughed at the unexpected display of humor, the first he'd shown since Carter had brought him back. "Fine—Dr. Gunter, please don't kill yourself."

"Fair enough." He was clearly relieved. "But in that case, what do we do now?"

"It says it's searching for a secure location," Zane pointed out. "Do you remember any of the criteria for that?"

Gunter frowned, thinking back. Then he brightened. "Yes! Yes, I do! It won't move itself outside Eureka!"

"What? Why not?"

"It requires a certain level of security in both technological safeguards and physical shielding," Gunter told them. "There are only a few places in the world that would qualify in both areas. And it also requires that the selected location be under the control of the United States Army! That eliminates all the foreign labs, and all the privately owned ones. Which only leaves here and Area 51!"

"So why won't it relocate itself to Area 51?" Allison asked.

"Because that site has been breached too many times, and has attracted too much public scrutiny, to be considered secure." He grinned. "The only place that meets all its criteria—is right here!"

"Well, that's something, anyway," Allison agreed. "But it could still put itself—and us—anywhere in town. What happens if it does?"

Gunter gulped again. "Relocating the vacuum chamber would be a very bad idea," he warned. "Those gases are held in perfect suspension! Any alteration—even being de-composed and reassembled elsewhere a nanosecond later—would unleash the full force of the chemical reaction."

"It'd blow up," Zane translated.

"Yes, it would. Just like a sun going supernova." Gunter looked up at the clock displayed in the upper right corner of the computer monitor. "Just like it's going to do in less than twenty minutes!" The clock read three twenty-one.

Allison looked at Zane, but he shrugged. "I'm fresh out of ideas," he admitted.

"So am I," she agreed.

"Fresh out of ideas about what?" All three of them turned as Carter stepped through the door. "Sorry, I got back as fast as I could. What's going on?"

Allison smiled. "Carter, perfect timing. I've got something I need to run by you."

CHAPTᴇR 30

"Uh-huh." Carter listened intently as Allison explained. "Yeah. Okay. Got it. So we need the MRS to think it's safest right where it is," he reasoned out loud.

"Exactly."

"And I guess we can't just tell it that's the case?"

"We tried that. It's kicked into a new subroutine, and this one won't allow direct input anymore."

"So that's a no."

"Yes, Carter, that's a no."

"Just checking." He scratched his head. "Look, I'm not the egghead—hell, I'm the anti-egghead! So why ask me?"

"Because Zane, Dr. Gunter, and I are all stumped," Allison replied. Zane and Gunter both nodded behind her.

"Great, no pressure," Carter muttered. "Hang on, did you ask Henry?"

"Not yet—I was going to conference him in."

Carter grabbed the lab's landline and dialed. "Hey, Henry?" he said when his friend answered.

"What's up, Jack?"

"We've got a problem. We need a way to make the MRS think pretty much all of Eureka is unsafe. Any ideas? And no, we can't just tell it so."

"Hm. It needs to think the rest of the town isn't safe? Can you bypass its sensors and input false data to skew the selection process?"

"Not in time," Allison replied after Carter relayed the question. "The security protocols are better protected, both physically and from hacking. Zane's trying, but we've only got less than half an hour left."

"Right. So it needs to be real data, not fake. How about an EMP? Fry every circuit in town, overload the grid, and make it think there's no place to run?"

"Yeah, but doesn't it have that crazy mini-sun power supply going on?" Carter asked. "So why would it care if the power's out?"

"You're right, Jack. Good point."

"Well, what would make it decide a place was unsafe?"

There was a pause on the other end. "Off the top of my head, poor security—"

"Which doesn't work here."

"—extreme temperatures, toxic fumes, dangerous radiation levels, seismic instability—"

"Hang on." Carter glanced at Allison. "Seismic instability? So if the ground's not stable it won't take the risk?"

"Probably not," Allison agreed. "This lab is carved out of solid rock. And I'm guessing some of the equipment here is pretty heavy, a ton or two at least. It could crash right through the ground if it's not stable, and that could put the entire system—and everyone for a few miles around it—at risk."

"We could fake seismic instability," Henry offered. "All

we'd need is to generate low-level tremors throughout town so the MRS's sensors pick them up. And if it's only for a few minutes, it won't cause any real damage—most of the buildings in Eureka are earthquake-proof."

"Great, so we just need to fake a few tremors. That shouldn't be a problem, right?"

"It wouldn't—if we had time," Allison agreed. "But we've got about fifteen minutes left. I don't think Zane can build something in time, and Henry's not here."

"Even if I were, my garage is gone," Henry pointed out. "Most of my tools were in there."

"Right, your garage got moved," Carter said, thinking fast, "but your truck didn't!"

"My truck!" Henry's excitement was audible. "That's right! And the fire hose uses compressed sonics. If it were aimed at the ground, it would produce seismic tremors. Nice one, Jack!"

Carter grinned. That was twice in two days—a new record for him.

"Where do we need it?" he asked Henry.

"Right by Café Diem—or the Elkhorn Café, rather. That's almost dead center—the shock waves will ripple out from there and trigger every sensor in town. You'll have your earthquake."

Carter frowned. "I'm at GD with Allison—I'd never make it back to your garage and then to the diner in time." He smiled. "But I know somebody else who's in the right direction." He put Henry on hold and dialed again.

"Fargo?" He bit back a groan as the researcher answered. He'd actually been hoping for Zoe, but there was no time. "Listen, I need you to do something. It's urgent. Get Henry's truck—it's parked where it always is, outside where his garage should be. Drive it to the center of town, right in front of where Café Diem was. Then grab the fire hose, turn it on full, and point it at the ground."

"I'm on it," Fargo assured him, and hung up.

"Okay," Carter told Henry once he'd switched back over. "I've got Fargo bringing your truck over."

"Yes, but, Jack," Henry warned, "you know I've got the fire hose set so—"

"I know—I'm out the door. I'll meet Fargo there."

"Perfect," Henry said.

"Thanks, Henry," Carter added.

"No problem, Jack. Let's just hope it works."

Carter tossed the phone to Allison and headed for the door. "Better get Mansfield on the phone," he suggested over his shoulder. "Let him—and the elusive Major Holmes— know we're about to have a small earthquake on our hands. And warn them to let Fargo and me do the fire hose thing or those tremors'll be the least of our worries."

"Go get Henry's fire truck, Fargo," Fargo muttered as he swung himself up into the driver's seat. "Drive it to Café Diem, Fargo. Turn on the fire hose, Fargo. Don't stop until I say so, Fargo." He slammed the door shut behind him. "Did it ever occur to him to say *Please*? Or *Thank you*? Or *The town is in danger and we need your help*?"

But no, of course not. Sheriff Carter just issued orders and expected Fargo to jump to it.

Which, admittedly, he always did.

Now, which gear was which on this monster?

It took a few minutes of grinding and groaning before he got the fire truck rolling, but after that driving it wasn't a problem. Steering was a different matter. "Oops," Fargo whispered as he took out a stop sign. "Sorry!" He struck a trash can as he turned, then flattened a bike rack.

Well, this was an emergency.

Finally he reached Café Diem—or the Elkhorn Café,

at least—and slammed on the brakes. For a second he thought that was it for him—the back of the fire truck skidded sideways and forward, twisting the entire truck to the side, and slid several yards, the tires crunching up to and over the curb. Then a sturdy tree got in the way and halted the vehicle's slanted progress. It shuddered to a stop, and Fargo turned off the engine, then sat there shaking for a minute, his hands clutching and unclutching the wheel.

He would have sat there longer—possibly all day—but Carter had stressed that time was of the essence. So Fargo steeled himself, took a deep breath, and climbed down out of the truck cab.

The fire hose was stored in a side compartment midway down the truck. Fargo yanked it open, removed the sleek metal hose, and examined it. It looked more like a futuristic rocket launcher than a traditional fire hose, all matte-finish metal with several stops and buttons and valves like an oversized flute.

Once he was sure he understood how it worked—fortunately Henry was a big believer in functionality, so the buttons were all in logical places—Fargo aimed the hose's business end down at the ground and hit the button marked On—

—and nothing happened.

"What? No! No, no, no!" Fargo tried again.

Still nothing.

He was about to panic when he heard—were those sirens?

Looking up, he saw Carter racing toward him, sirens and lights on full. The truck skidded to a stop inches away, and Carter was out of the vehicle half a second later. "Give it to me!" he shouted.

Fargo was more than happy to comply.

"Sorry," Carter explained as he took the fire hose.

"Henry has the thing set so only city officials can activate it. Prevents kids from stealing the darn thing." He glanced at it. "Now, how do I turn it on?"

"Right here." Fargo pointed. Carter nodded and hit the button—

—and a wave of pressure nearly knocked both of them off their feet. The ground shook, and Fargo staggered a second time. Was this supposed to happen?

But yes, that made sense. At least as much as anything did around here.

"Here, take this." Carter nodded toward the fire hose, still keeping it on and pointed downward. "I need to get back. Now that it's on, it should work for you." He edged to the side, and Fargo grasped the device, sliding his own thumb over the On button just in case. But sure enough, it kept working. Good old Henry.

"Just keep it steady, Fargo. And don't stop until I tell you." Carter patted him on the back—almost toppling him and making him clutch the fire hose tightly to keep its nozzle pointed firmly downward—and then headed back to his truck. A minute later, he was gone.

Fargo wondered how long he was expected to stand here. The vibrations were making his legs shake and his teeth rattle. But Sheriff Carter had said, "Don't stop until I tell you," and he'd saved the town too many times to count since he'd taken the job. Far more than his predecessor, Sheriff Cobb, had done. Not that Cobb had been a bad man, or a bad sheriff, but Carter was better. And Fargo trusted him.

So he'd stand here, shaking, trying to keep his balance, until he was told otherwise.

But he expected a thank-you when this was all over.

"Okay, listen up, everyone," Zoe called out. Heads rose from books and computer screens and iPods alike.

"I've just been told there's a gas bubble that formed from the leak, and they think it's about to burst. When it does, it'll cause a brief ground tremor, like an earthquake. We're not in any danger, though. It's actually a good thing—it'll help the gas disperse more quickly. But you might want to sit down, hold on to your glasses and cups, and make sure you're not sitting by a stack of books or anything else that could fall on you. Okay?" She started making her way around the bookstore, helping people get themselves situated. She hoped whatever was going on really would help, because the people she was minding were anxious enough as it was. Sitting through an earthquake was the last thing they needed.

"Check it out!" Zane's shout made Allison and Carter glance up and Gunter start. Zane was looking up at the monitor, and after a second Allison realized there was a new line of text on the screen:

"Warning! Seismic instabilities detected. Location C65Z3 deemed unsafe. Searching for alternate location, designated C65Z4."

"That's a good start," Allison commented. "Now we just have to hope the effect is widespread enough."

"I'd say it is," Gunter noted as the activity log updated to show the computer's continuing attempts to select a new location:

"Location C65Z4 deemed unsafe. Searching for alternate location, designated C65Z5.

"Location C65Z5 deemed unsafe. Searching for alternate location, designated C65Z6.

"Location C65Z6 deemed unsafe. Searching for alternate location, designated C65Z7.

"Location C65Z7 deemed unsafe. Searching for alternate location, designated C65Z8."

"How many times do you think it'll try before it gives up?" Allison asked Gunter.

"I don't know," he answered. "But this might help." He leaned in and pulled up the system log-in window, then logged out.

Allison and Zane both stared at him. Carter looked like he didn't understand what had just happened. "What are you doing?" Zane demanded. "Now we're locked out!"

"Trust me," the tall scientist told them, smiling slightly. Then he entered his access code again and let the computer scan his retinal pattern. All three of them sagged in relief as the large *Access Granted* banner flashed across the screen.

Zane was nodding. "You figured the system had classified your presence as suspect," he said, "but by logging out you wiped that connection. So when you signed back in, it was a clean entry, with no taints from the earlier access."

"Exactly." Gunter actually beamed at them. "Now the computer—and the security systems—know I'm here, and believe I had nothing to do with any of the potential security breaches earlier. And since the automatic congruence comparison circuits are still down, and the subroutine is growing desperate for a proper location, it's only a matter of time before—" He laughed and gestured at the screen. "Voilà!"

Turning back to it, Allison saw that the system had gotten as high as C65Z25 before giving up. Now it showed a blinking cursor again, and the words "Please input secure location, designated C65Z26."

"With pleasure," Allison said to no one in particular as she typed:

"Secure location C65Z26 selected: Laboratory number five twenty-seven, Section Five, Global Dynamics, Eureka, Oregon."

There was no response after she hit Enter. They waited. Then it replied:

"Location C65Z26 deemed unsafe. Please input secure location, designated C65Z27."

"Just enter it again," Zane told her. "Don't worry about it. Give it the lab, every time it asks." Gunter nodded.

"Okay." Allison typed it in again, and got the same result. And the same the time after that. And again after that.

She typed it in a total of eight times. Finally, the computer offered a different response:

"Please input alternate secure locations, designated C65Z34-38."

Zane whistled. "This thing adapts fast! It's not happy with the one location we're feeding it, so it's asking for five at once. That way it can select the one that's closest to its criteria!"

"What should I do?" Allison asked. "Put the lab for all five?"

"Exactly," Gunter answered. "Don't give it a choice."

She did as he said, and again they waited.

Allison glanced at the clock. Three twenty-nine. They had nine minutes left.

Zane's whoop startled her eyes back to the center display. "Yes!"

She wanted to cheer right along with him as she read the computer's decision:

"All locations deemed unsafe. Risk to system too great to continue. Total security lockdown required. Disengaging current program."

"We did it!" Gunter shouted, slapping Zane on the back. "It gave up!"

"Good to know we're more stubborn than a computer," Zane agreed, laughing. "That was close!"

Allison laughed, too, as she leaned back. "Close? You know better than that, Zane. We still had almost ten minutes left—around here, that's probably a record."

Just then the lights dimmed. "Wait, what's going on?" Carter demanded.

"Nothing to worry about," Gunter assured him. He laughed, though Carter didn't think it was aimed at him. "Quite the opposite, in fact." He gestured off to the side, and Carter followed the motion of his hand—and gasped. The sun had gone out!

Well, not gone out, completely. But where there had been a tiny miniature sun just a moment ago, blazing so brightly it had driven away all but the most stubborn shadows even in the farthest corners of the lab, now there was barely a flicker, a tiny glowing cinder like the leftover spark from a dying fire.

"It's powered down," Gunter explained happily. "The program disengaged, and so the system dropped down to only standby mode. Which means it's safe."

"Safe?" Zane eyed the vacuum chamber dubiously. "It's still a tiny baby sun, even if it is in nap time at the moment."

"Fair enough. It won't explode."

Zane nodded. "I'll take that."

"So will I," Allison agreed. She stood and stretched. "Well, it's certainly been an exciting day, but good job, both of you." She shook her head. "I don't mind saying, I could use some proper rest. And maybe a drink."

"Talk to Taggart," Zane suggested. He laughed at her expression, but didn't explain further. And right now, Allison just didn't care.

CHAPTᵉR 31

"Quickly!" Gunter suddenly ordered, breaking the moment's quiet. "Reboot the system!"

Allison stared at him. "And start the whole thing all over again? Not a chance!"

But after a second's hesitation Zane slid past her into the chair and began feverishly entering commands. "He's right," he explained as he typed. "We need to get the MRS up and running again, and fast!"

"What? Why?" The lab brightened as the miniature sun flared back up to full strength, forcing Allison to shield her eyes for a second. When she blinked the spots away, she saw screens opening across the monitors again. "Zane, talk to me!"

"We can bring the MRS back online," he answered, shuffling through the various windows, "without setting off that same loop. Gunter and I already restored most of the failsafes, so rebooting should have reactivated those again."

" 'Should have' isn't exactly my favorite saying," Allison warned him.

"It's what we've got," he replied, shrugging. "Anyway, I've got the MRS up again." That last was directed toward Gunter, who was fiddling with one of the data banks.

"I've got the circuits back in place," the lanky scientist replied. "Go ahead."

"What exactly are you doing?" Carter asked as Zane brought up the MRS activity log.

"We need to get all of the transplanted locations back where they belong," Zane explained. "They're all listed here in the activity log, so we can just trigger a recall and the MRS will reverse the process, from the most recent switch all the way back to the earliest one." He turned to grin at the others. "But with the power off, it only had a ten-minute memory life. The earlier transfers were stored to long-term memory, but the most recent ones might not have been written in yet—"

"And if it wiped those, we wouldn't be able to get them back home," Allison finished. "Okay, fine. You could have told me that right from the start."

"Not a lot of time." Zane shifted back toward the monitors. "But now we're all set, and I can send everyone home. Slowly, so we don't risk another overload."

"Not yet, you can't," Allison corrected. She reached for the phone. "I have to make a call, first."

Zoe answered her PDA on the second ring. "Hey, Allison. . . . Really? That's great! . . . Okay, I'll take care of it. I'll call you when they're all back—but remember, this is only the ones who weren't in Café Diem. I'll need time to get them back home as well, once we've got the café itself back. . . . Okay, thanks."

She hung up and turned to address the people she'd

started to think of as her charges. "Okay, everybody, listen up! Good news! They've fixed the gas leak! It's safe for you to return to your homes now. I'll be taking you back, one at a time—please be patient and wait your turn. You may still be experiencing some mild side effects from the gas, and I want to make sure you each get home safely. Thanks!"

Then she walked over to the nearest person, a tiny weathered woman with sun-bleached white hair. "Mrs. Gerard? Why don't we get you back to your cabin?"

"Great, thanks, Zoe." Allison hung up the phone. "Okay, everyone we still had here in Eureka is back in their original home or building." She nodded to Zane. "Go ahead."

"Right. I just need to push—" He paused his finger dramatically over the Enter button, and then stabbed downward.

"Wait!" That was Gunter leaping forward and knocking Zane aside, chair and all. "Don't!"

"Hey, what's up, Doc?" Zane demanded, rising to his feet. "This was your plan, remember?"

"Yes, but I just remembered something." Gunter leaned forward, studying the log, and then sighed. "Ah, good. I got to you in time." He smiled at Zane. "Sorry for the push. If you'd entered the command, though, we could have started the problem all over again."

"What? Why?"

"Think about it," Gunter urged. "We were going to trigger a mass recall. The MRS would have worked its way backward through the transfers, one by one. All the way back. Putting everyone back to where it found them."

Allison straightened. "Except you," she blurted out. "You were one of the first swaps it performed! In fact, it was your swap that shorted out the process, because it got confused when you tried to issue a recall and send yourself back!"

Gunter gave her the same nod she'd gotten from professors when she'd answered a particularly tough question, back in school. "Exactly. But I'm here, so it can't send me back."

"Which would have thrown it into a logic error all over again," Zane finished. He scrubbed at his hair with one hand. "I can't believe I missed that."

"I might have, too," Gunter assured him, "if I hadn't been the one it would have been looking for." He pulled the keyboard toward him. "We just need to find the right entry on the log—ah, here it is! C44!—and delete it. The rest should be fine."

"Not necessarily," Carter corrected, thinking back to the early incidents, what seemed like months ago. "At least one of those changes was also people—a high school student named Nora Allen and a GD researcher, Karl Worinko. I don't know where either of them is right now, but I'm betting they're not out in the woods."

"There's at least one more that won't work," Zane added quietly. He gestured to a line on the log. "That one needs to be deleted, too." Carter only caught a glimpse of it before Gunter removed it, but he thought the addresses involved looked familiar.

"There was a car, as well," Allison remembered. "Larry's car got swapped with Dr. Styvers's."

"Yes, that's here," Gunter agreed. "C41. I'll remove that one, too." He frowned. "Actually, it looks like the first building came immediately after that, at C42. Previously it was only locations and people. I'll start with C42 and that should solve the problem."

"There's that 'should' again," Allison muttered to herself, but she shrugged. What choice did they have? "Okay, do it," she said out loud.

Gunter reset the recall and activated it, and the three of them waited. Nothing happened for a second, and then the tiny sun flared even brighter and a new line appeared on the activity log:

"Targets C64A and C64B returned to original locations."

"Yes!" Allison hugged Carter, then Zane, then hugged Gunter as well. It looked like everything was going to be back to normal. Or at least normal, Eureka style.

"Hey, look!" Zoe pointed. In front of them, Ellen Witte High School shimmered, blurred, and vanished—to be replaced an instant later by a rapidly clearing, equally bulky outline. One that read *Tesla High School* above the front steps.

"They did it!" Lucas crowed. He had braved the military cordon to join her after she'd escorted the last transplant home. Now he glanced at Fargo's laptop—they'd brought it with them, since Fargo was still away on whatever errand Zoe's dad had given him—nodded, and swiveled it around for her to see. "Look!" The activity log was showing the high school's recall.

"Yes!" Zoe hugged him. "I never thought I'd be so happy to see school again!"

Lucas hugged her back. "Me either." Then he kissed her. "You were great."

"Thanks." She stood on tiptoes, raised her head, and kissed him properly. They enjoyed that for a second before Lucas stiffened and shifted away. "What?" Zoe laughed. "It's not like my dad is here to stop us."

"No, but plenty of others are," her boyfriend pointed out. She glanced around and saw more than a dozen soldiers, all watching them. All heavily armed.

"Eh, ignore them. They worst they can do is throw us in the brig."

He considered that for a half a second, then laughed. "As long as they put us in together, I'm okay with that." Then he kissed her again.

"We need to get ready," Zoe reminded him after a minute. "Once Café Diem's back, we'll have to bring each of them home as well."

Lucas smiled at her. "You're amazing," he told her, and leaned over to kiss her again.

"Thanks." She forced herself not to get too distracted. "Remind me to remind you to tell me all about how amazing I am at great length once we've gotten all this sorted out."

"Deal."

Allison and Carter had headed back up to her office so they could use their respective PDAs again. Allison was on the phone with General Mansfield, assuring him that the MRS was no longer a problem.

Carter, meanwhile, had his old cell phone out. He had to work fast. It wouldn't do to have the people he'd asked to help out see the house they'd been watching vanish, to be replaced by a completely different one. After that he'd call Jo and Henry, tell them they could head back home.

In the meantime, the phone on the other end was ringing. Then someone picked up, and Carter smiled. "Hey, Brad? Carter. Listen, good news. . . ."

"Take it easy, Jo," Tango told her as the rest of his squad marched back to their copter.

"You too, Tango," she replied. They bumped fists. "Come visit some time, and I'll show you what small-town life is like."

He laughed. "No thanks—I think Eureka's a little too active for my tastes."

"That's half the fun," she said, but she laughed with him. "Stay safe."

"Yeah, you too." He loped over to the copter and hopped onto the runner as it was lifting off, then hauled himself into the cabin in one smooth motion. "Don't shoot anybody!"

"Only if they deserve it!" she shouted back. She waved, then turned back to Davey and the waiting Night Wing. She'd gotten the word from Carter just as General Mansfield issued a full recall to the troops. Time to head back home. She wondered where Zane was right now.

She sighed. There was going to be a hell of a lot of paperwork on this one. Then she grinned. One of the advantages of being deputy instead of sheriff—she could always pass the buck.

It looked like Carter was going to have his work cut out for him.

"Glad everything worked out, Jackie," Lexi said, snuggling back against Duncan. "Sorry my visit got cut short."

"Come back anytime," her brother told her. And she could tell he meant it.

"We just might take you up on that," she warned, laughing. Duncan kissed her cheek. "Take care, Jack."

"You too, Lexi."

"You go to visit your brother and niece for a few days, and look what happens," Duncan teased after the phone call ended. "All kinds of craziness."

"Oh, that had nothing to do with me," Lexi assured him. "That's just Eureka."

"I'm on my way back now, Jack," Henry assured him over the phone. "I should be there in a few hours."

"Great," Carter replied. "I want to spend some quality time with Zoe before she has to head back to school, but I'll catch you tomorrow. Breakfast at Café Diem?"

"Sounds good. See you there."

Carter hung up and settled into his seat, concentrating on the road ahead to avoid all the Eureka residents streaming back to their homes now that the evacuation was over. He'd pulled all his old friends back off the job—most of them had been sent home by the military anyway, but he'd felt he owed each of them a personal thank-you. Things had gone surprisingly well in that regard, with so many agencies working together so smoothly across so many states. In some ways, this had been one of the best assignments he'd ever handled.

Which made him realize something. He hadn't lost any of his old skills—if anything, they were sharper than ever. And that was because Eureka wasn't like anyplace else. Yes, it was a small town, but a unique one with all kinds of unique problems. And he liked it that way. It kept him on his toes. It forced him to use all of his negotiating skills and team coordination experience, but it made him think on his feet and look outside the box as well.

And he was good at it.

Plus he realized something else. He was relieved. Not just about everything turning out okay, but about the fact that he was heading home.

Home.

That's exactly what it was.

Back in the old days, he'd been antsy when he wasn't working. He'd needed the excitement of being on the job, on the road, on the go. He'd never been able to relax at home, which was why Abby had left him. He hadn't really been there for her, or for Zoe.

That had all changed now. This had been an interesting trip, and in some ways a fun one—certainly it had been exciting to be back out on the road again, even if just for a little while. But he was looking forward to a nice quiet dinner with Zoe—and S.A.R.A.H.—and then maybe a movie or something.

He was looking forward to going home.

Because that's what Eureka was for him. It was home. Sure, Zoe was going to head back to college in a few days, and it'd be at least another month or two before she came home again. But even when she eventually graduated and found a home of her own, he'd still have a place in Eureka. He'd have friends all around him. He'd still have a sort of family. A crazy, completely dysfunctional family full of geeks and nerds, but a family nonetheless.

Maybe someday he'd decide to move on. But he didn't think it was going to be anytime soon.

"There really is no place like home," he said softly to himself as he drove. "Especially when it's all in one place."

Just then his phone rang.

"Sheriff Carter speaking," he answered. And as he said it, he realized he might never get tired of that.

"Sheriff?" It was Fargo, and he sounded like he was shaking. "Can I stop now?"

Don't miss the next Eureka novel

EUREKA: BRAIN BOX BLUES

Coming in December 2010
from Ace Books!

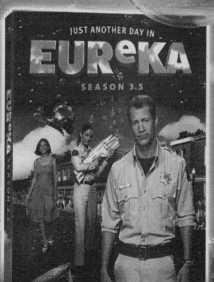